CHANGE: A NOVEL

JOE BALDWIN

For those fighting for a change for the better

Keep fighting

For dad

who would change his life in a heartbeat for those he loves

PART I: THE MOVIE STAR

Madeline Cross was on her way to becoming a movie star. Her road to Hollywood was paved with hard work and dedication to her craft. In 1993, she starred in a commercial for diapers where she had to crawl on the floor and pretend to love her fake mommy. She cited that as her easiest gig. But, after the advertisement faded away and the family house phone remained silent, she never got her big break.

Fast forward to 2016. Madeline was walking home from her 9 to 5 when a white paper stapled to a telephone post caught her attention. *Open auditions for an off-Broadway production of Annie,* read the heading. She was too old for the lead role, but she knew there was a mean old lady who hated the children of the orphanage, and she felt that would be the perfect role for her.

She was correct.

Madeline nailed the audition and got the part. It was a grueling year of rehearsals, after rehearsals, after rehearsals. But it all paid off in the end. What she didn't know about those performances was a movie executive attended the Sunday evening show and contacted the higher-ups to get her into her one true love: on-screen acting.

2019's *Love Audition* about a woman working hard to get the role of a lifetime who falls in love with the movie's director fit Madeline perfectly for the lead character. When she read the script, she viewed the film as a cheesy rom-com, but with internet hashtags, a certain "love" scene going viral featuring her face in GIF form, and Madeline with a stint in internet "cancellation" jail made the film millions, as did Madeline.

As she escaped the reverie of her life that felt like a dream, her small, yellow, two-story ranch home came into focus. The Ford Fiesta idled in her small driveway. Her chin threatened to hit her chest during the hour and a half drive from the airport, but she made it. The home in Los Angeles was closing in a couple days, so the cross-country flights back home to Connecticut would soon come to an end. Although, her two sons were not happy with the move.

Madeline turned the key in the front door, making as little noise as possible. The television glowed off the magenta walls. Individual pictures of smiling boys and an art project of hers from a wine and paint night adorned the living room.

"Sarah. Sarah, honey." Sarah was a live-in nanny and was on the final day of her four-week-long stay. Madeline wished she would have been awake at least on her final night, but she sympathized with Sarah, as it was three in the morning.

Sarah stirred, massaging her face with her palms, creating mascara raccoon eyes around her beautiful blue irises. "Oh, shit." Sarah shot up. She stared at the silent Rory and Lorelai having a couch conversation on the television as though she had never seen *Gilmore Girls* before. "Oh, shit." Again, she swung her face to Madeline. "I'm so sorry. I tried my best to stay up."

"That's okay. My flight was delayed for a few hours. I'll give you some extra to compensate." Madeline removed a checkbook from her purse, wrote out four thousand dollars, tore it off, and shoved it at her exhausted babysitter.

Sarah would stay over when Madeline was in California, bring the boys to school, feed them, play with them, and acted as a stand-in mother while she was away. And Madeline was forever grateful for her services.

"Oh, that's okay, Mrs. Stewart."

"Madeline, please. And it's Cross, never Stewart," she said with a shiver.

"That's too much for four weeks."

"You're going to take it and you're going to put it towards college," Madeline said and winked, but Sarah was so out of it, she seemed to barely recognize where she was.

"I—my parents have a college fund already and—"

"Spend it however you like, sweetie. Do you need a ride home?"

"No, I'm okay. It's only a few streets down. I—" Sarah let out a giant yawn as she stuffed the check into her pocketbook. "I can make it that far. Good night, Mrs.—Madeline."

"Text my phone when you're home safe, please. Your mother would kill me if I let anything happen to you."

Sarah gave an unenthusiastic thumbs-up on her way to the mouth of the cul-de-sac. She watched until Sarah disappeared behind the tall hedge splitting the main road and Madeline's quiet dead-end street. Quiet. Just the way she liked it.

Madeline cut the TV off and recognized for the first time how truly dark it could get inside her home. The yellow streetlights and the full moon were enough to get Madeline from the living room to the foyer, where she removed her shoes and took those fifteen exhausted steps up to her own bedroom.

At the top she read the "no girls allowed" sign taped to Brandon's bedroom door. "You are the only one allowed to break that rule, Mom. It's because I love you. But other girls have cooties," he had said when he first hung the unnecessary deterrent weeks ago. She used her "mom pass" to enter this early morning and saw him sound asleep with the heavy *Superman* comforter pulled up to his neck. She pecked a kiss on his temple and exited.

She was down the hall, standing outside of Leo's room. His door was as empty as the inside. Leo never made a fuss when he was smaller, and as he grew, that trend continued. She feared he was on the spectrum and even ran some tests. The doctors concluded he was "just a quiet kid." Anytime Leo had a question or a comment, he would lean in close to Madeline, pull her blonde hair behind her ear, and whisper his thoughts. Her quiet kid had thrown his covers to the floor and snoozed in the fetal position. She covered him back up, planted the same kiss on his head, but for Leo, she whispered, "I love you."

The door was placed back into its frame, and she was successful in not waking her two boys. Her anxiety grew as she approached her bedroom. It grew anytime Brandon and Leo popped into her thoughts. She left them for weeks at a time to pursue her lifelong dream. The move to LA was a good thing. Brandon wasn't happy to leave his friends and teachers, but she would be able to see him every night. She tried to reiterate that point, but he wasn't listening.

Before she left this previous time, Brandon and she had an argument. "I don't wanna go there," he had said.

"I know. But you can make new friends."

"You don't know that at all."

"I do know that," she said, her car idling in the driveway.

"No, you don't. I'm learning a lot of things and doing good at it."

Brandon was improving ever since his father left. He was a daddy's boy, and the divorce devastated him. Madeline noticed his confidence growing every school year as well. "I need to go. We can talk more when I get back."

"No. I never wanna talk to you again. I hate you." Brandon pounded upstairs and slammed his bedroom door.

That was a shot to the gut. Her throat was warning her of incoming tears, but she had to save them for the drive.

Leo had sat on the couch, invested in his video game. He never had an opinion on the move, but she could read his eyes. They were sunken, sadder than they were before. And his lovely whispers had ceased. She kissed Leo on the forehead. He never glanced up.

She thanked Sarah and took off for LA. Four weeks was the longest she would ever be away from them, and the attempted nightly video calls denied by her own children were devastating.

Her jet lag and lack of sleep should have drifted her into an immediate dream state, but her mind was struggling to shut off. The new movie she was working on, her kids, and the direction of the country were flowing through her thoughts. She never paid much attention to politics until it was something she couldn't escape. Every time she opened her phone, turned on a TV, or heard passing conversations on the street, she was bombarded with the information.

What really brought it to the forefront was *Love Audition*. When her face was plastered throughout the internet contorted in what was beautifully referred to as the "orgasm face," she was embarrassed. It got so bad she made a joke about it on her Twitter page, captioning the photo with: *When the dessert shows up at the table.* After her tweet went viral, she noticed the GIFs and memes began to subside.

Madeline was happy to see the spotlight shine from her and onto the movie. The movie was a flop in theaters, but the sales on *Love Audition* boosted millions in a matter of weeks when it hit streaming services. She loved seeing her bank account filling and other movie offers pouring in.

Her happiness fell apart when the pandemic hit, and her current film was shut down. She was able to be with Brandon and Leo for three months before filming resumed with a multitude of precautions. But with no income and virtual learning, it was affecting her mentally. Then came the riots and looting in response to social injustice. In her city, they destroyed a diner and blocked the highways.

In a moment of frustration, she posted a meme on Twitter that came across her social media pages. It was a picture of a man leaving a Target with a flat-screen television. The caption read, *A new TV. That just screams justice.* Minutes after she made the post, it had hundreds of thousands of retweets and comments by angry internet goers and likes by others who agreed.

She deleted the post only eight minutes after it first appeared, but it was too late. Screenshots lived forever. She subsequently apologized and made a sizeable donation to various charities supporting those in impoverished situations.

In the months after, nobody showed up at her home, nobody approached her at the grocery store. It all stayed online and in her DMs. Her account was still active, but she rarely used it anymore. It seemed to have been forgotten or overshadowed by the fight for the vaccine or a cat riding a skateboard. Going from a normal, everyday person to a noticeable figure in such a short amount of time came with a ton of responsibility.

Bang!

Madeline was woken from a sleep she hadn't realized she fell into. She tapped her phone on the bedside table. The screen's blinding light in the black room caused momentary vison loss. When she recovered her eyesight, she saw it was 3:47 AM. If she had fallen asleep, it would have been for a total of ten minutes.

Bang, bang, bang!

The sound was rapid now. She threw the covers off herself and opened the bedroom door. She peeked into the hall. Nothing. Nobody.

Bang!

The noise was coming from downstairs. She attempted to keep her breathing under control. One step, breathe in. One step, breathe out. Repeat. At the top of the stairs, she peered down at the green front door and the half pizza window looking at the front of the street. The front porch light was off. She couldn't see a thing. She had to move down.

Bang!

The breathing exercises failed her. She bit the bullet and pounded down to the foyer. Her back was against the door like she was preparing to enter a building on a stealth mission in Afghanistan. The bay window in the living room was her viewing access point to see who was at the door. She had a feeling this wasn't the US Postal Service.

Bang!

The sidewalk where the boys first learned to walk was as it always was in the early morning hours. Painted with yellow streetlight and deserted. Only… There was something. It wasn't there when she arrived home less than an hour ago.

Is that paint?

Bang!

This time it was matched with a faint, muffled yelp. Madeline took a cautious step, exposing herself further,   but being able to see her front steps became priority.

"Oh my god," Madeline shrieked.

She ran to the door and flung it open. "Oh god, Sarah." Sarah's body blocked the exterior door from opening, but Madeline was able to squeeze her way outside. The streaks of blood on the cheap plastic screen door were like a bad art project.

"What happened?" Madeline asked, not expecting an answer.

"Th-they did—watch—ou." The gibberish was not computing in Madeline's exhausted brain.

"Okay, well, let's get you inside." Madeline didn't want blood staining her floors, but somebody did this to her, and she needed to be out of harm's way.

Madeline rolled Sarah so she could open the plastic screen door. Her hands were red gloves stretching down her elbows. The cuts on Sarah's forearms and throat poured down the two steps and back into the trail of where she had crawled from whoever or whatever did this.

There were no other cars parked on the street. That was the normal protocol for Keen Street. And in that moment, Madeline wished she brought her phone with her. She dropped Sarah half in, half out and jetted up the stairs.

"What's happening?" *The boys. Fuck.*

"Nothing, sweetie. Go back to your room. Now." It was gentle but firm.

"You're bleeding." It was a phrase she never wanted to hear come out of her ten-year-old's mouth. She peered down at herself, and the 3x sized tee shirt she wore as a nighttime dress was a smattering of streaks. From his perspective, it must've been a mind-shattering experience.

"No, not me. I'm okay. Just go back in your room and stay there until I tell you. Okay?"

"But—"

"Okay?" That came out more than firm, but the insistent Brandon returned to his room.

Madeline yanked the charging cord from her phone and was able to unlock using her face and swipe up. But the blood smeared on the touch screen caused the apps to seize and become unresponsive to her touch. She instinctively rubbed it on her shirt, only further bloodying the device.

"Fuck."

When Madeline returned to the top of the stairs and looked down at Sarah, she wasn't alone.

"Madeline Stewart-Cross. So nice to finally meet you." A woman stood in her foyer, entering through the door Madeline left wide open. The woman looked to be in her late forties but was surely in her twenties. Her dirty brown hair was the definition of bedhead, and her clothes looked to be stolen from a hobo down on Main Street.

"Get out of my house," Madeline's voice cracked. She sounded weak. That was not a good first impression to the home invader.

"Well, I don't know if you know this, but you left your front door open. That indicates to me that you are open for business, Miss Stewart-Cross." The disheveled woman twirled a knife a bit smaller than a machete as she wandered toward the kitchen and out of view.

Sarah's head lay in the foyer staring at the white popcorn ceiling. Her neck wound waterfall had slowed down, and that meant she was running low on life juice. Madeline had a sad thought that the boring ceiling was the last thing Sarah would see in her short life.

"Hey," Madeline said, forcing some gruff into her voice. Being a single mother thrown in this situation was her worst nightmare. She wasn't going to move from this spot. She wanted her children at her back the entire time because if the crazed woman wanted to get to them, she needed to go through Momma first. "My husband will be home any minute."

"Oh, Madeline Stewart-Cross, we know your husband got tired of your twat when it became the size of an elementary school hallway and went on to fuck his co-worker because it feels better fucking a Pringles can, if you know what I'm sayin'," the woman said with a wink as she returned to the foyer, chomping on a piece of bread.

That wasn't entirely true. He had had an affair with his co-worker, but their marriage was falling apart eons prior to that.

"What do you want?" It felt to Madeline like they were having a western standoff, only they were at different eye levels and neither of them had guns. Madeline had always been against weapons until her husband left, and she had two beautiful children to protect. Although, acquiring a gun fell to the bottom of her priority list, even in the heat of her internet "cancel" debacle.

"Want?" the woman said and knelt next to Sarah, who surprisingly mustered up the strength to adjust her body away from the reaching hand of the nutjob. She pulled out the four-thousand-dollar check Madeline had given to Sarah earlier. "You probably think I'm here for your precious Hollywood money." The woman reached into her ratty jean pocket and removed a pink lighter. She lit it and watched the paper turn from yellow to orange to a floating black dust. "Fun fact: I'm not."

"Then what the fuck do you want?" Madeline sounded tired because she was. Not from her flight or lack of sleep, but from people being in the way of her trying to live her life.

"I'm here for *you.*"

"Me?"

"You." The woman ran at her. Her feet, blackened socks, were soft on the wood stairs. Madeline stood her ground. When the woman was two steps away, she was knife-ready to pierce Madeline's heart. Madeline grasped the banisters on either side of her and put a foot into the woman's chest. The knife hit the ground before the nutcase hit the first step. The woman barrel-rolled back to the foyer. Her head lay next to Sarah's. The sound was massive but quick.

"Let's go. Now," Madeline said, rapping on both the boys' doors.

Brandon was ready. He had even changed into his daytime clothes. Leo exited a bit slower, rubbing his eyes. He still sported his white tee and cat pajama pants.

"Don't pay attention to anything and move quickly." Madeline led the way, followed by Brandon holding Leo's hand. They got into fights often, but Brandon always helped Momma take care of his little brother.

"That's Sar—"

"I know. Don't look."

Brandon was looking, though. He loved when she stayed with them. They played board games, watched movies, and she even got Brandon to sit down and read a book. Leo joined in, but his shyness typically forced him back to his room.

They stepped over the bodies and ran for Madeline's car. In her tiredness, she had left the car unlocked, so she placed the boys inside.

She ran back into the house and grabbed the keys off the kitchen counter. When she was back outside, she took a glance at the quiet neighborhood where many were deep in their slumbers while Madeline fought for her life. Knocking on Mr. Franklin's door crossed her mind, but she wouldn't want to put her across-the-street neighbor in danger. Or any of her neighbors who had never bothered her in the years she lived on this street.

Even as she escaped what became her house of horrors, the silence of the street unsettled her.

I'm here for you, the crazed woman had said. Why her?

There was no time to solve that. She needed to be far away from here and find a phone or a police officer, whichever came first. Madeline climbed into the driver's seat and turned the ignition. The engine roared to life, and she felt a momentary relief period wash over her until she turned to comfort her sons, even though she was most likely more freaked than them. When her head whipped around, she jumped at the extra body in the car.

"Madeline Stewart-Cross. We've been looking for you." Another woman with the same disheveled look sat between her two boys, stroking their dark hair they got from their father.

Brandon and she had many spats, but he was a good kid who was going to grow up to do something great for the world. Kids who stood up for what they believed in were often world leaders.

The streaks of tears and bulging eyes tore her heart to pieces. The long blade was inches from Leo's neck. Madeline looked deep into Leo's eyes. They had a silent communication.

It's okay, bud. He seemed to have gotten her message because he split his trembling lips and whispered, "But I'm really scared, Mom."

The tears Madeline had tried so hard to hold inside during this entire scene had failed. She failed her boys, she failed Sarah, she failed everybody. Madeline wiped her tears away and whispered, "Me too, bud. Me too."

CHAPTER 2

The black boots of Detective Anthony Rawlings scraped on the rough cement covered in a streak of blood leading to the front door of 346 Keen.

"I need to check you in," a cop not much older than twenty-one said.

"Is this your first day on the job, son?" Ant asked.

"First week, sir."

"Well, nice to meet you…" Ant squinted at his silver chest nameplate. "Officer Small. I'm Detective Anthony Rawlings. I have been with this department for over twenty years, been a detective for fifteen of those. Now, you tell me if I need to be checked in."

The kid was a deer in headlights as Ant pulled up the yellow caution tape and entered the crime scene. "Hey, kid"—the baby face turned toward Ant—"keep up the good work."

Ant grew up on the east side of the city. The side of the city nobody wanted to go, including the police department. He would lie on his cot he shared with his two brothers, listening for the popping sound, so he knew the shooting for the night would be over and it wasn't his turn. Then he would drift off to sleep.

One of the days it happened just outside his momma's complex. A bullet entered through the wall and took the life of one of his two brothers. If the aim had been inches higher, Stanley would still be on the earth today.

Ant's momma called the police, and the dispatcher said they would send a patrol car through. Ant would never forget that night. Waiting from two in the morning, when the shooting occurred, to two twenty in the morning when a police cruiser rolled through. Ambulances and fire trucks followed. It changed his life forever: standing in stunned agony as his momma held her dying baby, trying to stop the bleeding while screaming through her sobs into the phone, running up the street and uttering horrifying screams to anyone who would help.

The fear, the frustration, the emptiness Ant felt that night was something he never wanted another child to feel. He worked hard toward his goal of becoming a police officer, and he did just that. He spoke with children after shootings in the same complex, and he felt he was making a difference in their lives. Now as a homicide detective, he was bringing closure to families. He'd had two hundred fifty cases land on his desk, and he solved every single one. It felt good to provide a small glimmer of hope to families who lost everything.

"What do we got, Chet?" It was a question Ant had asked the responding officer hundreds of times. But the look on Chet Morse's face told him this one was different.

"It's bad, Ant. It's real bad," Chet said.

Officer Morse was hired three years ago but was quickly in the good graces of his superiors. The cool blonde, slicked-back hair and mustache a firefighter would love made him look the part. But his willingness to participate and follow order placed him higher on the list of advancement within the department when the time came. With that, referring to Ant as any name other than "Detective" alarmed Ant to the depravity of the scene he was stepping into.

Chet's pale face and shimmering eyes sent his stomach sinking.

The blood pooled at the front door was a normal amount to him. His first assessment was multiple casualties. As he entered, he hopped to the right over the red puddle and into the kitchen. The kitchen looked virtually untouched. A bag of bread lay open on the island countertop with pieces strewn out the top. Unless the perpetrator cleaned, nothing occurred inside the kitchen.

As he guided his way through the home he had visited once or twice, he noted the yellow placards and crime scene technicians snapping photos and gathering evidence. He'd gone through the process on so many occasions; it was a task that became simple but never easy.

Ant walked through a threshold and into the living room where the action was. When he was training with his detective mentor, he was told to show no emotion. Especially when speaking with the family of the slain. Never show them you were upset.

The scene he stood in front of now made the task of holding emotions inside tougher than ever before. Three victims were in chairs that matched those at the living room table where Ant pictured the family eating dinner together. They were stripped of their clothes, and their hands were forcibly tied behind them. All three had life-ending slashes through their tracheas. In addition, all three had markings. Ant took a few steps closer. The blood surrounding the victims was impossible to avoid.

The woman, the mother, had a deep, near perfect line, intersecting with the throat cut down through her chest plate ending below her navel. Back at the collarbone, the cut started again, circling around her left breast, meeting and ending at the straight line. It wasn't hard to determine, even with the drying streaks of blood, the letter *P*.

Ant had come across ritual killings before. The killer would leave insignias carved into their victims. They wanted to become the next popular serial killer. True crime documentaries were not only disrespecting families of the dead but showing the mentally deranged they could be famous.

He never came across letters of the English alphabet carved into the victims until today.

He was having a rough time moving on to the next of the dead. He was struggling to even look in that direction, but this was his job. No matter the crime and its entities, he must study any and all clues. What helped him get through the tough ones was remaining laser focused on the job at hand. Piecing each clue, no matter how small, together and solving the crime at hand.

The ten-year-old boy's cut split the center of his torso in an impressively straight line. A second line went across the kid's collar bone from one shoulder to the other. The final line went straight across and under his navel. The deadly weapon had cut deep enough that the head of the snake of an intestine was hanging on the outside of his body. It completed the letter *I*. He couldn't stand to look any further, so he moved on to the final victim.

It was enough to be required to survey mutilated bodies, but it became impossible when he knew the dead. Ant had many conversations with Madeline at cookouts and parties thrown by the department. And Brandon was a celebrity. Anytime he walked through the halls of the headquarters, every officer, sergeant, lieutenant, captain, and even dispatchers slapped him five and asked how school was going. Ant loved that kid as if he were his own.

Ant prepared to look over the final victim and paused. He shouted through the front door for Chet. Chet walked to Ant, avoiding the trail of blood leading up to the home. "Was there anybody else inside when you arrived?"

"No, sir. Just the three victims in the living room."

"And you searched the entire home and surrounding areas."

"Sure did."

"Hm."

Ant returned to the room where he pictured Madeline on the couch, watching TV with her boys. Brandon engaged in conversation while Leo focused on his games or a book he was reading. A family now torn apart.

After Ant finished and was back outside, he allowed the crime scene techs to do their jobs. He pulled Chet away from the red and blue lights flashing off the façade of the murder home and the surrounding dwellings. Neighbors stood on their stoops in their pj's and bathrobes with hands cupped to their mouths, being as nosy as possible without interfering with the investigation.

Ant opened the driver's side door of his Ford Crown Vic parked a little away from the action and motioned for Chet to enter the passenger side. When they were in the secluded vehicle, Ant asked, "Was the third victim identified?"

"Yeah, Sarah Plax. She lives a couple streets over. Her mother panic called the station when she never returned from her babysitting gig. I bet you can guess who Sarah was looking after."

Ant nodded, thinking three steps ahead of that. "Then where is—"

"I don't kn—we don't know. Every inch of that home was searched. Under beds. Inside toy chests. The back of closets. The whole everything. An APB was put out, and every cop we have are keepin' their eyes peeled."

"Fuck," Ant said, slamming his hand on the dashboard. He never grew frustrated at a crime scene, but this was personal. "Does *he* know?"

"Multiple attempts were made to reach Chief Stewart, but as you know, he's on vacation with his new girlf—um, well, it's possible the killers knew that too."

"That's fine. But the number one priority for everyone right now is to find little Leo. Holy shit. I sure hope he's somewhere safe and not taken by the lunatics who did this. I really fucking hope so."

Ant turned the key in the ignition, and he and Chet sat in silence for a full minute. Ant wasn't thinking about anything. After what he witnessed inside, he wanted to clear his mind of anything and everything. He was curious what was on Chet's mind, though. Chet was first to arrive, and that was the worst position to be in because he saw victims at their freshest.

"What—" Chet said, then turned and looked back at the house. "What do you think about the bodies?"

"The bodies?"

"Like, the carved letters."

"What about them?" Ant knew what he was referring to and had already made up a solution in his head, including a possible lead. But he wanted to hear Chet ask.

"What were they trying to indicate?"

"Do you know the story of the Manson family?" Ant asked.

Chet turned away again and nodded to the rising sun. "Sure. The crazy mofo with the swastika tattooed on his forehead."

"Right. His sadistic family members, under his direction, murdered actress Sharon Tate and some others who happened to be at her home that night. They tried to trigger a race war by painting 'Pig' on the wall in Sharon Tate's blood. Trying to blame the murder on the Black Panthers and create chaos. It had zero impact whatsoever."

"There aren't many Panthers around anymore, so who—" Chet turned away ashamed when it clicked in his own head, then continued, "So, you think that's what's happening here?"

"A semi-famous movie star who said some not so…kosher things online. Yeah, I know that's what's happening here. Without question."

"And you know it won't trigger a race war of any kind?"

Ant rubbed the steering wheel, took a big breath, and let it out between pursed lips. "That, my friend, remains to be seen."

CHAPTER 3

Crossing over the Bridgetown bridge, the only way in and out of the city, Mac Pulaski's McMansion sat upon a hill higher than the rest of the city. It was a sight to behold for many passersby, but for the residents of the city, it was a stark reminder of how the rich got richer while everyone else suffered.

The home was more of a mansion inside a small city. A wrought iron fence kept those who didn't belong outside. At the top of the long, winding driveway, many attempted to climb the fence, but after a video surfaced of a teenager shocked to death by two hundred volts of electricity, that thwarted any other attempts to gain access to the property.

Inside its largest bedroom, Mac pushed himself from the hardwood floor, then down again and up again for the two hundredth time that morning. Exercising was a sign of strength and a sign of strength that meant nobody wanted anything to do with him. And that was how Mac liked his life to be.

Mac tucked hospital corners into his king-sized mattress and aired out the comforter over the top. Then he wandered to his desk where a laptop sat atop the thick birchwood desktop. He hit the space bar, and Beethoven's "Fur Elise" played through the home's built-in speakers. He opened a walnut wardrobe. Dark suit jackets lined the inside with hangers holding them in perfect alignment. He removed one and laid it on his bed. He pulled a white button-down from the hanger and shrugged it over his toned shoulders, covering his six-pack. He pulled gray dress pants on and buttoned them over the underhang of the dress shirt. He tightened a tie around his neck, and it dangled just above his gold belt buckle. He completed his look with the blue suit jacket. His shaved head required nothing more than a blade swipe every couple of days.

He exited his room and knocked at the adjacent door. No answer in five seconds gave permission to enter. Inside a smaller bedroom, though sizable compared to the rest of the world, lay Sadie. Her face was a bloodied and bruised mess, as were her elbows and knees.

"Did all go according to plan?" Mac asked.

No answer. Her eyes were open, unblinking.

"Did all go according to plan?" he asked again. Still no answer. No movement. He approached the bed and yanked her from her ankle. Her naked body thumped to the floor. Moaning indicated she was alive and well. "Answer me or there will be punishment."

"No," she said, wetting her cracked lips.

"What happened?"

"That bitch kicked me down the stairs."

"But is she dead?"

"I don't know. Ask Nat. I just woke up I think I need a hospital."

"You need no such thing. Clean yourself up with a shower, then eat some food."

"Where are you going?"

"None of your fucking business. When did you become so smart-mouthed? When your skull smacked the bottom step, it must've changed your personality too."

Sadie rolled away from Mac, pulling her jacked-up knees to her chin. Mac shook his head. When he first adopted her, she was an obedient girl, but now she was turning into a whiny bitch.

Mac exited the room back into the foyer. Every morning, he gazed at the fifty-foot-high ceiling mural of Michelangelo's God's creation of Adam. A beautiful reminder of why we live, why we are free, and why he is all-powerful. And most importantly, why Mac continued to spread his message. Mac passed the 24-carat gold statue of a bird extending its arms, ready for an embrace. He paused, said a prayer for those warriors and soldiers fighting for him every day.

Amen.

He disregarded the front door and entered the kitchen. There were constant attempts to snap photos of Mac. News crews showed up wanting an interview. Many attempts by CNN and MSNBC to have a sit-down exclusive. Fuck all of them.

They know my worth and they know my word.

"Breakfast?" Natalie said with a grin. She wore a black and white apron, her backside airing out.

"Depends. Tell me about last night."

Nat looked at the marble floor, swishing her white toes back and forth. "Well, she's dead."

"Excellent. We will celebrate her martyrdom later. And the boys?"

"Um, one of them kinda, sorta got away."

Mac's blood boiled in his gut. "Which one?"

"Uh, the smaller one."

"Ignore all other tasks for today. New task: locate the smaller boy and kill him. Capeesh?"

Nat nodded solemnly. Her brown curled bang hung cutely in front of her left eye. "So, no breakfast?"

"No time. Exciting day today. One day closer to my goal being achieved."

"I'm so excited for you. How about a bacon for the road?" She held out the pig meat, and Mac ate it out of her hand.

"A kiss for Daddy?" Mac said, and Nat planted a loud smooch on his right cheek. Her lips were crusted, and her face was distorted in a traditionally ugly woman. She was his task runner, and he needed her and the one upstairs, but they knew well they could be replaced in an instant.

As Mac grabbed his suitcase from the front hall closet, he yelled back to Nat, "Oh, and keep an eye on Sadie. She's being a little crybaby today." The home had wonderful acoustics. The white walls had tremendous noise bouncing ability. Even with the classical music through the speakers, he was positive Sadie heard his words. "Love you girls."

Mac exited into his garage, the size of a poverty-stricken family home that could be found on the east side of this broken city. Not broken for much longer, Mac thought. The child needed to be dead, but his girls had no option but to complete the task at hand.

The epoxied floor shone under the fluorescent lighting, showing off his Maserati, Lamborghini, Datsun, and Dodge Grand Caravan. He opened the sliding back door of the van, threw his suitcase in the rear seats, and as he started the car, listening to the idling engine, he said another prayer. It was a prayer to himself. He wanted all to work out in his favor. Because if that occurred, the world would be in good hands, and peace would be achieved.

CHAPTER 4

Mac Pulaski was a celebrity in the city of Bridgetown, but not a fun celebrity you may run into at a fancy restaurant or at the high-end grocery store. Mac had the type of celebrity status most in Hollywood tended to avoid but most political figures were drawn toward. The type of status where you were painted as the villain in the world of real life. Mac was the Bridgetown villain, or at least that was what he wanted all to believe.

Ant was not fond of Mr. Pulaski, as they had many run-ins. Ant believed he was responsible for at least ten murders in the city. Those crimes were solved, and the proper parties were arrested, but when Ant tried to lead the trail from his "henchwoman" to Mac, the physical evidence always went cold.

It was no secret who Mac "adopted" into his "family." He ran his own live streams from his McMansion, sometimes playing video games and talking with his "fans." Most of the time, though, he was chatting it up with two, sometimes three of his "henchwomen" sitting on his lap half-naked. How that didn't break any rules through the streaming service baffled Ant.

Anytime Ant thought he had Mac locked down on a crime, either the search or arrest warrant was turned down by the state or his witnesses decided to skip town after being cooperative with the police. Though Ant was aware where they ended up.

Back in the police academy, Ant was mesmerized by police work. The laws fascinated him, and he was called a nerd by his academy classmates for being excited for class time. The physical training and having a drill sergeant's saliva splatter his face as they yelled inches away was the easy part. It was mostly a psychological game they liked to play.

Ant's favorite class was Detective 101. The required hours were ten for the entire academy, but Ant felt he learned more about policing in that one class than in any other section. And he proved it to any doubters by being the first to record a perfect score on the detective exam in Bridgetown history. He was prouder to be their first Black detective, but the department didn't much care for that stat. However, once he entered the force, skin color, gender, and size didn't matter. You were one family keeping the streets safe.

He knew Mac's time was running short. In the detective class, he remembered a specific comment from the instructor. "The cases go cold, the bad guys get away, but it only takes one fuck-up for an arrest." Ant could feel in his gut that Mac's fuck-up was coming. But he feared it would be a spectacle.

The winding drive from the city's edge up to the McMansion was a scary one. Ant had driven in any and all weather conditions, been in high-speed pursuits, but circling the road with no guardrails and just enough blacktop for his beige Crown Vic was dizzying.

He made it to the top. Pulled up to the wrought iron gate and pressed the intercom button. This was his twentieth time sitting in his car facing the monstrous home, unable to gain access, but resilience was Ant's middle name.

"Hello, who is it?" a cheery young female voice chippered through the speaker.

"Detective Anthony Rawlings. I'm here to speak with Mr. Pulaski."

"He stepped out for the day. Please exit the way you came in and never return. Thank you!" The cheeriness in her voice never faltered.

"Early this morning, we had a brutal murder of three individuals and—"

"And you think my Mac-y had something to do with it?"

"As a matter of fact, he is my number one suspect."

"That is discrimination, Mr. Detective. You hear me, discrimination."

"I can tell you a thing or two about—"

"Your words bore me. Please leave. You have no business here."

"Actually, I do. I have a warrant for Mr. Pulaski's arrest." Ant lied. It was a tactic that worked on many criminals in the past. He had major doubt it would work with this girl. Mac's "henchwomen" were trained to handle any and all situations.

"Show me the paperwork. Hold it up to the intercom. I got a camera. C'mon, Mr. Officer man."

As she went on and on with her games, Ant surveyed the property. To his left was a four-car garage. The square peeking windows were sprayed the same white as the bay doors and the entirety of the home. To his right was a gorgeous overview of downtown Bridgetown. High brown brick office buildings, the minor league baseball stadium, and the bright red iron bridge leading people to and from the city where Ant was born and raised. On that late morning, the September sun gleamed sparkles off the Long Island Sound. A beautiful morning rising on a day of darkness.

"I'm waiting," the voice beamed again.

"How about this. You tell Mr. Pulaski I stopped by and pass along that I will be at the Galaxy Diner on Main at 7 PM. You know, where he ordered the hit on one of our officers three years ago? I will be at the first booth on the left. No weapons, just words."

There was silence for ten seconds. Ant was beginning to think she hadn't heard the previous thing he said, then: "I'll tell him. But don't expect him to show. He's very busy." This was the first time in their conversation where she toned down the pitch in her voice.

"Thank you. Oh, and one more thing to pass along."

A pause. "I'm waiting."

"Tell him I'll be chowing down on some peach cobbler. He'll know what I mean." A click indicated the talk was over and it was time for Ant to make his way down the death spiral.

He knew something about Mac's past. He knew something about him that nobody else knew. A phone call from his past. Something Mac didn't want to let out, and this was the perfect time to drop the bomb. A bomb so devious, Ant knew he would see his face at that diner tonight.

CHAPTER 5

"Will you hurry up and get inside before somebody sees us."

Mac took his sweet time, even swinging his arms and moving his legs in a slow-motion gesture. Something little kids did when they were doing their best to get on their parents' nerves. "Stop fucking around." Mac stopped, complied, and entered the building.

Mac entered through the rear door after parking his minivan down a side access road away from the street. He wasn't worried anybody would see him, and even if they snapped a photo or video of him walking into an old run-down warehouse, it would only add to the lore of Mac Pulaski.

Kevin Stewart slammed the heavy metal door shut and latched three locks into position. Unless somebody had an explosive device or remote access to the garage bay door, nobody was getting inside. "This may be fun and games for you, but this puts my livelihood on the line."

"Chill out, Kev, you could bunk with me if anything happens."

"If anything does happen, we'll be bunking in the state penitentiary up North."

"Pish posh bagosh. I may have lost many good girls to the system, but they can't hold me down. I'm untouchable," Mac said, giving Kevin a hearty slap on the shoulder.

"Nobody is untouchable. Remember that. Even me."

"Ugh, you're the chief of police. You are your own boss."

"You have an extremely skewed view on the chain of command," Kevin said, waving for Mac to follow.

They walked side by side through the open space. It reminded Mac of the city dump. He would routinely drop couches and chest drawers fifty feet into the garbage hole. Only they weren't ordinary couches and wardrobes; most of the time, they contained human remains.

"Holy shit," Mac said, trailing behind Kevin.

"Holy shit is right," Kevin said. "There are one hundred crates. Each crate contains three cannisters. Can you do the math on that?"

"Math was never my strong subject in school. Uh, one thousand?"

Kevin raised his eyebrows in disbelief. "Remind me to never let you near my taxes. Three hundred cannisters there, Mac."

"Okay, I was close."

Kevin shook his head again. "Anyway, let me show you how they work." Kevin pulled the top off a wood crate. Inside were cannisters two feet in width sitting snugly inside. A green liquid jiggled in each cannister like Jell-O. With both hands, Kevin cautiously removed the cannister and gently placed it on a folded comforter to his right.

Mac watched like a child seeing the true size of a roller coaster for the first time. Scared and intrigued.

"Now, this is extremely important. Do not get this green material anywhere on you. It can potentially enter through your skin, and you will be the one running around like a monkey on PCP." Kevin picked up the syringe from the comforter and stuck the needle through the top of the cannister. He pulled the plunger back, and it filled with the green goo. "Stick this in whoever's arm and push down. It will enter their bloodstream and will be in their brain within seconds."

"Then what happens?" Mac asked.

"The goo will fill inside their brain, and within minutes they will lose control of their body."

"Are you serious?" Mac asked, joy rising in his voice.

"Yes, this is powerful stuff."

"And all of it is mine."

"You did pay for it."

"So did you." It sounded more sentimental than he had anticipated.

"My wife took the two people I love away from me. Was I an asshole? Sure. I cheated on her. But taking the kids in the divorce was the final straw."

"You made the plan. I just got the job done. Well, except—"

"Except what?" Kevin's bushy brows furrowed, and he placed his hands on his skinny hips.

"Uh, I'm not sure how to put this, but one of 'em got away."

Kevin nearly stuck himself with the needle during his exasperated reaction. "Fuck. Who?"

"The little one."

"Little Leo? What happened?"

"The fuck does it matter? He got away and took off running, but don't worry, I have my ladies looking for him. He'll be dead soon enough." It was a partial lie since he pictured Sadie still lying on the floor in her bedroom. The bedroom he was paying for her to stay in. And the only reason she was staying there was to complete tasks he wanted completed.

"Then I am holding off on the transfer of things."

"No. I need this now. It's starting tonight."

"You lied to me saying the job was done. And besides that, we had a deal. Once your end of the deal is done, all of this"— Kevin gestured to the crates—"will be yours."

Mac rolled his eyes and turned to leave.

"Is the online post gaining any traction?" Kevin asked.

Mac held up his finger and removed his cell from the pocket of his slacks. He tapped the screen a few times and showed Kevin. He showed the full picture and not the cropped one he texted Kevin, missing the babysitter. He swiped, showed again. Swiped, showed again. Kevin nodded his approval.

On Reddit, the post gained five thousand upvotes and one million shares before it was taken down. On Facebook, it gained three thousand likes and four million shares. It was just recently removed from the site. On Twitter, it gained three hundred likes and a measly one hundred retweets before it was taken down. Fuck Twitter. It didn't matter, though, because Mac suspected the photo would gain traction from the aftermath. As Mac did, internet idiots took screenshots and would share it on their personal pages. The news would get wind, and it would be a major story on every network. He pictured a news anchor, probably an idiot on CNN, solemnly discussing how brutal the killings of those wonderful people were. Though the news freaks talking about it would only draw more coverage and more anger from the people of this already fucked country. And that was just what Mac needed.

"The kid will be dead within the next couple hours. If my bitches don't take care of it, I'll do it myself," Mac said.

Kevin nodded his approval. He left the tools inside the warehouse and as they both exited Kevin locked up. Mac was off to get his green goo. He would go where the kids went when they were on their own. A place Mac went when he was a kid. It was his safe place. And for little Leo, it wouldn't be any longer.

CHAPTER 6

Ant loved the drive over the metal bridge into and out of the city, driving under the red arches and peering out over the sound when safe to do so. He was four years old when the bridge was completed after years of construction work. On that same day, all other access points into and out of Bridgetown were closed. An underground tunnel, which Ant remembered going through once, was demolished into a small opening inside Veterans Park. "Hold your breath all the way through and make a wish," his mother had said. "If you hold it in until the end, your wish will come true." Ant had wished for his father to return home. His mother lied about tunnel wishing.

Living outside of Bridgetown was the best decision he made. Working as a police officer, then a detective, taught him to not shit where he eats. Sooner or later, your shit always dribbled into your food. He would be at the grocery store and would run into a kid he placed in cuffs on a marijuana charge. He was released the next day and approached Ant, yelling obscenities about how weed wasn't an arrestable offense. It was. Nowadays, weed was viewed as a safe and effective way to treat chronic pain and mental health. And it was beginning to be legalized recreationally in many states. Connecticut, as usual, was behind everyone else. Though there were talks by the governor to legalize, and Ant couldn't be happier. Too many times, he was putting away good kids who were carrying an ounce. Ant was always by the book, which got him known around the city as "the teacher's pet."

Brookfield was a quaint town where crime was a third of Bridgetown's and a third the size. Ranch homes were in the backdrop of fir and birch trees protruding from front lawns greener than a can of peas. It was a "nothing bad ever happens here" town. The only difference was, Ant had lived there fifteen years, and nothing bad had ever happened there.

His neighbors knew who he was, and his left and right neighbors had signs in their front yard screaming *Back the blue*. He appreciated the sentiment even though their views differed when it came to politics.

Back in 2018, Ant was partially thrown into the political pool when he was called into the office of Chief Stewart. When the chief called you into his office, it wasn't a good thing much of the time. "I'm gonna tell you like it is. I've been happy with the progress you've made since your rookie year. You are the most decorated detective this department has ever seen. I'll be retiring soon, and I want you to take over."

He was taken aback by the forwardness of Chief Stewart's offer. He thanked him and said he would need to think about it. A couple days later, after the question stewed in his head, and without telling anybody, he accepted. Chief of Police was a political position. You were in constant contact with the mayor and other political officials, while ensuring every single officer under you was performing to their highest ability and ethical standards. He knew it was a stressful job, but he could take it on.

Chief Stewart was overjoyed with his decision. He was told to keep the offer confidential until the day he was on the job. "Don't tell your wife, don't tell your fellow officers, don't tell your own dead momma. The day I retire, you will take over. Is that understood?"

Ant had nodded and completed the transaction with a handshake. Now, two years later, Kevin Stewart was still Chief, and Ant was solving crimes. And he never told a soul. Neither did Stewart. He knew that as fact, because once news like that reached the wrong ears (i.e., any officer in the department), it would be on the local news the following night.

The two-car garage at the end of the long blacktop driveway was not accessible for parking. Ant was a do-it-yourself guy. Mary wanted the gravel driveway turned to blacktop; Ant was on it. Ant had a vision for a back deck: he was at Home Depot every day and building what was now a wonderful wood structure outside their back door every night. Instead of vehicles, the garage stored the extra wood from that project, a table saw, and other tools strewn across the ground. But the one thing his wife wanted to trash since the day he bought it was his 1998 Harley Davidson. Ant rode it one time when he purchased the bike six years earlier, and then it broke down and had sat in the garage ever since.

Ant parked his Crown Vic beside his precious deck, and before he reached the deck stairs, he could smell the basil and tomatoes. Having an Italian wife came with its benefits. Exquisite cuisine was near the top of the list.

He was on-call twenty-four hours a day and seven days a week, but he went into the office at a normal Monday through Friday, 8 AM to 4 PM pace. A bit of an earlier start today, as the homicide call came in at four in the morning. And each day at four thirty, dinner was on the stove ready for their five o' clock eating time.

Today was no different, only Mary wasn't stirring the sauce, which had taken on a bubbly boil. Ant took a second to turn down the heat and stir the red goodness. As he crossed the threshold from the kitchen into the TV room, he heard faint sniffles. Mary's elbows were on her knees and her palms covering her face.

"What's wrong, sweetheart?" Ant said, rushing to her, ignoring the voice of the CNN news anchor. He embraced her, her red hair tickling his inner elbow.

"Oh, Ant, it's awful what's happened."

Ant was transported back to the day of September 11th. Mary, during their first few months of dating, had frantically called in patchy breaths as Ant clicked on the television at the station, watching the second plane barrel into the tower. That night, he drove home, kissed Mary, and immediately went back out to a waiting patrol car. A now retired sergeant sat in the driver's seat with Ant; a rookie, in the passenger seat, and a now retired officer in the rear seat drove down to New York City. It was

Ant's idea to go down and help in any way they could. Pulling rubble and debris in a now prevalent N95 mask until five the next morning was the toughest, most heart-wrenching thing he had ever done. But finding two people alive under the debris reminded him why his occupation and the occupation of firefighters and EMTs was so important and necessary. And why he was damn proud to wear the badge.

Back in the present, he felt that flutter in his stomach on a much smaller scale, but many more butterflies as he turned his attention to the television. He watched a picture of the very crime scene he left hours ago flash on the screen.

The headline read: *LOCAL POLICE CHIEF'S FAMILY SLAIN IN OWN HOME. "PIG" CARVED INTO THEIR BODIES.*

Madeline, Brandon, and the neighbor girl, Sarah. Their freshly cut naked bodies and injuries were blurred, but the blood spatter on their cheeks, foreheads, and lips were enough to make many people's heads whirl. The same crime scene he called so many different entities about. He asked for DNA evidence left on the bread bag in the kitchen as quickly as possible. He asked for any video footage from the surrounding homes that may have captured the assailants. This had to be the work of more than one person.

He knew who was behind it, and he knew the woman he talked with at that McMansion was involved. But the most difficult part of his rewarding occupation was solving the crime. Especially when your boss's family were the victims.

Mary had gone to every cookout and police event possible. She knew Madeline and her two boys better than Ant had. Madeline had even confided in Mary when she found out Kevin was screwing around with one of the few female officers (who was still currently employed).

"Those boys were—they were—" Mary couldn't collect her thoughts enough to get them out between the sobbing.

"Leo is still out there. I just know it."

"Do you, though? Do you know that as a fact?" It left her mouth in a harsh tone Ant had never heard from his wife.

"No." Ant told the truth. "But I've got my team on an around-the-clock schedule looking for him and catching who did this."

Mary had no response. She fell into his shoulder and cried for another fifteen minutes. That picture getting out to the public changed the case. Ant knew this would get people stirred up. He needed to go back to the station and help his team with the anticipated chaos control, but first he had a date with a killer. A killer who was behind the murders and spreading the disease of a picture that would change the world forever.

CHAPTER 7

Veterans Tunnel was accessible by all who travelled to and from Bridgetown from 1902 through 1986. The demise of the tunnel began with Randall Floyd. He was born in the hospital two miles toward downtown and was raised in the Trumbull Gardens apartment complex. There were thirty separate housing units, each of which held two families, one on each side of the unit. On the west side of the complex was a basketball court. Randall was a master in the paint. At six feet, eight inches, he would stand under the hoop, and his two teammates would steal the ball and toss it to the waiting Randall, and a small leap later, two points were awarded. When he got the chance to drive toward the hoop—this one with no net and faded backboard—he perfected the hook shot he watched his hero Kareem Abdul-Jabbar float over defenders. The three on the other team would argue that it was unfair to play against somebody with Randall's stature, but he couldn't help the genes he was born with. His father at six foot six and his mother at six foot one, they knew what was in store for them.

"Yo, Limb, that was goaltending," one of his opponents said. Limb was the nickname he was given since he was built like a tree. After pleas for years to stop calling him that, he reluctantly conceded.

"The ball was airballing," Randall said. "And this is street ball, we called no goaltending months ago. You even agreed to it, bro." The same six friends played three on three for the past eight years. The jawing back and forth was the fun of the game.

"Well, either way, its your turn to check up."

"I gotta go," Randall said. "Sorry, y'all."

The moaning and groaning and complaints of not being able to play with five faded as Randall was across Pembroke Street and headed for East Main Street. The friends met in middle school, and even after graduating high school two years ago, they still met for their weekly games. Without them, Randall would be lost in the world.

He refused college and worked as a waiter at a place called Missy's one town over. It was a twenty-minute walk from Trumbull Gardens, but he didn't mind the exercise. Though his friends would mock his skinny, lanky body at the mention of exerting energy.

When his mom died in a plane crash three years back and his dad died of a heart attack last month, he was left to pay the rent at the Trumbull Gardens apartment his parents held his whole life. And the restaurant was his way of having the money each month.

Walking his way through Bridgetown was interesting. He would get looks from guys leaning against the outside of convenience stores, smoke billowing from their mouths and noses. Then he would turn the corner and see a high-rise in the process of being constructed. An office building surrounding blocks of George Washington Carver, PT Barnum, and Greenfield Hill apartment complexes. Surprising considering two miles west was downtown with the same structures. He could feel the way the city was pushing those less fortunate out without saying a word.

Veterans Tunnel terrified him. The open-mouthed entrance invited any trouble to happen inside. The mountainous convergence of trees above felt ready to collapse once he entered. Inside the bookbag he carried an apron for work, a change of clothes so after his shift he could change into something that didn't smell like French fry grease and sizzling meat. But before he entered the tunnel, he had to take out his Walkman cassette player and place his over-ear headphones on, blasting his mixtape. If his basketball buddies knew he was listening to Madonna and Wham!, he would get relentlessly bullied for the rest of his life. Even the Chaka Khan track wouldn't be approved by them. He didn't care; he liked what he liked, and it was what got him through the tunnel walk.

He placed his orange felt headphones and grasped his Walkman, but before he pressed the play button, he heard, "Hey."

Randall turned to find a police officer standing in the center of the road. This wasn't a commonly used road, but there was no police vehicle in sight.

"What?" he said, dropping the headphones to hang around his neck.

"Where you comin' from?" the officer asked. He recognized him as a Bridgetown cop, dark blue uniform, shined black boots, star badge shimmering from the afternoon sun, and a utility belt, the gun clasp undone.

"My home." He kept his responses short and to the point.

"Had a robbery at the jewelry store, said it was a tall, skinny Black kid."

"Well, I hope you find him," Randall said, flipped the headphones back over his ears, pulled the Walkman from his pocket, and pressed play. "Wake Me Up Before You Go-Go" pumped his eardrums as he turned into the tunnel.

Randall Floyd was dead before the bullet left the officer's gun. It entered the rear of his head, impacting his cerebellum and exiting through his right nostril.

The officer claimed Randall was pulling a gun on him, but all he found was a portable music player.

Between the time of checking for a gun and not finding one, the officer leaving the scene to figure out how to get away with murder, and returning to scene with a plan, the body of Randall Floyd was gone.

Speculation over the next several months was rapid and unfounded. Randall's five basketball buddies reported him missing the next day after the officer kept the shooting to himself. When the police investigation was taking too long, the friends followed his route to his job, and once they entered the tunnel, shivers rippled down their spines. They could hear the click and whine of a Walkman and the cries of George Michael.

Some said they found nothing odd, but some ghost experts said the readings of paranormal activity was "off the charts."

It wasn't until three months later that the officer's guilt racked up to its highest point and he admitted to shooting a kid inside the tunnel, but the body vanished. The officer was placed on administrative leave, and the tunnel was shut down to all foot and vehicle traffic, leaving the bridge the only entry and exit access point.

As word of the shooting spread, protestors marched outside the tunnel while investigations were being conducted. The story even reached the national news. The mayor at the time, looking to save his image and the perceived image of the city, called for the tunnel to be imploded.

The destruction was completed the following week, and in the following years, the mouth of the tunnel was a cave that was said to be three feet deep, but when anyone dared to enter, strange noises could be heard from beyond, scaring off the trespassers.

In the future years, urban legends and ghost stories surrounded the cave inside Veterans Park, but nobody knew what or who called from inside. A voice broken and silenced but understood by a select few who connected with the man in the cave.

***

Mac wasn't fearful of the tunnel.

He stood in the grass field where many had died by his hands or the hands of his angels. The drop-off into the Saugatuck River was the perfect height for jumping and feeling the rush of life. It was also the perfect body-dumping site. Nobody swam in the dirty, needle-infested, polluted water, and Mac was grateful.

Away from the water and a half mile into the woods was where Mac spent most of his childhood. His mother lay on the couch in the heat of her heroin dreams, and his father cut his time between sharing needles with his wife and working his life away all while whoring it up with the local prostitutes. They acted as though they never had a child. Sure, they fed him and changed his diapers, but when Mac turned eight, his father told him he was old enough to be on his own. Upset, Mac ran through the park, cowering into what remained of Veterans Tunnel.

His cries were matched with the screams of a man. Hoarse and muffled. Mac made no effort to enter the dark depths any farther. Instead, the man came to him. Mac's body shifted when a thin, brown, snakelike branch slithered from the hole and snapped at him like the teeth of an unseen monstrosity.

He was scared. Of all he witnessed around his mother and father. Of all the abuse he took at school—locked in a bathroom stall after the bully flooded the toilet with an entire roll of toilet paper and a turd floated across his bare foot; the same bully who followed him home and choked him until his face turned a shade of purple and let go because his hands grew tired; and the same bully who flung an unopened soda can at Mac's face and broke four of his teeth. Then he went home, and his dad blamed him for letting the kids push him around and knocked out a fifth of whiskey. But the thing that lived in a place that felt like an escape, Veterans Park with a grassy hill leading to the beauty of the Long Island sound he could stare at for hours. Ruined by tendrils that chased him out of the park, looking to snatch him and bring him into a place from which he feared he would never return.

Mac was pulled from his reverie by the sound of a snapping twig. He poked his head around the cement mouth of the former tunnel. After hearing the backstory and exploring the tunnel many times after a body dump, he feared nothing except his own failure.

It was the kid. It was little Leo. His bowl haircut swung around his egg head as he kicked rocks and smacked a stick against a pine trunk. Just a bored kid without a care in the world. But he should be caring. His mommy and brother were killed mere hours ago.

Mac was filled with instant excitement. This was it. This was his ticket to controlling the world. First this shitty Bridgetown, then the state, then the country, then the world. Control would be his.

Mac loosened his tie and pulled it from his neck. Little kids had small necks and lungs. It would be an easy kill. Send the pictures to his pop and—

Buzz buzz.

Fucking phone. It could have been Kevin telling him he would pass on the serum to Mac after all, so he viewed the screen.

Nope.

Natalie. *Why is she calling right now?*

He pressed the sleep button and slid it back into his pocket. He wrapped the black tie around his hands like a football player taping his hands before a game. This was his Super Bowl.

He peered around the corner again and the kid was gone. The woods stretched for miles, and Mac wasn't searching for him as if he were a dead body. He did the killing, not the strenuous work. He needed—

Buzz buzz.

Natalie.

"What?"

"Um, sorry to bother you, Daddy, but, um, that detective came by earlier and—"

"I don't care. He's probably gonna come by every single day, just do what I told you and—"

"Well, he said to meet him at the diner."

"Fat fucking chance."

"Uh, he did say something about peach cobbler. I don't know—"

"Fuck."

"Are you okay, Dad—"

"Find that fucking little boy like I told you to. Right now. Veterans Park. I just saw him here. Bring that other bitch with you. Get it done."

Mac ended the call and spiked the phone into the hard dirt ground. When he picked it up, his screen was spiderwebbed. "Fuck. Fuck. Fuck."

He slid the phone in his pocket and took off for his Caravan.

CHAPTER 8

There was fear in Ant's gut it would all happen again.

When an officer in a neighboring city or across the other side of the country went beyond the expectation of policing, it automatically dropped the respect citizens had for that individual department. Each officer in the Bridgetown Police Department must gain trust back from all citizens whether they never had a run-in with the law or had trouble staying out of trouble. They sat on their couches and watched in horror as an officer of law murdered somebody in broad daylight. It took months for certain storeowners, residents, and even the homeless to speak or look at Detective Ant again.

He was attacked by White folks for not sticking up for his fellow officers. He was ostracized by Black folks for working a White man's job, and even some fellow officers took him to the side to tell him he wasn't building morale. Ant felt the morale boost should come from the chief who didn't say a word about the incident. Even when rocks came flying through his office window and the windows of his home, he remained silent. Ant supposed all his co-workers could sense he was next in line to the political throne—which he was—so that many of them turned to him for support.

Ant eventually gave a talk to the force. He reminded them of all they knew. "Stay vigilant from any attacks. Be smart even when your adrenaline has taken over your brain cells. But most importantly, protect yourselves out there," he said as they donned armor and picked up the clear shields to contain the acts driven from the acts of another. There was no blame thrown at the citizens. They were angry and rightfully so. When the ones whose sworn duty it was to protect and serve were performing the opposite, then the world had turned on its axis and the citizens all over the country had every right to be angry.

The eight broken windows were replaced three weeks ago, and Ant feared they would be knocked out again. The fear in Ant's stomach as he made his way up the mostly deserted Main Street stemmed from a gift he possessed. A gift of predicting what came next. And he predicted chaos. Those mutilated bodies plastered on national news networks would cause chaos. From whom, where, and when, Ant had no idea. It was a frustrating scene, as Ant knew the carved word was a setup, but he wasn't certain all would know the same.

Ant pulled into a front slanted parking spot, staring up at the Galaxy Diner signage. He didn't expect Mac to show, but he figured he would get food out of the deal regardless. The peach cobbler message would ruffle his feathers, but was it enough to get him here?

"Anthony, so good to see you, hon. Your usual spot is open," Jill, the waitress, said. She wore a baby blue shirt and brown khakis beneath a white apron. Ant enjoyed the old-school outfits and vibe of the diner.

"Thanks, Jill, smells great in here." It was a line Ant used each time he entered. The maple smell, mixed with the vanilla of the pancakes was the same every day, but it was one he couldn't get enough of.

Jill waved, saying she'd be over in a minute as Ant slid into the booth facing the front of the restaurant. He watched the few cars travel north and south to and from their usual life duties. A man in a bucket hat and Hawaiian shirt exited the tire retailer across the way. Quiet was good. Quiet for too long was bad.

"Your usual?" Jill asked. The notepad she used for writing orders poked out of the apron pocket.

"Actually, I'm gonna just get dessert."

Jill placed the back of her hand on her forehead and fell back into the adjacent booth in a dramatic showing.

Ant chuckled as she climbed back to her feet. "Peach cobbler."

She whipped out her pad and jotted down in giant letters *PEACH COBBLER* and showed Ant. "Just so you know I won't forget."

Ant shook his head with a grin as she sauntered away.

Ant fiddled with his phone and peered out at the mostly vacant front spaces. He watched with anticipation for a grand entrance from the resident cult leader. A Black cop meeting up with a White supremacist sounded like a sitcom just dying to be aired.

This had to be the one that put Mac behind bars. The compartmentalizing after walking out of a crime scene that vicious and personal on top of what he witnessed in his twenty-five-year career was beginning to affect his daily life, but retirement wouldn't come until Mac was locked up.

"One peach cobbler," Jill said, placing the slice in front of him.

"Thanks, Jill."

She stood by his table for a moment, staring out the front window. He couldn't pinpoint her exact thoughts but was expecting something in relation to the news. The question was answered with a question of her own. "What do you think will happen next?"

Ant remembered his first time back at the Galaxy. Jill was terrified. Kids had thrown napkin holders, salt and pepper shakers, sugar containers off the tables. They went into the kitchen, and within minutes, the entire food supply they had for the week was unusable. She confided in Ant, and he helped with the clean-up efforts, even taking money out of his own pockets to replace what had been damaged.

He peered around the current, pristine diner. There was an elderly man reading the newspaper as his yellow eggs got cold.

The only other patron. "It's going to depend on a lot. So, it's unknown at this point."

"Shouldn't you—" She hesitated to possibly rethink her question. "Can't something be done to prevent that? Like a proactive approach."

"Not much we can do. We're investigating as we speak, and the city is calm, as of right now. As somebody who witnessed the victims firsthand, quite frankly, it pissed me off. I am aching to take action."

"So, who do you think did this?"

"I can't really say until—"

Before Ant could finish, he heard trouble from a mile down the road. The soft shush of tires had been a normal Main Street sound, but the rumble of a V-10 engine was unmistakably jolting. The unspoken answer had arrived.

A fresh-off-the-lot glistening white Lamborghini skated into the open spot next to Ant's Crown Vic, making his car look like it was free for the taking. A group of passing teens looked on as the driver's side door flew up into a winged position and a bald-headed man in a suit stepped out. He shut the door and honked it locked with the key fob. Mac was a local legend, and those kids knew him, but they knew not to mess with him either. When you made it clear that you were carrying a full arsenal of weaponry, people tended to shy away from your presence. And that was what the group did. They took themselves to the other sidewalk.

The jingle of the bell startled Ant. He wasn't nervous. He had faced worse criminals than Mac, but this was the closest he had ever come to him, and it was unnerving. Jill skirted away as Mac slid into the booth across from Ant. His gold ring clicked on the table, and the matching gold necklace hanging by his sternum gleamed in the light of the restaurant.

Mac stared down at the peach cobbler. "How did you know? I kept that a secret."

"The police know more than you think." Ant wasn't backing down even though his heart was going to burst outside his chest, creating a topping for his cobbler.

"Heh." It was halfway between a laugh and a grunt. "Y'all don't know everything. I know that as fact."

"There's a difference between knowing and proving."

"And what do you know, Mr. Officer?"

"I know you are behind that attack of the chief's family."

"And what can you prove?"

Ant moved his gaze from the round head to the dessert. "I can prove you have a weakness." He picked up his fork from the white napkin and cut the cobbler. He stabbed it and shoved it into his mouth.

Mac appeared uneasy for a moment, then regained his cocky composure. "That was a long time ago. That was a different me."

"Then what are you doing here?" Ant asked.

"I'm here to prove my innocence."

"That's done in a court of law."

"From what I seen, you officers don't do much of the innocent till proven guilty thing."

Ant jerked his head, cracking his neck.

"I can only speak for myself," Ant said, returning the fork to the table.

"And I only speak for me, so stop talking with my girls. You wanna talk to me, then talk to me."

"What do you think I'm doing right now?"

"I think…" Mac paused, cleared his throat. "I think you're hopin' I break down and confess all my sins. But the good lord is who I confess to, not some chump on the police force."

Ant had been called worse. "Why not come down to the station and take a polygraph."

Mac didn't chuckle or grunt; he busted into a full-on laugh, causing the elderly gentleman to peer over his paper. Jill poked her head out from the kitchen, the sound of clanking spatulas against metal bowls and the sizzling skillet gaining frequency. The other waitress ignored the sounds to ask the other patron if he needed anything. Ant nodded to Jill, and she ducked back inside.

Mac quieted and directed his attention outside. Ant knew he wanted him to look outside, but he bored his eyes into Mac's temple. "Hm, let's hope nothing gets out of hand with a pig family killer on the loose. That's gotta piss off some of those people. We don't want a replay of a couple months ago. And wouldn't it be a shame if it never ended? Wouldn't it be a shame if they couldn't be stopped, no matter how hard you and your comrades tried? That would surely be a shame. Wouldn't it, Mr. Officer?"

Ant felt a sting at the corner of his eyes. He hadn't cried since his best friend was murdered in an ambush a few years back, but he wasn't going to now. He had too much damn pride for this city. He had too much damn pride for himself. "Wh—" He swallowed his tears down but still got hung up on his words. "Tell me what your plans are."

Mac didn't answer. He wasn't even paying any mind to Ant. His facial expression had changed. Mac wasn't in the conversation anymore. Ant could tell his mind travelled to another dimension. Mac silently slid out of the booth, walked out, got into his rich man car, and zoomed away.

Something had changed. Ant knew the TV and the elderly patron were behind him. The television was always muted. Ant turned, and he felt he had the same expression plastered on his own face that Mac had seconds earlier. The local Channel 12 news was on with a Breaking News report.

REPORT: BRIDGETOWN POLICE CHIEF KEVIN STEWART DEAD BY SELF-INFLICTED GUNSHOT WOUND

Ant's phone buzzed, and he had a feeling it wasn't going to stop for quite a long time. He was the new head honcho. He was the one they called.

Anthony Rawlings was the new Bridgetown Chief of Police.

CHAPTER 9

2018

Kevin Stewart ran his fingers from the face cheek to the rear cheek of the twenty-two-year-old blonde lying beside him. Her soft skin and fit body chased away the images of his wife's body scars from her c-sections and zero desire to have sex. Their sex life used to be on fire. Every night, sometimes two times a night. She fulfilled his every want and desire, then those rascals were born, and she made it all about them. He was lucky if he got an unenthusiastic tug job as she fell asleep. And she wondered why he had an affair. Because when you neglected your husband, you got what was coming to you. Any man would leave any woman who wouldn't give him the loving he deserved. Plus, he had a good thing going with Officer Miles.

Karin Miles was one of three women on the force, but Karin stood out to the chief. She was great at her job. She was head of community relations and improved Bridgetown with her voice and good deeds to the children in the impoverished neighborhoods (which made up most of the city). He loved going to the toy drives and seeing the smiling faces of the children as they were handed a monster truck or Barbie dream house they would never receive from their parents. And Chief Stewart had a wider grin seeing his department in good light and his blonde superstar the center of attention. Though when the sun went down and the weapons came out, Bridgetown's murder rate remained steady at three homicides a week. All the community work for nothing.

After one of those events, he noticed Karin sitting in her squad car, her hair a tousled mess, her face drooped, and tears black on her cheeks. Stewart sat in the passenger seat to comfort her. She vented about how the city wasn't improving despite her unbelievable efforts. He wanted to fix that too, if not to get with her, then to at least get the mayor off his back.

His first real contact with Karin was in that police car. A hug. Nothing sensual. It was in broad daylight in front of other officers and a community of residents chatting it up. A comforting embrace to reassure one of his best officers how good a job she was doing. And he reiterated that with his words.

It became more than a boss comforting his co-worker after a night at O'Malley's, the local cop bar, when she asked him to help fix her boiler at her home. She initiated the contact. She wanted it. She placed her hand on his chest. She rubbed herself on him. She planted a soft kiss on his lips. He had no choice but to comply with her wishes.

Now, two months later, she wanted him nearly every night. It was his escape. His escape from his family. His escape from those kids. His escape from everything. He would go back to Karin's place after his workday, do his business, then go home to the miserable Madeline, who would greet him with: "Where have you been?" and "I've been taking care of these two for the entire day." And other questions that made him feel more awful than he already did. Not about the affair or being a father, but about her not doing anything for him and him needing to be there for her. It was a fucked up, mismatched thing to go on about.

It was a good thing, keeping those two lives separate, until one of the other female officers, who knew Madeline the best, somehow found out (Stewart believed there was a leak in the department from one of the officers who knew what was going on), and Madeline made that final phone call. He didn't do much investigating into who the rat was because he had already mentally checked out from Madeline. She and the kids were already dead to him.

"I've got a meeting with the mayor, sorry." Kevin attempted a slide out of his new resting place, but Karin tugged on his arm to stay in bed longer.

"But it's four in the morning," Karin, drowsy, whined.

"Yeah, the perfect time for a quiet meeting. I'll be back in about an hour. I sure hope you'll be waiting." Kevin kissed her on the forehead. "Maybe in that red lingerie I like so much."

Karin was half-asleep and mumbled something unintelligible.

"Exactly," Stewart said, winking at her. Although in the dark bedroom she surely didn't see.

Her soft breathing assured him Karin was back asleep as he slipped out the front door.

The flashing yellow streetlights splashing his face as he sped down Main reminded him of the overnights he worked as a rookie officer. Crime was one-third back then compared to 2018. It was a never-ending cycle of homicides, assaults, robberies, and any other major crime you could conjure up in your mind. That was the topic of this meeting with the mayor. He was going to lose his 2020 election if the crime didn't dissipate by then. "As if it was my fault these idiots can't control themselves," he had said when he called Stewart on a private line a couple weeks ago to set up the meeting. "I've got a surefire way to cut crime and improve things for years to come. Bridgetown won't be looked at as the crime capital of Connecticut but viewed in the same lens as Fairfield and Greenwich."

The words of Mayor Higgins swirled in his head as he reached their meeting place. Back in the 50s, Bridgetown was a major manufacturer of many products. Rifles, brass, and carpenter steel were just a few things pumping out of the city and shipped off to other parts of the country. The economy was booming, crime was down, and it was the time to live in the big city. Now, the old factories sat abandoned, some were turned into affordable housing, some were demolished and replaced by an open field serving no purpose.

One of those brick buildings on the east side of the city, RELLINGTON ARMS FACTORY, remained on the façade in stenciled white spray paint high above the silent city street. This was where Stewart pulled into the rear. A narrow alley led him to a dirt plot. He parked, shut his engine down, and approached the rear door. He was beginning to suspect he had arrived at the incorrect building. Until the bay door swung up, and Higgins was a silhouette in the threshold.

"C'mon. Hurry," Higgins said.

"It's dark in here," Stewart said.

"Well yeah, I can't exactly turn a light on. We are trying to be discreet. Did you listen to anything I said?"

"Yeah, yeah, just tell me what you need to tell me so I can go back to my love."

"Your side squeeze or main?"

"They're the same person now."

"Ouch. Sorry."

"I'm not. Hurry up. It's cold."

"Okay. As you know, this year has been the worst in terms of crime. The worst in the city's history. I've got the governor breathing down my back. So, he's forced me to breathe down your back."

"Unless the governor wants to supply me with thousands of officers for every street corner round the clock, there's not much I can do about that."

"Oh, but there is." Higgins swiped a flame on his lighter and walked deeper into the oversized room. The smell of cordite mixed with a sulfuric stench reminded Stewart of what used to be. "This," Higgins said, glowing a yellow flame on a floor-to-ceiling stack of wood crates.

"What am I looking at?"

"Our way to a better life."

"Can you just explain instead of giving me the runaround?"

"Fine. You are no fun. You know that? I'm trying to make this a big presentation. Anyway. Inside these crates are vials of Cromisaul." He paused.

"Which is?"

"Which is a chemical agent that acts as a mental deterrent. Meaning"—he held a finger toward Stewart before he could open his mouth—"the agent enters intramuscularly, travels into the veins—the bloodstream if you will—then enters the brain. The serum is activated only when a bone in the subject's body is broken. Then the person will enter a zombie-like mode."

"So, you want to be responsible for a zombie apocalypse?"

"No. Well, a controlled zombie outbreak. Not those you see on that *Walking Dead* show, but these are smarter. They still have their human intelligence. It only attacks the motor part of their brain, forcing violence toward others. They aren't able to help themselves."

"How do you know this actually works?"

"You'd be amazed what the president of the United States can do."

"The president created this?"

"Are you kidding? The guy's a nitwit. He had scientists create it in a lab. Then volunteers were brought together for a"—Higgins made air quotes—"'scientific experiment,' then oh my god, it goes terribly wrong. Yeah, fucked up."

"Okay, but how is this going to help our crime situation? Are we just gonna infect everybody?"

"This will be an organized effort between you, me, your willing officers, a handful of EMTs, and unsuspecting residents."

"We can't just release zombies into people's homes. It would cause mass hysteria."

"Gentrification," Higgins said. Stewart thought he tuned out for a portion of the conversation and reentered.

"What?"

"Gentrification. It means to take—"

"I know what it is. What does it have to do with what we're talking about?"

"The old factories, such as this one, as you know, were destroyed or turned into projects. That affordable housing is what is dragging the city down. Ninety-five percent of crime comes from those areas. Ninety-fucking-five."

"I know."

"So, how do we fix that? We force them out. Take control back of these properties, build high-rise apartments, restaurants, and maybe even a fucking casino. Bring the rich back through who left all those years ago, and watch the crime dwindle down to close to nothing. And as a plus, watch Bridgetown's economy shoot back up. Take back our city. What do you say?"

"Won't that cost a ton of money?"

"Money shmoney. Gotta spend money to make money, as they say. Yeah, it will take a while to get that going, but once it does, we will be heroes."

Kevin Stewart never wanted to be a hero. He wanted to get the job done. And Mayor Higgins's plan sounded like it would work. But he had one last question. "I can control my officers, but if the deaths go way above my head, and past yours, to say, the FBI or the governor's office, I can't help you."

"You let me worry about the fucking governor. He's been in my back pocket since my first day in office. As for the FBI, they won't have time to hear what's going on until the damage is done. This will be quick and efficient. And most importantly untraceable."

A fever of excitement shivered through Kevin.

"I'll get my people in place. But this is important, so listen. This needs to be executed at the perfect time. It needs to be done in a time of chaos and panic. We slip this perfectly in line with that, few would bat an eye. It could be tomorrow; it could be years from now. You will know when to pull the trigger. Trust me."

"But I can't do this on my own."

"You won't be. I've got backup plans and many friends."

"Friends?"

"Yeah, Chandler, Rachel, Joey," Higgins said with a smirk and a wink. Stewart wasn't smiling, and Higgins recognized that fact. "There's a guy who lives up on a mountain in a big house."

"Mac?"

Higgins nodded, then shook his head as if he were thinking how crazy this all was.

It was more than crazy. But it just may work.

PART II: The Blackout

CHAPTER 10

2020

"Fucking asshole. Fuck, fuck, fuck." Mac's voice bounced off the walls of his McMansion.

"What's the matter, Daddy?" Natalie said, running into the foyer. Her five-inch heels clicking on the floor were at about the same register as Mac's yells. The apron she wore fluttered upward as she ran farther, exposing her nakedness.

"This fucker took the coward's way out. What a shit."

"Who, Daddy?" Her cutesy voice dropped to a serious tone.

"That fucking chief. We had a deal. We had a plan to execute. Now he's…" Mac trailed off. "Fuck it. Fuck the kid. Fuck the chief. Fuck the mayor. This is my city now. I'll take care of this shit on my own."

"Please be careful. That police guy is looking for—"

"He ain't lookin' for shit. I just had a dinner with him."

"Was that a good idea?"

"Are you questioning me?" Mac said, stepping closer to Natalie.

"No, of course not, Daddy."

"Good, because I can easily throw you back on the streets where I found you. You could go back to your miserable garbage life. Do you want that?"

"No, not at all."

"Good. Keep an eye on the news because this happens tonight. Any reports you hear about those neighborhoods, you call me right away. Got it?" Mac extended his arm and wrapped his long, bony finger around her neck. Her mouth was open, gasping for air. Like a car trying to start up. She was trying to say something, but when he let go, she fell to the floor; sharp, rattled exhalations released from her. "Don't ever question me again. Where is the other one?"

Natalie couldn't speak. Pointed to Sadie's bedroom. Mac moved swiftly through the large foyer, to the west hall, and flung the door open. Sadie wasn't fighting to stay conscious or pretending to sleep any longer. Her bed was made. Her room was clean of her own blood. The cleanest he had ever seen it. Her window was open, letting the cool autumn air waft through.

And Sadie was gone.

***

Mac took the Caravan. If he got even a micro scratch on one of his big boy cars, as he called them, he might as well burn the mansion down. Sure, he could get it repaired. Money was like leaves on the trees; it would always grow back into his bank account for hundreds of years, even after he was six feet underground. The cars were of sentimental value. He loved Kerry, Mary, and Teri. They were his true loves. No living human being could equate to them. The Caravan, however, was his working car. She did the dirty work, and she was going to work the hardest she ever had before. She may even die tonight, but it was a risk he was willing to take.

The '98 Dodge Caravan just fit down the alleyway to the rear of the old gun factory. The fog from the dirt parking lot settled as he pointed the van's headlights at the bay garage door. "Dear God, I know you're watching. I know it looks bad now and I know it will look worse later, but I assure you once the dust settles, it will be for the better. They are the ones committing sins. They are the ones killing. They are the ones who think they

62

are fighting for a cause. They are wrong. And they deserve to be punished. I'm sorry for yelling, God. My passions are blinding me. But I see clearly with you in my view. I do this for you. I do all for you. Amen."

He opened his eyes and pressed the gas pedal to the floor. He had about twenty feet to work with, so he needed a good head start. The rear tires kicked up dirt into the large rear stone wall, and the van fishtailed for a moment before correcting herself. She hit the bay door at thirty miles per hour. Her front bumper tore straight off. Her headlights smashed, dousing as they entered the darkened factory. She came to a stop at the far side of the open space. Luckily, opposite the side of the stacks of crates. Her front end was smashed up and her sides sported new lines of missing paint. But her engine still ran strong.

Mac slumped over the steering wheel and began to stir after a momentary loss of consciousness. His head was throbbing, and he patted his forehead. His fingertips came away with red. A small cut, he hoped. He didn't feel dizzy, just tired. He needed to kick the driver's side door to get it open. Once he did, he stepped out. He walked around the van and stood at the base of the crate mountain. He peered up and smiled. It didn't matter if blood was dribbling into his mouth or that he wobbled as he looked up. It was all his. He now controlled Bridgetown. This stupid fucking city was finally all his.

Mac's laughter may have been heard by the few passing cars or even by the druggy neighborhood a few streets over, but it didn't matter. It didn't matter because laughter was now the second-best medicine. This took over the number one spot.

How do you fix a city's drug and murder problem? Sit down and Uncle Mac will give you a free demonstration. Now, who will be the first volunteer?

CHAPTER 11

Ant's phone had turned into a pollinating bumble bee.

When he received his work phone on the first day, they informed him that if he ever purposely shut it off or made any attempt to avoid calls from his superiors, it would result in immediate termination. The constant vibrations in his pocket were ratcheting up his anxiety with the thoughts of losing his job, but he was going to do his sergeants, captains, and lieutenants one better: he was going to face them in person.

The death of Chief Stewart rocked everyone. When Ant entered through the back entrance, he typically heard the hooting and hollering of officers chatting about a call they returned from or some personal life banter.

Today, though, something Ant never would have expected no matter the circumstances, silence. Not even a soft whisper. The front desk guy, who always had a *Sports Illustrated* magazine in hand, was staring out into the front lobby, his eyes boring into the plaques and awards lining the brown wood board walls. As he walked through booking, into the area of classrooms where officers completed training exercises, and up the stairs to the important offices, they all had the same look. Shock.

"Cap, I'm sorry I haven't answered the ph—" Captain Anderson held a palm to Ant. The hair from his knuckles curled to the lines of the bottom of his fingers. Ant hadn't noticed how hairy Anderson was until now, hair everywhere except for his distended head.

"Sit." Ant did.

"Look—" The palm again. Captain Anderson wasn't allowing Ant one word.

"I'm doing the talking. Okay?"

Ant nodded.

Anderson took in a large inhalation, held it for five long seconds, then released and began. "Chief Stewart's death came as a giant shock to everybody in this building. Absolutely unexpected. But what I just found out was more shocking, more revealing. When the news came through about Kevin, and by the way, I don't know how the news station found out before the police, but I suppose that's for another day." Anderson fidgeted with one of his many pyramid glass awards lined on the front of his desk and continued, "I was expecting to take the reins and perform my duties as next in line. I even began preparations to make improvements I felt Stewart was lacking. But that was when the mayor's office called. And they instructed me to get into contact with you since they were struggling to and begin the process for you, Anthony Rawlings, as Chief of Police."

"I can expl—"

"Shut the fuck up, Rawlings." Anderson's voice rose fifteen octaves, and his slamming fist shifted his accolades and nameplate. The door to his office was wide open, peeking out at the sergeant's and lieutenant's offices across the hall. They didn't come running or sound alerted in the least. This sounded like they had heard the news already and Captain Anderson's anger was to be expected.

"This should be a violation of department policy, but Stewart, the fucking bastard, set it up with Mayor Higgins two years ago. Said you signed a written agreement to take over when he retired or died. What the fuck, Rawlings?"

Ant felt himself slump in the poorly padded chair. He wanted to get away from this situation. He wanted to run away. Maybe start over in a different city at the bottom as a beat cop and stay there until he could retire. But he was here now and couldn't move if he tried. Frozen with fear and cowardice. When he accepted the transition two years back, he had a brief blip in his mind of Captain Anderson. He was supposed to take over, but Stewart never mentioned him. Now, Ant came to the realization he may have done that on purpose.

"Now is the time you speak," Anderson said.

"I guess I really don't know what I was thinking. It felt like a one-on-one thing between me and Chief Stew—"

"Former Chief Stewart."

Ant nodded. "It wasn't any disrespect toward you or anybody else."

"Then why does it feel that way? Fuck. A detective promoted to Chief. What a fucking time we live in."

Ant didn't know what to say. So, he said nothing. They stared at each other for minutes.

"So, what is your first order of business, Chief Rawlings?" Anderson said his name in a snotty tone a six-year-old would use when mocking a friend.

"I—well—"

"You don't know. You don't know because you are unaware what a chief even does. Am I right?"

Ant gave away his answer with his body language by staring at the green linoleum floor through his spread legs.

"That's what I thought. God, this department is fucked."

"Clean up the crime." Ant didn't even recognize the voice as his own.

"Oh, and how are you going to do that? Don't you think that is what every chief in every city across the fucking planet is trying to do?"

"Yes, but I have a plan. And it will work." Ant was lying from his lungs and through his lips, but something he would do would be to get out to the problematic neighborhoods and communicate with the troubled youth who were causing the majority of issues. Get them off the streets and into round-the-clock programs. As silly as it sounded, Ant believed boredom was the main root cause of those kids acting out. If you got them to school, then to an after-school program, and kept them places other than the streets, crime would be improved. Also, giving those kids a parent who didn't have one. Discipline would keep them on the straight and narrow and on to great things. It wouldn't only improve crime but boost morale for those in poverty who felt like they were at the bottom of the shit stick.

"Okay, and what's that?" Anderson asked.

"You'll see."

Ant exited Anderson's office and cut right toward the end of the hall. He entered what was Chief Stewart's office and closed the door behind him. Kevin had plaques on the wall commending him for his great work for the city of Bridgetown. On his desk was a picture of his two boys. Madeline was conspicuously missing. He knew they were separated, but he could have made it look like they were on good terms.

It felt odd to sit in his beige wingback chair, the same chair he sat in to ask Ant to move to Chief after he was gone. "You won't regret this decision. Trust me. It's a rewarding job but a tough job. Everybody is down your throat all the time. When it's not the mayor's office, it's the media. And with social media, the platform for everybody to give their unsubstantiated opinions, is the worst of all. Because apparently opinions matter more than facts these days. But I digress," Stewart had said, wandering his large office. Ant still remembered his gruff smoker's voice and perfectly styled black hair swooped to his right side. His comically square jaw as he spoke. It was something Ant hadn't thought about since then, but it came rushing back as soon as he saw the news report.

"But I want you to do something for me," Stewart had continued. "Once I'm gone"—and gone was a more powerful word now—"I want you to lock yourself in this office, sit at my desk, and underneath will be a strip of black tape. Remove the tape and there will be a key. There aren't many locks in here, so you'll figure out where it goes to. Open it and remove the paperwork inside. It's something I've been working on for a while. I like you, Ant. I truly mean that. And I trust you more than anybody else in this department. That's why I made you this offer. Now, when you read this, you will be shocked and shaken, but you need to understand the bigger picture. Can you do that?" Ant had nodded even though he was skeptical of what he was getting himself into.

Ant patted his hand on the underside of the desk until he found the black tape. He peeled it and removed the key from the sticky. He attempted the three drawers on the right side of the wood desk. Nothing. He tried the filing cabinets. Too big for the keyholes.

He strolled the office, his phone still vibrating—with what must have been hundreds of missed calls—searching every nook and cranny for a keyhole. He even pulled some books from the shelving for maybe a trapdoor. With the phone calls momentarily ceased, he took it out of his pocket, and the screen was filled with missed call notifications, text messages, and a useless notification from Facebook. A bunch from his wife. A few random numbers. But one stood out from the rest. Thirty-five missed calls in the past couple hours. On cue, that number was calling again. He answered this time.

"Hello?"

"Finally. You gotta answer when I call now."

"I don't even know who this is."

"Your new boss."

"Oh, Mr. Higgins. I'm so—"

"Yeah, yeah. Enough with the pleasantries. Let's get down to it. We gotta talk. So come down to City Hall right now and I'll get you all squared away with the technicalities of the job. Whaddya say?"

"Yeah, sure. I'll be there in ten."

"Perfect. Oh. And Chief Stewart was so damn proud to run Bridgetown, just so you know. He loved that job and everyone inside of this piece of shit city. He showed off that damn plaque to anyone who would listen. Anyway, see you then."

The call went dead, and the search would need to continue later. Ant opened the door to leave when the gold framed plaque caught his eye. He approached it and read it over. An award for Kevin Stewart's bravery and twenty-five years of service. He placed a hand on either side and removed it from the wall. Behind it was a safe. A keyhole and a handle. He stuck the key in. Perfect fit. He turned it and pulled it open. A stack of papers lay neatly in a yellow folder. Ant removed it and sat back at the desk.

He pulled the flap of the folder open. In big, bold letters, the heading read: *OPERATION SAVE BRIDGETOWN.* Ant skimmed through the pages and grew increasingly angry and upset with each word. This wasn't Operation Save Bridgetown; this was Operation Destroy Bridgetown.

He untucked his polo shirt he wore on workdays, stuffed the papers into his rear waistband, and tucked his shirt in over it. He adjusted his service firearm and detective badge, though he realized he may not need those things any longer, and left for City Hall. Once there, he would confront Mayor Higgins with his findings. Because he knew Higgins was the true mastermind behind the destruction, which, according to the papers, was coming soon.

CHAPTER 12

"Higgins. Operation Save Bridgetown is a go," Mac said into his phone while shaking the cobwebs of the self-inflicted motor vehicle accident from his head.

"Not yet. Wait a few more hours. We can't have zombies roaming around until after midnight."

"Well, I've already gone too far, so it's a go."

"I have our new chief coming over for a visit. After I speak with him, we can get started. Please don't do anything stupid."

"Mr. Mayor, stupid is my middle name," Mac said and pressed the end call button. Higgins made an immediate call back, but Mac had made up his mind.

Mac approached the crates and kicked the top off the first one he came upon. He had forgotten everything the now-dead Stewart had explained to him about the safety measures. The "don't do this," "don't do that" of the whole thing. But who cared? His heart might as well be on the cement floor in front of him. He was a kid standing in line for the ride of the century. Excited to get on and feel the rush of wind and breathlessness. Anxious to get off and be a goddam hero.

A syringe sat on a soft pillow beside an open crate. He wasn't even close to a medical professional, but he had watched them on TV. He examined the green liquid floating in the cylinder and gently pressed the plunger. The needle leaked a dribble onto the floor, and the cement floor sizzled, turning the green liquid to a solid. It reminded him of the silly putty his drugged-up mom supplied for his entertainment as a kid. Then like a hit to the back of the head, he was infested with the voice of Stewart. "Don't touch the liquid unless you wanna turn into one of those things." Mac patted his white button-down (he had forgone the suit jacket, too formal for the occasion) and found no traces of the goo.

The needle was long, and the cylinder was girthy, but he was able to temporarily hide the syringe from the view of suspecting passerby as he chose one of them for his experiment. *A guinea pig if you will.*

Mac exited the side door after unlocking the five industrial latches, keeping the public and squatters from his equipment. Although they were obsolete since Mac's destruction of the garage door. He wandered casually down the alleyway between the old factory and a rusted fence covered in climbing vines, blocking any potential view from the residents of the disastrous homes that in fact stored humans. Most of which were communes for the heroin addicts.

Few people walked by the eyesore of a building. You had your usual cast of homeless bums, doped-up karate experts, and people who made a wrong turn away from the nice side of town. He preferred the bums. Long gone from their families and the ones who few people knew were the targets when causing devastation.

After fifteen minutes of waiting and quiet, a rise of voices rose from his left. It initially sounded like a large group. He wanted to avoid any such unit of humans. One was the go-to; two he could probably handle. Lucky for them, it was a couple. He wasn't positive they were dating, but it was a man and woman. The man was having a great conversation, only the context was lost in the gabbles. The woman responded with some natter of her own, but the infection of the drugs they surely injected were the root cause.

Mac slid back into the shadows in the mouth of the alley as they approached.

"Psst." They were so lost inside themselves that they didn't hear Mac's snake sounds.

"Psst," he tried again to no avail. They were beyond him, heading for the deserted Cannon Street cross.

"Hey," Mac said in his most baritone voice that sounded nothing like his own.

That got their attention. They returned to the alley and peered down, squinting through the natural darkness. "Come closer. I got some H if y'all are interested."

They both knew the drill. In unison, they checked the street for the cops, even though Mac had the police in check, nor did they often patrol this area of the city. "Aint no po-po over here." As if that were permission, they approached Mac.

When they sauntered into the streetlight, Mac could make out the details of their faces. The man was Black and had the creepiest eyes he had ever seen. They were a light brown and glazed over. His pupils were the size of walnuts, but he appeared alert despite his mumbled speech. His thick beard was black with white strands poking out, matching the mop on his head. Bugs skittered through his facial hair. When he spoke, his teeth looked like he had just finished a job as a carnival game. "How mush?" the man said, asking for a price.

Mac remained quiet as the woman came in behind the old man. She was a scary thin White woman with blonde hair, most of which had fallen out, and clothes that draped on her like she was a scarecrow.

"Twenty," Mac said. He had not the slightest clue of the asking price in this hood. He was strictly a weed and coke guy. Watching his parents zombie out on heroin was enough to keep himself off the stuff.

"No," the man simply said, and they began to walk off together.

"Okay, five."

The man looked back, incredulous. "Five? For how mush H?"

Mac was growing impatient with the man. *If it's five bucks, who cares.* "A whole needle full."

"Let's go, Mart, this guy don't got nothin' for us," the woman's deep voice startled Mac for a moment.

His blood was boiling. As the couple turned, Mac ran up behind the guy and stuck the needle into the side of his neck. He let out a terrifying yell as the woman turned and put on a face of terror. Mac pushed the plunger all the way down and removed it.

"Help. Somebody help."

Mac panicked.

The crook of his arm snuggled nicely around the woman's scrawny neck. He used the same bloody needle to jab her in the center of the chest. He was positive she was used to sharing dirty needles. Probably with her boyfriend who lay at Mac's feet. There was no juice left for her, but after the sixth stab, it didn't matter much. Her body thumped to the ground, and Mac dragged her limp body into the dark of the alley.

The Black man was having a convulsion session, and a green pus leaked from his neck wound as well as his mouth. After standing there watching like a bystander witnessing a lion wrangler being chewed on by its own pet, Mac left him. He hiked Skinny Susie onto his shoulder like a bag of mulch and carried her to the rear of the building. He plopped her down and returned to the man, who had stopped moving. The woman's blood soaked his white shirt to a black sticky mess and a trail that led any curious bystander to the new house of horrors.

He made a cautious approach. He looked at his chest, and it wasn't going through its normal up-and-down motions. Had he just killed the man? Did he give him too much juice? Did he jab him in the wrong place? He didn't know. What he did know was it looked like the serum didn't work. All that work. All that time. For nothing.

Fuck.

CHAPTER 13

Ant had watched Mayor Higgins many times through his phone's screen or on his home television, but this was the first time he was feet away from his pale, marked-up flesh from what looked to be years of fighting with acne. He attempted to cover it with a brown thinning beard that made him look like an evil movie villain from an 80's action flick. And that was what Ant thought of him.

He placed the paperwork found behind the plaque in deceased Chief Stewart's office on the desk that split the two men.

"Are you going to explain yourself?" Ant asked.

Higgins kept his pointer finger to his lips as though he were shushing Ant, but his perplexed face showed he was thinking. He leaned back as his chair screamed for oil. "Yes. But first you'll need to know that this is far from the original plan."

Ant wasn't interested in the original plan. He needed the plan to be cancelled.

"Chief Stewart, as I'm sure you're aware now, had a difficult job. And as I'm aware, this godforsaken city is a fucking mess. A six-year-old was killed by a stray bullet last night. A fucking six-year-old." Higgins was whisper-screaming. "There are bad people living here."

"And Chief Stewart's wife and young son along with their young babysitter were brutally murdered in a ritualistic way. There are bad people living here and everywhere."

"Everyone knows that to be true. But no other place in this country is like Bridgetown. There has not been a passing week in the past three years without a murder. Place that into your thick skull and ping it around in there for a bit. Three fucking years."

The cell phone next to Higgins buzzed on the desk. He peered at it and cancelled the call with a press of the side button.

"You don't need to lecture me about the statistics of this city. I was born and raised here. I have solved every homicide that has landed on my desk for the past fifteen years. And damn proud of it," Ant said with veracity in his voice.

"So, you should be first in line to want to go through with this." Higgins tapped the white pages with his three middle fingers.

"My line of work is to keep every soul in this city safe, not the purposeful killing of innocent lives to improve the fucking economy." It was rare for Ant to curse, but he felt he needed to match Higgins's demeanor.

"This has little to do with money and more to do with safety. Once those people are removed, we can improve the city. Crime would go—"

"Those people?"

"Fuck you, Anthony."

It was weird to hear his full legal name come out of his mouth, but there wasn't time for those thoughts. "No, I know what you're doing and—"

"And it will work."

Ant couldn't deny that fact. On his drive from the department to the City Hall—albeit a short one—he thought over the aftermath if (hypothetically) the plan succeeded. With the correct funding and development, it *would* improve the city. But Ant felt with the same time and money, he had a plan to reach the same goal by also keeping residents housed and reducing crime and, not to mention, alive.

Higgins cancelled his buzzing phone again and continued. "Listen." He brought his voice down to his lowest register like he was convincing an old friend. A political tactic Ant wasn't falling victim to. "Chief Stewart was really the brains behind this operation. When I saw the news, I wanted to cancel the whole thing."

"Great. Let's do that."

"I wish I could. There are already too many moving pieces to this chess game. My job was to supply the drug, explain how it worked, and he would handle the rest."

"So just knock the pieces off the board and call for a game-over."

The phone buzzed again.

"You're not understanding. It's already in motion. The plan."

Higgins answered the phone this time. "Can't talk. Okay. Yeah. Okay. We'll be there in a few." He hung the phone up and stared at Ant.

"We?"

"Like I said, the first piece has been set in stone. There's no going back now."

"And you think I'm just gonna go along with your evil plan, because…"

"Because I've made a deal with the devil, and that devil is holding the key to this city's destruction."

"I can take you in right now based solely on this plan you've devised here. You know that, don't you?"

Higgins scratched his uneven beard, making a sandpapery sound, and said, "From the second I agreed to this, I could have been taken in. But what you're really not doing is looking at the bigger picture here. If you really wanna save the people of Bridgetown like you say you do, then you need to come with me."

The last thing Ant wanted to do was go with this monster. Ant trusted the criminal justice system. Innocent until proven guilty in a court of law. He trusted the jailing system. Sitting in a five-by-five cell for a majority of the day made anyone crave the freedom they once had. And Ant knew the moment he walked out that door with this political monster, he knew he would be crossing over that line he had been so afraid of since he was a child: a criminal.

"No. I can't do that. I won't arrest you, and I won't even spread the word of what you're doing here, but I will not be involved in your criminal activity."

Higgins shrugged. "Suit yourself. But you will be involved one way or another. In a matter of hours, you will see a shift in the city. Not one for the better at first. But this plan is going into action, and if you want those deaths on your conscience, then by all means, leave."

When Ant was small, and he would search the aisles of Blockbuster, his mother would allow one movie and one movie only. He would stand there with two VHS boxes, one in each hand. His mother would hover over him and say, "Looks like you're in a pickle, honey."

And that was what Ant found himself in at this moment. A pickle.

"I have a plan for your plan."

"Let me guess. You are going to post your officers outside every halfway house and poor neighborhood to guard against this. Only problem is, these monsters, these things being released. You or anybody else will not stand a chance against them."

"We have an arsenal. I'm not afraid."

Higgins surprised Ant by laughing. A great big laugh that went on for ten seconds. "Oh, if only you knew what they have. If only."

"Then tell me," Ant prompted.

Higgins leaned forward, his chair screaming once more. "We have your police force under our wing. They're already on our side. Every last one of them."

"That's not true."

"Think about it, Anthony. We worked with the chief, and the chief makes orders. And we have the great equalizer. Cash money."

"I don't believe you. I know my guys, and I don't believe they would agree to this."

"What if I told you they had no choice? What if I told you I am above the law? This city is as corrupt as the United States government. All the way up the ladder rungs."

"Then why am I only finding out about this? I was part of this department for twenty-plus years."

"Because we needed a scapegoat. Somebody to blame. Somebody to take the heat."

"Why me?"

"C'mon, Anthony. You know very well why. It was an obvious choice."

Ant did know why. The thing that made people cross the street when he was walking toward a young family. The thing that made people view him differently because of historical events. The thing Ant never really thought of growing up. The thing Ant ignored through the taunts and name-calling. The thing that automatically made him a scapegoat to the world the second he entered.

The color of his skin.

CHAPTER 14

Mac made two phone calls since he arrived at the old factory. And that was after he had a trial run of his new drug that went very wrong. His first call was home. Natalie picked up on the first ring (good girl), and he instructed her to walk down the twisted drive, then gave directions to where he was. He reiterated to make sure nobody spotted her. But she was good. Mac had trained her right. Sadie was better at keeping a low profile, but she had abandoned him. He had something lined up for Sadie, but for now, this was much more important.

Higgins, his second call, was more difficult to get in touch with. Mac needed to call him four times before he finally answered. He knew he was meeting with that cop prick who thought he knew Mac's life story, but he was doing his routine bullshit cop act. When Higgins answered, Mac went on about how he ran into an issue with his test and how his drug didn't work and how angry he was about it. Higgins just gave routine, "sure," "uh-huh," and "yeah" responses. But he informed Mac "we" would be there soon. Why would he drag the cop into this?

In addition to the wide-open space of what used to be filled with men on assembly lines putting rifles together, there was a catwalk surrounding all four sides of the building. Up on the catwalk were offices where Mac imagined the supervisors sat handling logistics and work management. That was a job Mac always longed for, but when he found out those supervisor jobs would always have somebody above him, bossing him around, Mac took a different approach. Mac was his own boss now, and nobody told him how to act or what time to wake up in the morning.

This old factory looked to be about thirty floors high, but each level was narrow in space. The main floor was where the assembly of the weapons would take place, then the floors above were the office spaces. Mac looked up at the square design and was dizzied by the rafters at the top.

He made his plan and leaped over the rubble of twisted metal and broken wood boards of what used to be the flooring and made it to a treacherous staircase. The railing was contorted and hanging off to one side. This place existed prior to elevators being a requirement, so the steps were his way up. The cement that had presumably set over a hundred years ago was broken, and even an entire step was missing. But Mac still made the climb. One foot in front of—

The third step from the bottom shifted under his feet and he made a windmill with his arms as he tried to keep his balance.

He failed.

The metal railing wasn't broken enough from being cemented to the steps so that he was able to put his entire weight into it. And thank God for giving him the strength and mental power to commit to his morning push-up routine. For a moment he was dangling over a drop of about seven feet. A fall that wouldn't kill him but could possibly incapacitate him. And for Higgins to find him unable to get off the ground would crack his ego immensely.

He righted himself, hopped over the missing stair, and made it to the top platform, which was surprisingly intact. He searched the offices from long ago until he found what he was looking for. A rolling desk chair was tucked into a desk like somebody had just left work earlier in the day and would return tomorrow. Since this factory had been closed for fifty years, he didn't see that being the case.

Mac forwent niceties with the chair. He lifted and launched it off the catwalk, and it landed on the hard ground below. Maneuvering it down the death stairs would be a hassle. Now it was down where he needed it to be, and lucky for him, it remained a functioning tool.

After a leap, hop, and skip to the ground floor (an elevator would have been nice), he righted the chair and rolled it near what used to be the garage bay door before Mac rammed his van through. She remained idling on the far side of the room. He didn't want to shut her off for fear of never getting her started again.

The dead (maybe?) body of the drugged Black man was heavier and a real chore to pull up the alleyway and to the rear of the building. Luckily, the forestry in the back divided by a fifteen-foot-high fence blocked any view a druggie resident or potential wandering soul would have spotted of him dragging a couple of human bodies. He had dragged the woman inside already, and she lay just inside, out of view. Although the trail of blood from the front to the back was a dead giveaway that something was up. He had been doing this killing thing for a while, but this one hadn't been formulaically plotted and executed. It was too quick and too messy.

Mac propped the man into the chair; he fell off, and the wheelie chair went flying. Mac nearly chuckled at the rocket style the chair shot off in, but he held it together. He had a job to do. He stuck the back of the chair against the far wall opposite the stack of crates and was able to twist the dead weight into the red chair. It wasn't until now that Mac noticed a javelin piece of bone protruded from what used to be the man's functioning elbow. It must've collapsed under itself when Mac couldn't handle the weight of the body.

"Fuck, that can't be good," Mac muttered to himself as he thought he saw the man's finger twitch.

After settling the man on the chair to where he wouldn't fall, he ran to his van and retrieved some tape. *Always keep tape in your car. You never know when you'll need it.*

He stuck one end of the tape to the chair and spun it. After the man was properly secured and partially mummified, he ripped the tape and returned it to the van.

"Holy shit."

Mac jumped at the voice. He had a flash of being caught, placed in handcuffs, and locked up for the remainder of his life.

But it was only Higgins.

"You scared the bejeezus out of me," Mac said.

"Bejeezus? What are you, ten years old?"

"I have a bit of a situation."

"I would say so. You've got a blood trail leading to a dead body, and you have the last mummy taped to a fucking office chair. Is this how you handle things when left to your own devices?"

Mac felt ashamed because ol' Mayor Higgins was correct. He always failed when he was on his own. And all he had right now was Higgins, and Natalie. A lonely life for the most successful man in this city.

"Either way, you need to get this mess cleaned up," Higgins said.

"Aren't we getting ready to make a mess? Isn't that what all this is about?"

"Yes, but if this is traced back to the original source of the act, you'll be the one they'll be after."

"Who? Who will be after me? I am above all."

Higgins let out a hearty laugh. "You really believe that?"

"You told me that. When you called me to get involved with Stewart, you said this would go off without a hitch. You said I would get off scot-free. Those were your words."

All the joy he once had drained from Higgins's face. "I told you that because it sounds good. Sure, we have the backing of the Bridgetown Police Department, but the surrounding towns, states, the feds. They'll all be here once word goes out from the media, or worse, social media. The pics of the Madeline slaying can only hold for so long as a distraction, since it didn't cause the chaos we needed. There's always somebody watching. What did they say in that old book? Big brother or something?"

"Then why are we risking our lives for this city?"

Higgins looked at him like he had just taken a jab at his mother. "Tell me who lives up on that hill in that big house? Who?"

Mac wasn't positive if that was a rhetorical question or not but answered anyway. "Me."

"Exactly. And you think you live up there because it was just handed to you? No. It's because of money. The entire city can be like that. You're comfortable up there, are you not? Of course you are. And being Mayor, I can tell you if the trend continues the way it is, you are not going to be living up there much longer. No matter how much cash you have in your bank." Higgins was heated. "This city is headed for disaster, and I am planning on saving it. Now are you with me or not?"

"Am I interrupting something?" a tinny voice came from the outside. They both turned, and Higgins looked seconds away from an aneurism.

"No, baby. Just take the van back home, park it in the garage. All the way on the left," Mac said.

Natalie creaked the busted door closed and backed the van out of the factory hall. The busted car was a giant waving red flag, but he suspected the five-mile drive shouldn't be an issue.

"Girlfriend?" Higgins asked, back to an inside voice.

"Something like that. And to answer your question, yes, I'm in. Always have been."

"Good. We're gonna be heroes. You know that, right?" Higgins said.

Mac nodded. His body warmed at hearing the word "hero."

"But the thing isn't working like Stewart said it would."

Mac watched the blood drain from Higgins's face when he saw the dangling arm for the first time. Mac's body did the same when the presumed dead man's body twitched and pulled against the poor tape job. The moonlight was all they had now that the single headlight from the van was gone, and until the morning sun, he wouldn't see the true nature of the damage he caused.

"Fuck, Mac."

"What? I'm lost. Why are you freaking?"

"I'm freaking because injecting the serum doesn't activate it. A broken bone does. This shitty tape is not gonna hold. Help me wheel him out to my car," Higgins said.

Before Mac could reply, the previously unconscious man's full unbroken arm twitched, and he became conscious. "Where am I? What is happ—"

The heroin man's face contorted. His mandible jaw looked to be unhinging from its top compatriot. His eyes rolled into his skull, leaving white scleras. The scream that released from his lungs sent Mac through a small wave of anxiety. He had turned into a madman in a matter of seconds. "Plz. Wht is hap—"

"Uh, Higgins. I think he's—"

"Yeah, yeah. Help me lift him."

Higgins and Mac grabbed each side and hoisted the man, chair, and all into the rear of Higgins's Mercedes SUV and slammed the door. The gnawing, grumbling noises made their way through the closed car door.

"What now?" Mac asked.

"Now we begin the blackout."

"The blackout?"

Higgins grinned again. This time it wasn't saying "I have political power." It was saying "I have the power of death and I'm not afraid to use it."

CHAPTER 15

2018

It was midnight, and Kevin was out late again. He was Chief of the Bridgetown Police, and she thought when the promotion came with normal business hours, it would mean more time at home with their children, but he was away more. She had an inkling tapping at the back of her skull that it wasn't work related. But he would insist it was beers at the cop bar after their shift, and it would go late into the night. And often early into the morning. However, during the many police functions throughout the years, she had nonchalantly mentioned to the officers she knew he hung around with how they kept Kevin out late so many nights. Madeline could see the obvious fear in their eyes and sweat forming at the pores. They were the police, so they were good at hiding that stuff. But Madeline could read people.

Just as she did every night he was out, she took up the parenting role for both of them. She bathed the children, although Brandon was now old enough to do that himself. It was more so he told his mommy to leave him alone while he showered. She had a sting of tears on that day. You never wanted your babies to grow up. You wanted to hold them and love them forever. But she could picture Brandon hoisting his bags into his car and driving off to college many, many miles away. The thought made her sad, even though Leo would be by her side. She still felt she had an impact on their lives by placing food on the table every day. She wasn't the breadwinner yet, as her movie *Love Audition* was still in post-production and she was in talks to star in a new movie to begin filming in 2020.

One of the few positives about Kevin was that he fully supported her in her pursuit of becoming a star in Hollywood. It was on their first date where she ranted and raved about acting. She droned on about her fifteen stage plays—all of which were small local performances—and how acting in front of a camera was her ultimate dream. He sat there, his hand on his cheek, his elbow on the table at the fanciest restaurant in Bridgetown. She knew he wasn't listening to any of her incoherent rambling, but in the following years he bought her plane tickets to LA for auditions and was her biggest cheerleader. As her boys snoozed away upstairs, she sat on the couch watching classic movies, paying particular attention to the actors' expressions, nuances, and anything she could pick up from the best of the best.

Tonight's film study was *Casablanca*. She wasn't studying just the main stars but the full cast of characters. Although it was difficult to shy away from the chemistry between Humphrey Bogart and Ingrid Bergman. The follow-up movie she was in talks to star in was a romantic comedy with a serious twist. Though in her real life, Madeline felt a real connection with Kevin, nothing in real life was like it was in the movies. Acting was being a different person somebody else had written. In real life, you were just you.

Just as the climax of the movie approached when Rick Blaine and Ilsa Lund were giving their final monologues, Madeline was startled. If she had been watching a horror movie, she would have hit her head on the high ceiling.

The creaking stairs should have been a warning upon any descent, but Leo was standing at the arm of the couch. His stuffed bear he called Honey was tucked in his small armpit. She had placed him in bed, making sure to shove the covers under his small body, wrapping him like a burrito.

"Leo, honey. What's wrong?" Madeline asked. When either of her boys were up and out of bed, it meant something had happened. So, her first thought was: what did she need to clean up?

Leo, in his normal fashion, stood there not saying a word. He had "the whispers," as Madeline liked to call them.

"Come sit next to Mommy," Madeline said, patting the cushion next to her.

She paused the black and white flick, which she didn't think was playing too loud.

"Did the movie wake you, honey?" Madeline asked.

Leo shook his head in a slow, calculated manner.

At first, he sat like any ordinary human with his leg splayed out, hanging over the front of the seat. Then he jumped to his knees and shuffled over to Madeline. She knew he was preparing to tell her something.

Inches away with his hot, semi-stinky breath, he said, "Bear."

Madeline was sure he was referring to Honey, but when she asked, he shook his head.

"What about a bear, Leo?"

He cupped his hands around her ear and whispered, "Grill."

Now she was really confused. "You want to put your bear on the grill?"

Leo slowly shook his head again.

"Please just tell me what you mean, love."

Again, a whisper. "Daddy."

Daddy, bear, and grill. This was like playing *Blue's Clues*, trying to navigate through what he was saying.

Daddy, bear, and grill, she thought to herself again. Bear and grill. There was Tony's Bar & Grill downtown where they used to spend family Friday nights.

"You want to go to the restaurant downtown with Daddy?"

Leo shook his head. Now she was becoming frustrated. But as a parent, you had to hide that. Bottle it up and save it for a private time.

"Now," Leo whispered.

"You want to go now?" Madeline asked, trying to keep her voice even.

Leo shook his head.

"Daddy is there now?"

And a miraculous breakthrough.

Leo nodded.

"How do you know that?" Tony's wasn't a typical cop bar. In fact, it wasn't a cop bar at all.

Leo shrugged his kid shoulders.

It was always a prickling sensation she had that Kevin was cheating, and she knew it was crazy. Was she crazy? Her husband was gone all day, and Leo was home all day. There was no way—

But there was that small possibility her curiosity had to solve.

Madeline carried Leo up the stairs and knocked on Brandon's bedroom door. He groggily answered. "Watch your little brother for twenty minutes."

"Can I go back to sleep?" he whined.

"No, if you are sleeping, you can't watch him."

Brandon stomped his feet and angered a grunt. Leo shuffled into his room and shut the door. Leaving an eight-year-old in charge of a six-year-old was probably against the law, but she would be gone for a short period, and it wasn't the first time.

Madeline climbed into her car and drove seven minutes into downtown Bridgetown. The brick buildings housing law offices, shops, convenience stores, and the baseball stadium in the near distance were not on her radar. Tony's Bar & Grill was squished between a few other food establishments in the center of downtown. It was a Thursday night, so the typical medium-sized crowd shuffled to their seats and raised their food or beverage to their mouths.

She whipped into a parking lot adjacent to the restaurant with her tiny Ford Fiesta. At the back of the outdoor lot up against a chain-link fence was Kevin's obnoxious pick-up truck with his modified tires and lift kit. Why were men stupid enough to brag about their infidelities? And she—well, Leo, really—hit the bullseye. Her eyes were wider than her mouth. He had lied about where he was.

Strike one.

She slid into the spot next to his monster truck, turned off the engine, and sat there for a few minutes.

She was battling with herself like a tennis match. On one side of the net, she was his wife, somebody he agreed to be loyal and trustworthy with. But when she got the green ball to the other side, there was his own personal privacy. She didn't want to become the crazy wife bursting into a place, breaking up a romantic infidelity.

The winning decision happened to be by a long shot. Forty to love, Kevin. In tennis, love meant zero, and that was going to be how many lovers he had remaining.

Madeline felt awkward sneaking around the few remaining cars so she wouldn't be spotted through the large glass window. She was at the rear of somebody's busted Toyota 4Runner, and she could see the back of Kevin's head. It was undeniable with the largest bald spot in the New England area. When his egg head moved to the side, he saw a gorgeous blond woman opposite him.

Strike two.

Madeline hated admitting her beauty, but it was unmatched. Perfect golden bouncing curls on her shoulders, makeup that looked like it was applied by a professional, and cleavage deeper than an Olympic-sized swimming pool in a low-cut shirt. Then recognition struck Madeline in the face. She worked with Kevin. She had met her at one of the functions. She didn't know her name, but she was positive he was hooking up with a co-worker.

Madeline felt a sadness penetrate her. Sadness and pain. She had done so much for him. She raised the boys essentially on her own, while he was out working or apparently shacking up with those on the front lines with him.

When the whoosh of passing cars and movement of the few patrons inside the restaurant pulled her back to the reality of the situation, Madeline had eyeballs on her. Bright blue, blazing, bookended by spider leg eyelashes. She hadn't realized how far she had drifted from her car cover. Why were the police so vigilant?

Madeline froze as though they couldn't see her when she remained still. Blondie had gotten Kevin's attention, and the look on his face wasn't one of shock or surprise. He was angry.

"What are you doing here?" Kevin asked.

Victim blaming was strike three. *You're out.*

"What am I doing here?" Madeline said, aghast.

"Yes. You should be home taking care of those kids. You really left them alone? Are you stupid?" Madeline had gone into total shock. She wasn't processing his words anymore. She was only watching the jowls jiggle under his chin. He wasn't even fat. Who had jowls but looked flatter than a stop sign?

Madeline had played this very scenario in her head many times. She had thought she would cry and say things like "how could you do this to me?" or "I never want to see you again." And large gasping sobs would come between each word.

But none of those things happened.

She simply returned to her car and went back home.

On the whole ride home, she didn't think of Kevin once. The only thing on her mind was: how did Leo know his daddy was at that restaurant?

PART III: LEO

Leo tried not to think about the previous hours on the two-mile walk to the cave. He told himself it wasn't healthy for him. His mommy—

His mommy.

With every passing second, it sank into his small brain how he would never have his person any longer. He would no longer have that person who cooked him up some scrambled eggs and crispy bacon—just the way he liked it—each morning she was home. He wouldn't have that person who comforted him with an embrace before sending him into the school of ungrateful children. He would never have that person who tucked him into his heavy blanket so he could drift into sleep with ease. That person was cut with a knife across the throat to never walk, speak, or love again.

Sarah did those things for him when mommy was away. But she was a stand-in who he didn't feel a total connection with. And when mommy was rushing them out of the house, she told them not to look at the bottom of the stairs and Leo squeezed his eyes tight. But he had a feeling Sarah was dead.

He had another person.

His daddy.

His daddy wasn't his number one or his number two—even his older brother came before daddy—but he was a person in this dark, cold, lonely world he was thrust into.

When Leo thought of good times he had with his brother, he could count those times on his two hands. When it came to his dad, he could count the number of times he saw him.

His parents broke up when he was six years old. Leo didn't remember what happened before his sixth birthday. His sixth birthday: the day he was drawn to the man in the cave.

Now, at eight years old, he was stronger and wiser. And he had the power of a million men.

Kossuth Street was the final stretch of road before reaching the entrance to the park. He was lucky enough to be on this walk in the early morning when most of the Bridgetown community was sleeping except for the people who were working or had insomnia. The only occupation Leo could think of who had to be awake all the time were police, fire, and hospital workers. Although, his mommy told him that firefighters got to sleep all night anyway unless they got called to an emergency.

After the traumatic experience he went through, he couldn't have stayed to watch his mommy, his brother, and Sarah cut to pieces. That was what the angry lady kept saying. She said, "Imma cut all you to pieces and eat y'all one bone at a time." Leo didn't let that happen to him. He wished he could have helped his mommy and his brother in that car, but he just lost all his strength. For a lady, especially a crazy, angry lady, she was really strong.

At the end of Kossuth and past the row of boring homes with boring trees in the front lawns that did nothing but make his eyes itch during the spring was the wrought iron sign welcoming him to Veterans Park. He was tired. He was only drifting to sleep when his momma got home from her trip and the crazy lady came inside their home. The whispers in his head didn't stop until he went to his happy place. Leo's happy place was thinking about his brain games.

Little Leo's brain was made up of puzzles. Every day was a new game. Getting up in the morning and avoiding the cracks in the hardwood floor, then the grooves in the kitchen tiles, then the eroding earth cracks, then the space between the linoleum tiles in the school hallway. If you stepped on a crack, you broke your momma's back. But as he walked across down the long drive of the park, he was looking for cracks to step on. She didn't need to worry about breaking her back now.

As Leo approached ever closer to the grassy area leading to the edge of trees, the brain games had ended, and the whispers in his head returned.

"It's open twenty-four hours. You can get me what I asked for right now!"

"Yes, baby, deeper, deeper."

"How long have you been married?"

Leo had been dealing with that for years, and he was at his last straw. He was in Veterans Park to release the voices from his head and back to their owners. He was there to ask the man in the cave to release him from this nightmare and bring his family back together.

A sting of fear and anxiety crept into Leo's stomach as he grew closer to the mouth of the cave. He had only been at this very spot once before, and this time, his fear of the man inside grew exponentially. The power the man held was beyond any person's realm of reasoning.

"Hello?" Leo's greeting.

"Enter, Leonardo. Let us go back into the depths."

"No. I don't wanna go there again."

"It's not a choice, young boy. Who will you run to now? Who will you go to for food and comfort? Who, Leonardo, who?" The gruff of the man's voice reminded Leo of an elderly talking owl.

"How do you know what—"

"I know all. I see all. And you know this very well, boy. Now come with me and I will show you the way. I will lead you to the better."

Leo had been inside the depths of the cave one time—on his first visit—and he never wanted to return. But what choice did he have?

"I will go to my dad. I don't know where he lives. My mom never told me. But I can find it. He's Chief of Police. He'll know what to do," Leo said and turned to leave.

"Oh, Leonardo. You poor boy. You don't know." The man's voice shrank to that of a boy Leo's age.

"What?" Leo paused but didn't turn back.

"Your papa is—well he's—"

"No. No, he's not dead."

"I'm afraid he is."

"You're lying. Stop lying to me. You have lied about everything."

"Have I, little Leo?"

No. The man in the cave was the most honest person Leo had ever come in contact with. Even his mom would lie to him about certain things. He just didn't want to interact with the man any longer.

"I'm on-only here t-t-to—" Leo couldn't hold back the sadness creeping into his Adam's apple as it quivered. "You need to fix everything. Make my family okay again. Bring them back. I know you can. You said you can."

"I don't know. Only mere seconds ago, I was blatantly called a liar by an eight-year-old boy."

"You're not, okay. Are you happy?"

"Well, you know the drill. Step into my office, little Leonardo, and I will see what I can do."

Leo was swallowed by the darkness of the cave for the second time, and in the back of his mind, he had a niggling thought that it would be his last.

CHAPTER 17

This visit to the man in the cave differed from the first one for little Leo. He was older now and had more of an understanding of the world. The first time sneaking out of his house, wandering the streets of Bridgetown and skirting the edges of the dangerous east side was a risk he hadn't feared back then. Now, he knew what death was, he knew what bad people looked like; the event hours ago had changed his perspective on how he would live the remainder of his life.

"Welcome back," the floating voice said, drifting to Leo. He had an urge to yell as loud as his voice would allow so he could hear himself in surround sound, but he wasn't ready to expose himself yet.

"Tell me, little Leo, how has my spell been working out for you? No, don't answer, because I know. It helped save your life, didn't it?" There was no face any longer. Glancing back at the mouth of the cave and the corners of Veterans Park's green lawn and a wink of the early morning light peeking in off the sound didn't help with seeing the man in the darkness.

Then a laugh caused a shiver in Leo. A dismantled, choking chitter. Like the man in the cave wasn't able to breathe but needed to let out one more ounce of joy. "Oh, yours was a good one. I hope for my spells to be used for good, but sometimes…well, sometimes free will gets in the way. But I know you are a good kid. You will…already have used it for good."

Hours passed since Leo was sitting in his mommy's car with the smelly, dirty lady holding a knife at his throat. It was the last thing he wanted to remember. On his walk to the park, he would point out every little sign, car, or person to himself as a distraction. Think of anything else but that. A *Jake's mechanic shop* sign hanging outside of an old garage. Twenty-four (he counted) vehicles parked in their respective spots probably waiting for their turn to be fixed so their drivers could get to their destinations. The Galaxy Diner where a lady in a blue outfit was placing silverware and placemats on a table. The woman stopped and saw Leo, he was sure of it. Her eyes were brown, the same as her hair, then she returned to her job, and he continued down Main Street.

It wasn't a far walk for a grownup, but for a small legged human like Leo, it took him almost an hour to get to the park. He was tired and hungry, but he had a question for the man in the cave.

"Why did it work?" Leo said in his softest tone.

"Sorry, I couldn't hear. Speak up."

"Why did it work?" Leo was feeling as though he would never be able to move his octaves above a whisper again.

"It worked because the spell worked. When I died all those—
"

"You're dead?"

"Yes, little Leo. You think I'm all mystical while being alive. There's no such thing as that."

Leo nodded as though that explained everything.

"But as for an answer to your question. All the incantations I use cater to that person's individual personality. Do you understand?"

An uncomfortable feeling washed over Leo, not for any particular reason, just that someone was watching him. He spun around, and a figure stood at the mouth of the cave. They weren't immediately outside but five or six steps away and facing the opposite direction.

Fuck, fuck, fuck.

He knew that word to be the worst of the bad ones, so that man might be a bad one. The figure turned and walked off and out of view.

"Are you listening?" the man in the cave asked.

A numb nod confirmed he was and whispered, "How is my pers-on-al-ty-ty?" Leo couldn't get the word out just right. Not in a childish gabber, but the shadow on the outside had rattled something on his insides.

"Kind, caring, compassionate," the voice said.

The lump Leo caught before and swallowed down had returned, and he was unable to pause its formation to tears. He tried his best to be those three things for his mommy, and even for his older brother, but he couldn't save them. He saved himself, and it wasn't fair.

"But," the man continued, "when those traits are broken, when you stand up for yourself, when you use your most powerful asset, your voice, you can defeat anyone."

CHAPTER 18

The voices Leo heard constantly chattering in his head had been happening as far back as he could remember. The first time was that night when he was six years old and was lying in bed, trying the counting sheep method to drift into slumber. Mommy taught him to picture white fluffy sheep with different-colored collars bounding over a white picket fence. The idea was distracting the sleeper so much from other thoughts keeping them awake that the counting would easily conk you into dreamland. "You won't even get to forty before you're asleep," Mommy had said that night.

But Leo was so enthralled by the sheep that it kept him up later than he typically did. He wasn't sure what came after one hundred, which caused him to stop counting and stare at the boring ceiling for another hour before—

"You're married," a woman's sultry voice stated.

It jolted Leo from his prone state of insomnia. He was sitting up, and to his right was a window that looked out over Keen Street. It was a quiet neighborhood living on a dead end, so there weren't many people entering and exiting unless they came out of the woods at the end, and that scared Leo more than anything. A forbidden forest of the unknown.

But as he surveyed the Millers' goofy purple two-story home across the way, he noticed the top-right light on. He was never inside Mr. Miller's home. Nobody went in, and he never came out since Mrs. Miller died a year before. Even if Mrs. Miller had said that statement, there was no possible way Leo would have heard it.

"We are in the process of a divorce." The man's voice sent a shiver of chills through Leo's body. It was undoubtedly his father's rough tone. Mommy informed Leo that Daddy had an important job keeping the bad people off the street and in a cell where they couldn't leave for twenty-three hours a day. Leo

thought that to be nice since he only left his room for school and sit-down family dinners.

"Family is important to me." The woman again.

The window crack Mommy left open to let the summer nighttime air in through the protective screen wasn't emanating any sound other than restless chirping crickets and a periodical car cruising down Main Street a couple streets over. He knew it wasn't super late, but late enough to be fully dark and way past when a six-year-old should be resting.

"It's more important to me. That's why I'm leaving my wife. She is destroying my two boys' lives by leaving them for long periods of time to pursue a useless career path," Daddy said.

When Leo had a thought come to him, he viewed it as a second voice inside his brain. A little person the size of a lightning bug using his pink, squishy brain as a couch and saying any thoughts out loud right into Leo's ear. But these weren't thoughts; these were conversations.

"That's what I mean. I don't want to interfere with your boys' lives," the woman said.

Scared, Leo threw the covers off himself and headed for his bedroom door. He stepped over the Legos he had strewn across the floor, squeezed Honey, his teddy bear, against his chest, and opened the door as silently as possible. Mommy was downstairs watching a movie on a too-loud volume, and he knew Brandon stayed up past his bedtime playing his video games on mute.

"You won't have to worry about that for much longer." The air-conditioning dropped thirty degrees, and the tee shirt and pajama pants were no longer sufficient warming devices. The callous phrase of his father's voice coming from inside stopped him just outside of Brandon's room.

"What do you mean by that?" the woman asked.

Stairs three, five, and seven from bottom to top were the creaky ones to avoid for a quiet descent to the ground floor. But as he got closer to the landing and front door, the old timey movie came more into focus and Mommy sipping wine out of her glass was in his sights.

"Oh, I just mean she'll get custody. You know how the court system treats fathers."

Leo wanted to play a game with his mommy. How long could he stand in her line of sight without her noticing? He started counting the sheep again. He wasn't trying to go to sleep. He was so awake, he wasn't sure if he would ever sleep again.

"I have seen many cases go both ways. It just depends, but I'm rooting for you," the woman said.

When his feet got tired of the spot, he adjusted them and didn't need to worry about getting past one hundred. He never accounted for the snap of the wood floor on the crest between the foyer and the living room. Mommy snapped her head, and he felt bad for startling her.

"Thank you. I love you. Since you moved here from Texas, how does this bear and grill compare?" Daddy said.

He knew what a bear was, and he knew what a grill was, but putting them together confused Leo. It was tough to describe to Mommy, but something clicked inside her—potentially her little lightning bug in her brain spoke to her—and left Leo and Brandon home alone. He knew when Brandon was left in charge, two things would happen: Brandon would tell Mommy he would watch Leo, and then as soon as she left, he would go back inside his room, shut the door, and continue his game. And once his older brother evaded his only responsibility, Leo would sit and ponder what all this meant.

Without a minute passing of Mommy leaving and Brandon in his room, Leo had no time to ponder when another voice popped into his head.

"Leo. Leonardo. Leeeeeeeooooooo."

He never liked anybody calling him by his full name, except for Mommy of course. And the new voice came out raspier and deeper than Daddy could ever make his. Only this voice had a jolly, sing-songy quality.

"Leonardo. Come by and visit the park. I've got a special gift for a special boy like you."

The only park Leo knew of was Veterans Park where he would have the time of his life rolling down the grassy hill. But he couldn't leave the house. What if Mommy came back and he was gone? She would send Daddy's work friends to search for him.

"I can do this allllll night, Leonardo. I know you're upset, and I have that release you need. That push you need."

Veterans Park was a short car ride but a long walk. And once he got there—being guided by the voice—he met with the man in the cave for the first time. And when Leo left a few minutes later, he felt different. He felt stronger, wiser, and braver. He was handed a power he was shown only a glimpse of before the man vanished with the dust of the cave. The glimpse was of a violent, ear-shattering siren and someone with the unpleasant full-force reception of that noise.

It wouldn't be until two years later when he would use it for the first time. But that regret of not using it sooner, of not saving his mommy and older brother, was haunting him as he exited the cave for the second time with tear-soaked and dirt-grimed cheeks. The memory of his slain family as fresh as the blood that stained the windshield of Mommy's car.

There were no more tears to fall. It was his turn to be brave. The face of the killer was just as fresh, and he would find a police officer and tell them exactly what the evil woman looked like.

When he was into the daylight of the morning, though, it was a different world than when he exited last. He could feel his rigid body stiffen further with the weight of the city pressing down on him. And all he could think was, *this has something to do with what I saw.*

PART IV: The Beginning

CHAPTER 19

A mother's love was like no other.

Any man, without reproductive organs, could never experience what pushing a real-life human being out of a barely expanding hole would ever feel like. The pain, the anguish, the exhausting nine months beforehand, none of it. And furthermore, holding your child to your chest, that first skin-to-skin contact and how the small hands grasped at any part of your skin like they knew as soon as they entered the world who they were meant to belong to.

Sherrie Stevenson only got to experience that feeling once, and it was enough. Instant love for the rest of her life. Her sweet Shonda would outlive her and go on to do great things. Shonda was only in the third grade, but she was the star of her class. During parent-teacher conferences, her teacher would praise Shonda's A's and B's in each respective subject. And she was the most well-behaved student Mrs. Kelly had seen in her twenty years of teaching experience.

Though that didn't mean her angel wasn't still a child.

"Ma, tomorrow's Friday," Shonda said, blocking the view of the television. Walter never wanted to be involved in the parental decision-making and was bobbing and weaving to see the next pitch from the Mets game.

"Exactly. It's still a school night, and you need sleep if you want to get through the day."

Shonda whined and stomped her feet. Ms. Kara, the elderly downstairs neighbor, must've heard the clomp as she fell into her nightly reading ritual.

"Shonda Stevenson, I know you did not stomp your feet at me. It sounds like you want a whoopin' and not come out of your room for the weekend," Sherrie said.

Her only daughter rolled her eyes and ran to her room, then slammed the door. Sherrie bored her eyes into Walter's left temple, willing a migraine to drum his mindless brain into caring about more than a useless baseball game.

"She is going to wish for sleep when she gets older," Sherrie said.

"Mhmm," Walter breathed out.

"Can you put in a little effort when I'm having a disagreement with our daughter?"

The game was between innings, and Sherrie finally received Walter's full attention. "You had it under control," he said and sipped his late-night coffee.

"No, I didn't. And you know that. You just didn't want to get involved like always."

This struck a chord in him, and that was what she was prodding at. "No, it was just a stupid argument, and there was no reason for me to say anything."

A sigh more abrasive than intended exited Sherrie, and Walter flipped his legs down and stood. "I'm gonna go talk to her right now, okay?"

Before she could say any more, Walter was down the hall and into Shonda's bedroom.

He was in there for ten minutes before emerging with a smile plastered on his face. Sherrie couldn't help but keep the grin off her own. "What?" she said in a *what-are-you-so-giddy-about* tone.

"She said she was glad to have such an understanding father." His chin was pointed to the ceiling, and shame crept onto Sherrie's burning cheeks.

"Understanding is just another word for kiss-ass," she said as the sides of her lips curled up.

Walter forwent his recliner and joined his love on the open love seat. "It also means she likes me better."

"It also means she's getting everything she asks for," she said with a playful slap to his bearded face.

"Isn't that what having a child is about? Giving them everything that you couldn't have?"

Tears slipped from the ducts of her eyes, and she muttered, "Asshole."

"Oh, Sherrie, I didn't mean it like that," he said, using his thumb to clear the streaks.

She collapsed into his comforting arms and knew he meant no harm. But he also knew that her past was fragile to her and to never use it as a weapon against her.

"It's okay. I'm getting tired anyhow. Tomorrow's another day."

Sherrie slapped a kiss on Walter's cheek and slipped into their bedroom. She would be here alone until the game ended and then some. The bottom bedside table drawer slid out to reveal old DVD cases, books from when Walter had an urge to read for a week, and miscellaneous papers that looked important but were out of sight, out of mind. Underneath all the junk was an 8x8 notebook she was sure Walter knew nothing about. Inside were lines of phrases, one underneath the next.

She saw a therapist on the side once a month behind her husband's back. Her therapist suggested an exercise to heal from her past was to write down what Sherrie feared the most. The daily exercise added up to almost an entire book full of sentences. They each had a similar context: Shonda dying, Walter leaving her, the housing complex kicking them out on the street. Today's statement was a bit different. Something she thought of each day but refused to write down. But today she needed it out of her mind.

Don't let Shonda make the same mistakes I did.

CHAPTER 20

"Whatdowedowhatdowedo?" Mac said, focusing on the back seat where the man he injected was pulling and trying to tug the duct tape restraints free from himself and the chair wedged across the rear seating in a silly manner. Mac held the man-monster down as much as he could while Mayor Higgins used the safety belts from both sides of the rear bench, crossed them over one another, creating a harness Mac feared wouldn't hold the entire car ride.

"Shut the fuck up," Higgins said, leering at Mac. "And sit the fuck down. This is your fault, so you shouldn't be the one freaking out right now." The phone never left the ear of Higgins as he scolded Mac.

"Who are you calling?" Mac said, lowering himself into the passenger seat, refusing to use his own safety belt in case the snarling monster in the back broke free from its hold.

"Pick up the phone. Fuck."

Higgins peeled out of the rear of the abandoned factory into the early morning of the abandoned east side of Bridgetown. Mac asked Higgins what the plan was next, but he wouldn't say; he repeatedly called the same number to no avail.

"Here." Higgins shoved the phone into Mac's hand. "The number at the top. Call until somebody picks up."

"What do I say when—"

"Nothing. When they answer, you hand me the phone. Fuck, Mac. You messed this up so badly. We had a plan, and you had go and—"

Higgins didn't finish his statement, and Mac knew his frustrations weren't allowing it.

It took ten more cycles of five rings until a groggy voice said, "Hello?"

"Yes, I—"

"Give me the phone now," Higgins said and yanked it from Mac's hand. "It's on." A pause. "Yes, now. Get your ass out of bed." Another pause. "Because some people don't know how to follow instructions." An evil mother glare at Mac. "Meet me on East Main and Tucker." A pause. "Yes, the Barnum's first." A beat. "Bye."

"What's the plan?"

And as though it were an answer to his question, "Wha are ya doin' dis to meh," a jumbled marble-mouthed mess came from the back. The mind clarity to ask a question shook Mac. Before Mac injected the serum into the man's neck, he was a druggie who could barely stand on his two feet. And those feet took him to and from his next hit. Had the serum given him a sobering effect before it travelled through his bloodstream and into the brain?

"The plan is," Higgins continued as though nobody was in a frantic struggle for their lives inches behind him, "to meet with an EMT friend who does favors for me. We will hand him off to the EMT friend, who will use steel reinforced straps to hold this one." A thumb to the rear. "And when they are good and ready will pull up flashing red lights, no sirens. Wheel our subject into the Barnum project and let him run wild on all their asses. Then the police will set up a two-mile wide perimeter of the project, so nobody leaves and nobody enters."

"And when someone inside is bit, do they—"

"Plez, I have a fam'ly," the one from the back said.

"I thought the chief and I explained all of this to you." Higgins's violent nature was settling, and the panic lifted from him as he felt back in control of the situation.

"Are we going to talk about how 'the chief' took the coward's way out and screwed us over?" Mac asked.

Higgins took a left onto East Main Street and pulled over to the side of the road, extinguishing the headlights. All the streetlamps were either broken or purposely turned off and kept the two—three—of them in full darkness.

"Kevin—"

"What?" Mac said. Their floating voices with glimpses of movement caused Mac to think the monster man could escape and attack either one of them.

"Fuck Kevin," Higgins said.

"I'm not really into necrophilia, Mr. Mayor."

A rattling breathing was all that could be heard in the small space.

"It's getting closer. We may run out of time," Higgins said.

"Time for what?"

"Our friend to change over. After thirty minutes, the serum takes full control after the activation through the broken bone."

"Then what does that mean for us?" Mac asked, adjusting his exhausted ass.

"It would mean the end for us."

Silence was the choice between the two in the front for the next several minutes. Varying grunts and coughs from the back startled Mac in the dark his eyes were struggling to adjust to.

"Did you know Kevin was—" Mac said.

"Seriously, Mac, we have bigger things in the back seat to worry about. Fucking drop it." His tone was that of Mac's mother when she was between heroin shots and couldn't be bothered with such menial tasks as taking him to school.

"Ahghhgghaghg," the thing garbled.

"I'm calling again," Higgins said but didn't need to as headlights flashed in the rearview.

An ambulance pulled in behind them; its sounds of metal clinking underneath and hissing to a stop may have woken a few of the residents that inhabited the area.

"Here for the transport. And how has our patient been behaving?" the EMT said. He wore a barely fitting white tee shirt stained with what looked to be drool and pajama pants dancing with *Hello Kitty*.

"Nice trousers," Higgins said.

"You said to get here fast. And the girl I'm fuckin' is obsessed with this freakin' cartoon cat. But she is so fucking hot. A freak, I tell ya. And her body—"

"Okay, can you just get the job done," Higgins said.

"If the money is flowing, you know I got you covered."

"It's already on its way. Now, how do you suppose we get the patient from the back of the car to the stretcher?" Higgins asked.

Mac was in awe of the preparedness of both of them. Like he was enjoying a tennis match between two calm competitors. Mesmerized, he bounced his head back and forth.

"Well, I figure there's three of us—I'm Rick, by the way," the EMT said, holding out his fat hand slimed with sweat. Mac nodded as his "how do ya do." "I'll get the gurney ready while you two get one side of the guy. Then we can strap 'em in and be good to go."

Rick was back with the squealing gurney, and Higgins was ready on the door handle. "On three. Ready." Higgins confirmed with Rick and Mac before pulling the door open. "Unlatch the belts and hold his ankles."

The two seat belts crossed back to their respective sides. A momentary whack of the metal buckle gave an open window for Mac to grasp the flailing legs. He took a couple blows to the chest, but nothing he couldn't handle as he yanked the guy out and watched as he landed on his spine. Upon impact, the rolling chair split from the wailing patient.

Due to the dark, Mac hadn't gotten a chance to get a good look since they left the factory. His skin was peeling into pepperoni-sized meteors on his face. It was as though someone dug two fingers into a part of the dermis and separated it with ease. Teeth were leaving their gums and collecting in the back of his throat. That may have been the cause for the garbled talk. He was far past talking; the fight was on.

"Here. Dump him on as best you can," Rick said as Higgins had the guy locked in his arms. Like they were holding two ends of a jump rope, they swung the guy freely and threw him onto the stretcher that fell to its side with the improper weight distribution. The thing tried to get up and run free, warning all the citizens of Barnum housing of what was to come.

A leap from Rick surprised Mac, as was Higgins. "Bring it over here," Rick said in the calmest tone. Mac wheeled the gurney over as Rick, who looked about as athletic as Tony Soprano, lifted the man-thing from the ground and slammed it face down. He secured the reinforced straps as Mac and Higgins did their best to hold it in place.

The thing looked on its way to breaking more bones than just its arm the way it was bucking and clawing, being loaded in the back of the ambulance.

"Y'all gonna stay for the show?" Rick asked.

Mac thought after all that work, he at the very least deserved to enjoy the spectacle.

"No. We have other business to take care of," Higgins said. "I assume you made contact with your police escort."

"He's on the way, but I'll get started," Rick said.

"Then the replenishment should go smoothly."

"I will find a good candidate, hold them until tomorrow when we do it all again."

"Good. Bring them to the factory. Mac and I will meet you there around the same time. Where it should go much smoother," Higgins said, shooting another eye dagger at Mac.

"Sir, yes, sir," Rick said, saluting them off as he climbed into the ambulance. He flicked the lights on and went on his way.

The longest sigh left Higgins as they settled back into the car. "What are those things we need to do now?" Mac asked.

After a few beats, Higgins said, "Clean up more of your fucking mess. And if you don't follow my orders again, you will be out of your McMansion and into the next housing project we hit. Do you understand?"

Mac nodded and rested his aching head as Higgins navigated them back to the factory. He was exhausted. He was hurting. But God dammit, he was making a change.

CHAPTER 21

Ms. Kara had lived in the George Washington Carver apartments for the past twenty years of her life. Sherrie, Walter, and Shonda had lived directly above her for eight of those years. However, it was two years ago when they met for the first time.

It was a cold winter evening, snow was piling up outside, Shonda was home from school on a snow day, and Sherrie called out of work because there was no way she was driving in that storm. Walter worked down the street and could walk. An hour before Walter arrived home, there was a knock at their door. Sherrie was careful of whom she opened the door for. Deliveries—food or otherwise—were dropped in the mail lockers in the lobby or on a table between the open outside door and the foyer where drivers would buzz the apartment number, and the resident would go down and retrieve their Chinese takeout without fear. So, in Sherrie's mind, there was no reason for a rap on her door.

"Who is it?" Sherrie grew up in the PT Barnum complex down the road, a place and time much worse than this. This was living in luxury to her, but she remained vigilant.

When she heard the weak, strained sounds of someone attempting to get words out, Sherrie knew it could be a setup but opened the door with the dangling chain still attached. In the hall was a wizened face plastered with agony. Gray hair haphazard like twines of yarn a child had finished fiddling with. Her short legs were held by a wood cane she leaned on for support.

The door was closed and opened full in a flash that surprised Sherrie herself. "What happened? What can I do to help?"

"My pill-pills fell, and I can't—"

The words flowed like mud, and she couldn't finish.

"Shonda. Get out here now," Sherrie said.

Thinking she was in trouble, Shonda creeped her way of her room until she spotted the old woman at the door teetering. "Oh shoot."

"Where do you live?" Sherrie asked the woman.

"Right bel—"

"Shonda, go downstairs right below us and get the pills on the ground. Bring as many as you can. Do it fast."

No other words were needed, and Shonda darted to the stairs. Sherrie hooked an arm with the woman's and guided her and eased her onto the love seat.

"How many do you take?" Sherrie felt she was hounding the old woman by hovering over her and took a couple steps back.

A withered, shaking hand showed a pointer and middle finger. Two.

"Okay. When—"

"Got 'em," Shonda said, dumping a handful of red and white pills into her mom's palms.

"Water," Sherrie demanded, and as if they'd done this a million times before, Shonda was ready with the cup. The old woman swallowed, and a few hours later, Walter was home, she joined them for dinner as though she were a long lost relative.

That was what Ms. Kara became as Sherrie and Shonda visited her each Thursday night, kept her up on her pills, did laundry, washed dishes, and kept her company she never got anymore. It was a mother-daughter tradition Sherrie never got to experience. And even though Shonda wasn't too keen on the idea. To her, it felt like charity work she was forced to perform. But, based on Sherrie Stevenson nee Stark's dark past, Shonda would grow to understand and appreciate their time spent together.

"Sher, it is past midnight. You are not goin' anywhere," Simon Stark said.

"I'm goin' to the corner store. For fuck's sake, Dad," Sherrie said with one hand on the exit from the apartment.

She was sure the entire complex could hear their arguments. People woken from their slumbers, people trying to concentrate on whatever mischievous activities occurred at night. The lashings happened when it was dark, and they happened often.

The police were called one night when they went back and forth for over an hour. The authorities detested stepping foot inside the Barnum complex. Sherrie referred to them as "the complex," but the outsiders called them "the projects." Like if you lived there, your life was an ongoing failure until death succumbed you. It wasn't like it was portrayed in movies and television. It was a group that lived together even though some were working three jobs and barely spent time in the bed they were fighting their life to keep.

"Everything alright here," the sour cream officer said in a condescending tone as though he had more important affairs to respond to. It was probably true since Bridgetown had their fair share of homicides.

"Fine," Simon said and slammed the door in the officer's face.

There wasn't another knock. The footfalls drifted away, and that argument was never brought up again.

This new one was Sherrie's way of meeting up with her new boyfriend, Matteo. They passed each other in the halls, but Sherrie, a freshman, and Matteo, a fifth-year senior, was no bueno in Dad's eyes.

"I don't care what you say. I'm gonna go anyway," Sherrie said.

"What would your mother say if she saw you with a boy four years older than you?"

"Doesn't matter. She left your ass. So, what do you care?" Sherrie's words were a shot to the heart of her father. Mom was around until Sherrie turned two years old. Simon wouldn't tell her what the final straw was, but it had to do with thinking she wasn't fit to be a mother. Sherrie blamed Simon for egging her on and forcing her out. He insisted it was far from the truth. He insisted he used every tactic possible to hold on to her. But her mind was made up.

"Ya know what? Do whatever the fuck you want," Simon said. The grimace on his face told Sherrie he was on the verge of tears and was doing all he could to hold them in. Her father stomped away and slammed his bedroom door.

With her own feelings in a pot of boiling water, she grabbed her leather jacket, pulled her tube top down so Matteo had a nice show, and pulled her tight jeans higher, showing off her best asset.

The corner store was a half-mile walk once she exited the lobby of the Barnum apartments. She wasn't afraid of the testosterone creatures that lurked just outside the doors and along Tucker Avenue where the walls in front of houses were littered with them. The "hey, sweetie" and "damn, sexy" never fazed her in the least. It made her feel good about herself, and the confidence exuded through to Matteo.

A messy mop of reddish blending with brown drooped out to make it look like he had a flying saucer sitting on his head. A long white tee hung down by his kneecaps, and blue jeans surely hanging off his ass complemented his one true love: his white Nike Airs he paid three hundred for. She told him he was crazy for wearing them at all, let alone outside, but he wouldn't listen until somebody did something.

Flanking Matteo were two Black teens she didn't know well but had met on two other occasions. She received nothing more than a head nod from them.

"Damn, you look good." Matteo was the one with the flattery this time. She pecked him on the lips and scooted her arm so her hand rested on his toned oblique.

"What you gettin' up to tonight?" Sherrie asked, checking her three-inch dark red manicure on the other hand.

"Can you drive?" Matteo asked as though the previous question was unheard.

"Wh—I don't have a license if that's what you wanna know. Why?"

"But do you know how to drive?"

Sherrie separated herself from him. In the three months they were dating, Matteo would drive her to all the destinations when he would swoon her on dates. Was this his way of telling her it was her turn to take him out?

"I know the pedal on the right is go and the one on the left is stop," she said.

"That's good enough. Here." He tossed her the keys to his second-most prized possession to his sneakers. A 1985 silver Chevy Cavalier even Sherrie knew wasn't a hot rod, but it was a nice enough vehicle.

"What—"

"You're askin' too many questions. Get in and meet me at the corner of Bank and East Main. It's five blocks that way," he said, pointing past the corner store.

"Okay, but you still—"

He and his two friends were around the corner and gone before she could think about what was happening. She could chase him down and demand to know what the plan was, but she hadn't seen him do anything bad in their time together.

Her stomach tightened as she pulled the squeaking door shut and started the engine. As the car trundled to the intersection, she was cautious, looking both ways five times at the steady flashing yellow lights that stretched beyond where she could see. Counting each street and arriving at Bank took about three minutes, and she pulled into an empty parking lot of a shopping center. She cut the lights off but kept the engine running. An eerie feeling crept from her knotted stomach up to her throat. This didn't feel right.

Matteo never said how long she would need to stay at this intersection. She searched the street corners and in front of the dark shops for a pay phone but couldn't see any. Who would she call anyway? As she made the final decision to take off, three figures grew closer in the rearview. Matteo's bouncing hair was unmistakable, and the two friends flanked him.

"GO. GO. GO," Matteo said, still hanging out of the passenger side. Without knowing if the two were in the back, she was onto East Main Street without direction. "Slow down and turn the headlights on." She followed his orders and for the first time peered over at Matteo's previously white shirt now soaked in black. She was staring down at his well-kept, well-loved sneakers, exposing red in the yellow streetlights as they passed.

"Holy shit. What happened?" Sherrie said, taking her eyes off the road for too long. Matteo grasped the steering wheel and adjusted her to her side of the road.

"You're a lying bitch is what happened," Matteo said, and she looked to the two in the back as if they would give her some clarification to his response.

"Matteo. Tell me why you are covered in blood."

"It's not mine. Keep going down here until you come to Veterans Park."

Cold and calculated was his tone, and it scared her more than him freaking out. The dark faces behind her were in shock. It looked like they were dragged into something they didn't want to be a part of. Or it went differently than originally planned.

There was not a word spoken for the next five minutes until she entered the park, and Matteo showed her where to go. He exited the vehicle, walked down a grassy hill, dropped the bag he held in his lap, and climbed back inside. "You can get out now."

Sherrie's mouth was agape. "I live far from here. So, fuck no."

He reached across the center console and squeezed the tendrils of her neck. She used her nails to scratch him, and it took fifteen cuts and lightheadedness to release his grip. "Now on top of being the getaway driver, your DNA is mixed in. Get the fuck outta my car, cunt."

Her gasping breaths didn't stop until she was halfway back home. And as she reached the front door of the apartment, her lungs seized again. The door was caved inward, and the place was ransacked. The drawers in the kitchen were pulled out, and silverware was scattered into the living room. Couch cushions were thrown into the dining room. The television rested face down on the floor, glass surrounding the base. Sherrie ran to her father's room, and she broke down before she stepped one foot inside. Blood smeared the walls. He wasn't decently covered. The blanket was on the ground, and he lay supine with his right arm dangling. Blood dripped like a faucet that wasn't all the way off.

Hearty, gasping sobs would get the cops called again, but she didn't care. She didn't care who came through that door. She wasn't ever going to leave the ground. She wasn't ever going to leave her father's side. She knew who did this. One conversation when she was trying to impress Matteo came shooting back. "My dad has a ton of money. We just live in the projects because my dad says his childhood lives there."

One part of that was a lie, and the other part was the truth. Simon Spark's childhood lived in these apartments, and it would live on forever and ever.

CHAPTER 22

There were no words spoken between Mac and Mayor Higgins on the drive back to the factory. Mac was left to his own thoughts and imagination of what occurred and was still occurring in that Barnum project. He thought he would get the pleasure of being able to see the serum working at its highest degree. The garbling maniac tied in the back still had some level of conscious brain activity slipping through.

When he was introduced to the green liquid years back, Chief Stewart explained the stuff lived inside the victim's head while their cognizant thoughts remained. He used the example of dementia. Those elderly folks knew they were human and living, but their brains were telling them something different. The one in the back of the car said he had a family. The situation of the housing in that area of town didn't equate to working a full day and going home to a family. Plus, when he found him wandering the streets, he was already zonked out of his mind. He brought that problem upon himself.

"What happens to them after?" Mac asked as they pulled down the alleyway to the rear of the factory.

"Who after what?" Higgins said, and his exhaustion showed through red bags under his eyes, lines on his face that weren't there before, and the nodding Mac caught a few times. Prior to meeting Higgins, he had seen him giving talks on the news and on the streets for a parade, tricking the town into thinking he was a standout candidate. In person, he was a different person. The makeup that cleared his blemishes didn't mask his raw look. He looked almost goofy in a *Metallica* tee shirt and blue jeans instead of a neatly pressed suit. He was pale but even more so close up.

"The—uh, guy we—you sent into the housing project. After he does what—"

"Kill 'em. That's what the cop is there for, along with making sure nobody gets out alive. If this goes according to plan, within the next fifteen minutes, that will be cleared out and we can move on to the next late tomorrow night."

"And the EMT guy—"

"Rick."

"Rick is going to bring a new one here," Mac asked as a statement.

"Correct. And fuck do we have a lot to clean up."

Mac and Higgins exited the car and assessed the damage.

The steel garage door Mac drove through was crumpled like an oversized ball of tinfoil and off its rolling bar stuffed in the corner opposite the mountain of crates. Bricks from the main structure spread the space like broken teeth, and Mac worried if that would impact the integrity of the building.

The dead woman lay in a position where her legs and arms rested at a ninety-degree angle. Close to the universal crime scene chalk on television shows. Her blood pooled beneath her but wasn't a large puddle. Wood pieces from the abandoned desk in the center of the painted cement floor shot up every which way into jagged shards.

"Can you tell me about the plan coming together at least now that it's moving?" Mac asked. Higgins grunted a frustrated groan and shook his head. His graying temples—colored for TV— shimmered in the moonlight.

His tiredness shone through when he closed his eyes for longer than was comfortable for Mac and said, "We had this plan in motion since Kevin was a captain at the department. Five freaking years ago. Of course, I made sure he was Chief so there were no hiccups. To make the plan fully work, we needed backing from the entire department, or most of it. We settled for most at first. Slipping the trusted officers and higher-ranking officials money into offshore accounts was a tasty deal for most. Corruption is easy when you have the funds."

"Couldn't you have used those to, ya know, kick them out and build new nicer apartments?" Mac asked.

"You don't have a full understanding of offshore accounting. Plus, whose side are you on anyway? When we brought you in, you were the one getting your rocks off about ruling the world."

"I'm on your side. I'm just playing devil's whatever they call it."

"The plan is in motion, no thanks to you. The devil has already grabbed hold of everyone involved and will drag them down. But dammit, I love this city, and if this improves them, in the years after, my name will be chiseled to a plaque underneath my statue."

The way Higgins stood made Mac think he had turned into that statue. He held an honorary general pose like he was imagining winning the war.

"But, to answer your question," Higgins continued. "We tried that at first. Kevin, a state senator, and I set up a program where we would do our best to relocate the residents of those buildings. But those people didn't want anything to do with the politicians or the police and refused to leave the properties. There was even a short picketing session that lasted a week. Bottom line: they weren't going anywhere."

They started a short clean-up process of the factory, but they were slow moving. "We need some wood to cover the bay opening. This door is trash now. At least you knocked it all the way off. That makes our life a little easier," Higgins said.

"Do you want me to get some?" Mac said.

"It's"—Higgins looked at his watch—"ten minutes to midnight. There is nowhere to get wood at this hour."

"So, what do we do?"

The question was answered without saying a word. The mayor of Bridgetown lay on the cold floor of the old factory with the early spring breeze billowing in. Waiting till later in the morning was the only way.

"Since we need to kill time," Mac said, taking a seat with his back against the crates. He was protecting his stash. "You never finished—"

"Fuck, Mac. I am so tired. I am tired of talking, and I'm tired of you asking all these fucking questions. I have to go to the elementary school and give a talk about how to stay safe in the city in seven hours. Then I have a dinner with some asshole and his wife. Then I need to make a speech about the butchering you did of Kevin's family. So, please just let me get some rest."

He used his forearm as a pillow, and his eyelids closed. Mac wasn't tired and was amped up to do something further.

Turns out Mayor Higgins was getting fifteen minutes of rest when an ambulance pulled round back, and Rick hopped out.

"Next one up, mothafuckas."

Higgins grunted at Rick as he wheeled in a Black man bucking and weaving against the gurney straps, his mouth taped shut.

One more joined the all-night murder party, and they were going to be the ones doing the killing.

CHAPTER 23

Helping Ms. Kara on Thursday nights was Sherrie's favorite recent tradition. She loved seeing her elderly neighbor sit silently in her high back chair reading her current paperback when she wasn't feeling like talking, or hearing her talk her ear off about her life growing up in Bridgetown and her family who all moved far away from the city. Sherrie made a connection she desperately needed, aside from Shonda and Walter.

"Would you be a dear and grab my pills and water glass from the counter," Ms. Kara said to Shonda. Without rolling her eyes, she got up from the couch and retrieved the items. Shonda never complained about being dragged into the weekly help, but Sherrie knew when her daughter was not in favor of completing a task.

"Oh, I'm sorry, Ms. Kara I didn't notice the time," Sherrie said, lifting her wrist. It was five minutes past eight. Tonight was one of Ms. Kara's talkative nights, and the minutes had slipped past pill time.

"Oh, stop. It's my damn responsibility. I just wish I didn't need so much goddamn help getting around."

"Ms. Kara, we are more than happy to assist you with whatever you need. You know that already," Sherrie said. "Isn't that right, Shonda?"

Her daughter bowed her head in a gesture Sherrie didn't take as an affirmative, but after their argument earlier, Shonda hadn't said two words to her mother.

Eight was an impressionable age. Her memories would begin to stick when she grew older. Sherrie found her father dead on his bedroom floor when she was a newly turned teenager, and that vision was forever in her memory. In several short years, Shonda would be that age, and Sherrie tried her best to make all memories good ones starting now. And sometimes as parents, they had to force decisions on their children to keep them away from the bad decisions they made in their youth.

On the worst day of Sherrie's life, she made a terrible decision in the days after.

The police had asked their incessant questions. "Do you know who may have harmed your father?" Did you see anyone come in or out of the complex you didn't recognize?" "Is there anyone inside this complex that would want to do harm to your father?" Sherrie answered "no" to all their questions.

When those negatory responses left her mouth, stomach pangs would shoot from her intestines to her heart. She pictured the spirit of her father taking the hunting knife he loved so much and drawing a blood-soaking line through the entirety of her organs. She didn't deserve to live after that. She didn't deserve the cold-blooded heart that beat in her chest.

After the investigation turned up no leads and Sherrie moved in with her aunt and uncle, Matteo reached out to her. It was a twenty-second phone call. Exactly twenty seconds. Probably the same amount of time it took him to kill Sherrie's father.

"Yo, why didn't you rat me out?"

No reply.

"Thanks for not snitchin'."

No reply.

"You wanna meet up at our spot?"

No reply.

Twenty minutes after the call ended, she was in the back seat of the getaway car she drove from her own father's murder, his blood still staining the seats, and had twenty seconds of sex with Matteo. It didn't satisfy either of them. That was the last time she heard from him. Every so often, she looked at articles related to the cold case of Simon Stark. After twenty-seven years, nobody was arrested in connection to the crime.

On the day Shonda was born, in a haze of hours of labor and the exhaustive nature of giving birth, she rang the number she had for Matteo. What would she say to him? She didn't know. She didn't need to know. The automated voice informed her the number was no longer in service.

The regret, the sleepless nights, the constant merry-go-round of thoughts pinging in her mind cost her a normal life. Sure, she had a steady job that paid the bills. She had a husband to cover for her anytime she got out of hand. She had a wonderful daughter. A daughter she so desperately was there for every second of her life. If Shonda veered along the same path as Sherrie, there was no way she could live much longer. A failure was what she was growing up, but the thing with failure was there was time to turn that around. In the eight years of Shonda's life, she felt like she kept her only child on the right track. Which in turn kept Sherrie in the caboose along for the ride.

"How about one more story before you go?" Ms. Kara said.

Shonda looked up from the phone Sherrie told Walter she was way too young to have and rolled her eyes, but Ms. Kara was asking Sherrie. Loving all her stories, even when Shonda loathed them, she ushered her to begin.

She hoped the stories and the time would be a great learning tool for Shonda. A way to make real connections with people who could tell her about the old times. She had the urge to yell at Shonda, who was tapping away at her screen, but Sherrie knew her daughter would keep an ear perked up to listen in.

"The year was 1975, and I was home from Vietnam, as was everybody else. The war was over, and some were happy, some were mad. It was and is the way of the world. So much death and destruction, and it's forgotten with time. Time is a funny thing when you think about it."

Ms. Kara was never linear with her stories. She would go off on tangents, side stories, and yammer on about whatever popped into her head.

"I married John in 1979, and we had our firstborn one year later. Popped out two more the following three years," Ms. Kara continued. "Couldn't keep him off me." She let out a guffaw that stuck in her throat and hacked until Sherrie thought it would just about kill her. She recovered after a few sips of water Shonda provided.

"Anyway, I won't bore you with the details. At least until next Thursday night. You know, dear," Ms. Kara said, placing a cold, wizened hand on Sherrie's forearm, giving them no time to stand. "My mind is going places I've never been before. I think I've got dementia or one of those brain diseases."

"Don't say that about—"

"Oh, fuck all hell. You and your particulars. I know what my brain is supposed to be doin'. But, when you and your lovely daughter come here on Thursday nights, my thoughts come back, not all of 'em, but it just feels like I can think straight. Ever since my two sons and daughter had families of their own livin' in Christ knows where, they call two times a year. Christmas and my birthday. And do you know when that is?"

Having helped Ms. Kara for two years and hearing the family drama many times, Sherrie knew it well.

"The day after Christmas. Can you believe that?"

"That's one inconvenient birthday," Sherrie said with feigned shock.

"The presents I was gypped as a kid. Ugh. I can go on and on, but you should get back home."

Shonda leapt from the couch and said, "Have a nice night, Ms. Kara." And was out the door before a response could come.

When they were alone, Sherrie scooted to the edge of the recliner Ms. Kara let her sit in and reached a hand out to her. "Shonda really does like coming here. She's just young and—"

"Oh, please. When I was her age, I was cutting up the colored dance halls with all the boys. She doesn't want to hear an old coot like me go on for days about the days gone by. Let her have a little fun. Explore. It's what life's all about. If it's just you next Thursday, it's all the better. She's a good girl with a good heart. Take after her."

"I try my—"

"Don't I know it. Now let me get back to my book. It's a good one."

When Sherrie was back up to her own apartment, she closed the door and collapsed onto Walter's lap.

"Something bad happen at Ms. Kara's?" Walter asked, waiting for the local news to go live with a mug of coffee in his hand. If Sherrie drank caffeine before bed, she would be awake until the following night.

"No. In fact it was the best night we've had there. Shonda doesn't think so. Doesn't care to know. But I think there was a breakthrough with Ms. Kara's mind. I really think so."

"That's good. You two going over there helps. It has to," Walter said and kissed her on the forehead.

Sherrie sighed in agreement. Another good deed to go in her book of bad. Her task was to even out the good with the bad.

What Sherrie failed to realize was, the worst was yet to come.

CHAPTER 24

3 AM wake-up calls—or in this case text—were not what new Chief Anthony Rawlings expected. He anticipated a normal 9-to-5 gig where he could go to his new office and handle the business of the day, then go home to his wife each day of week. In the first sixteen hours of becoming chief, Ant did all he could to stop the mayor and the now dead former Chief Stewart from unleashing havoc on an already deprived city, tried his best to bring Mac Pulaski down, and recognized how he was set up from the moment he was asked to be Chief of Police. This was all a calculated, disturbing plan, and Ant was their black sheep.

Mary was still asleep; her soft breathing was the most calming sound he'd heard in days. Being a detective for so many years, Ant never got sleep. He was told by his constituents that he wouldn't sleep another day in his life. Between the all-night phone calls and weekly murders, there was simply no time to get any shut-eye. So, the illuminating cell phone glowing in the dark of the room was seen by his eyes only.

What a difference hours made, between receiving the most phone calls of his life in a span of one hour to radio silence from the entire department. The conversation with the captain rattled in his brain. The anger, hostility, and volatility he received felt like part of the plan. Captain Anderson playing a part for Mayor Higgins. A plan was in motion, and being the loner on the outside looking in, there wasn't much he could do before they took action first. The ceiling wasn't giving the answers he desperately needed, but the text on his screen might have.

Barnum—hit 1 of many—no other info

The number of the sender wasn't a typical ten-digit number, but five numbers crammed together. He attempted a call, but the phone wouldn't even allow that as a viable option. He typed back a predictable response: *Who is this?*

As though expecting an immediate retort, Ant stared at the two text bubbles hanging there like detached thoughts. He decoded the message he received within seconds of first seeing it. The Barnum apartments were a common call for homicides and left a personal hole in Ant's heart and gut. In fact, that complex had the most murders of any other spot in the city. But what happened there? And why was he receiving that message?

The tapping in the back of his head wouldn't let him forget about the "Operation Save Bridgetown" and the devastation started. From what he skimmed, he couldn't determine a particular plan of attack, just that the residents of these buildings would be killed. The paperwork was something Ant was intended to discover and not know more than he should.

He had to find out what was happening himself. Without waking Mary, he slipped out of bed and into a button-down, jeans, sneakers, badge, and pistol.

The streets of Brookfield were quiet at three in the morning on a Friday and every other time of day. The bridge that separated Brookfield and Bridgetown stretched exactly half a mile. 2640 feet was the difference between living a life free of crime and bullet holes plastered into the siding of your home.

Once over the bridge and entering the north side of the city, it was a dumbed down version of Brookfield. The houses were nice, it was where the residents were comfortable getting their groceries for the week, and the crime was close to zero. Until the Madeline Cross, Brandon Stewart, and Sarah Plax massacre, there was discussion to eliminate the bridge and have the north side join Brookfield. Ant imagined those talks were untrue rumors floating around the city, but from what he read of the plan he was guided to in Kevin's office, they were doing a bit of reorganizing of their own.

Each soul that crossed that bridge was forced to lay their eyes upon the majesty that was the Mac Pulaski McMansion. Up on the mountainous hills between the north and east sides of Bridgetown, it was as though his place was the meeting point for the middle class and poverty folks to begin the war of sides. A thirty-foot-high stone wall protected the perimeter of the property with a wrought iron gate the only entrance and exit after pushing a vehicle up the winding driveway to the top. Spotlights that were always on must cost Mac thousands a month for electricity. The shining pale light matching the shade of the moon made sure everyone who came through Bridgetown knew who was in charge.

Ant passed the bottom of Mac's drive without even exhausting a glance at his mailbox. He didn't deserve any of what he had. He was the poster child for hate and greed. Ant was forced to mind-numbingly wade through all his YouTube videos, Twitter feeds, and live streams to find a slip-up or mentions of any of the goings-on in the city. He was smart enough to keep his mouth shut on such topics.

Entering the east side was going from royalty to a war-torn country within minutes. There were homes to see and there were homes next door not standing any longer, cruising through Main Street past convenience stores with metal gates in the down position and gas stations who knew well enough to close when the sun was down.

He was in the department-owned Ford Crown Vic the residents, especially those on the east side, knew and avoided when it came rolling through. There were groups huddled in a couple dark corners. Three men on the corner of Main and Capital Avenue stood in a circle, shadows hiding their faces until the winking red glow showed their identity for a split second. The white smoke that followed revealed their eyes trained on Ant as he passed. Flanked in the background was the prison where so many were living due to Ant's arrests. He wasn't concerned with them or anyone else in the area. Word hadn't spread to the media yet that he was now Chief, and it needed to stay that way until Mayor Higgins could be dealt with. Having a corrupt mayor for a boss was any employee's nightmare.

Recognition piqued in Ant's mind when a sedan similar to his sat on a side street with its lights off. It was another officer's car.

Ant failed to get the tags. Someone on his team was watching all who travelled towards the Barnum apartments. Ant wasn't stopped but judging by the next two blocks of nobody on the sidewalks or cars on the road, all others wouldn't be granted access within the radius of the apartments. It told Ant this was a setup but laying in bed and doing nothing was sending him into a dark spiral and he needed to do whatever it took to help the citizens of this city.

All was quiet when Ant pulled to the front curb. Was the text a scam? Or worse, was it a ploy to lure him to an unsafe place to take him out? He tapped the gun on his waist, and that was enough self-convincing to exit the vehicle.

He looked up at the towering building. Twenty stories tall and twelve apartments on each floor. The glass double door stared back at him like it was warning him to stay away. To go back to his comfy bed in his cozy hometown. But this was his to protect, even if he was all on his own.

A buzz at his hip paused his movement to the apartment entrance.

You don't want to go in there—all police corrupt—they will use fingerprints to frame—will give more info—go home

Ant circled around the surrounding area to spot any movement to who could be watching him. Warning him. The streetlights that would paint the blacktop a light beige were inconspicuously extinguished. The vacant homes in the mile circumference were a great blockade to any witnesses to see whatever had occurred.

From the outside, there was no movement through the windows he could see. On the inside, any amount of hell could await whoever would be the first to step foot inside the Barnum apartments.

Way back when, Ant made a promise to the town that under any circumstances, he would fight for them and their safety. He even had a teary-eyed, tough discussion with his wife about the possibility of putting his life on the line for a complete stranger. Mary understood and accepted with a strong embrace.

Ant took two steps, hand on his service pistol, not drawn yet, when a shuffling of feet against the pale path leading to the front door came from his left. In keeping with the caution, he kept the building in his peripheral as he watched the small shadow approach.

A gasp that must've come from his late mother released from within before speaking.

"Leo," Ant said and ran to him, leaving the complex in the rearview for the time being. "Where have you been, bud? We've been looking for you." A twinge of pain poked him in the chest at the lie. The interdepartmental corruption was enough for a grown adult, let alone an eight-year-old child.

He elevatored down to Leo's level. It made kids feel grown, and he looked about ready for a grown-up conversation.

Leo leaned close to Ant's ear, his hot breath tickled Ant's neck, and he whispered, "Danger."

"Danger? Where is there danger?" Ant asked, followed by a quick scan of the dark surroundings.

The kid moved his head left to right like a pitcher shaking off a pitch he didn't like from his catcher. Ant nodded in understanding. "Who is in danger?"

Little Leo, whom Ant knew for many years. From going to Chief Stewart's home for a summer party he threw each year. From Bridgetown funded events. From times Kevin would bring Leo and Brandon by the station. After all those times, "danger" was the first time he heard Leo speak. And the second word sent splinters of chills zigzagging down his spine.

"You."

CHAPTER 25

The sobbing, air-sucking wails of an infant bounded off the walls of the home. It was a crying rampage Mac thought was never going to stop. He waded, exhausted, through a long, never-ending hallway. Doors connected with other doors, and the ceiling was too high to see a top. The floor was a redwood pine that was not red in the past. Bright blotches of crimson weaved into the flooring underfoot. There were no door handles to try, and his attempts to ram his shoulder into the wood rectangles would break his arm off if he tried anymore. So, he continued walking until he saw a light in the distance. The illumination replacing the dark looked like a train full speed ahead preparing to run through his body without adhering from its destination.

When he came to a four-way intersection, Williams and Long Hill, stop sign at each stretch of road, his mouth went dry, and the process of saliva ceased to exist. It wasn't a train in the hallway of a home. It was the headlights of a car. It was—

His ears rang with the shattering sound of a car's horn going and going and going and never stopping. His hands couldn't get past his waist. They were held down by rope strung around him like the beginnings of a mummy wrap. His ankles were taped together and forced into the most terrifying one-legged race of his life. There was nowhere to go. This was his fate. The fate he caused so many years ago. The rope tightened around his neck, and his breath left his body. He frantically grasped at his throat as though his hands were the answer to continuing his life. His sinuses burned with saltwater and choked the rear of his mouth. White lights flashed as there was no more life to live. And now—

Slivers of sunlight poked through the few holes perhaps made by gunfire a time ago. This was a gun manufacturer at one point in history. That was the extent of his knowledge, especially being pulled from a sleep where his body forgot to breathe. As his lungs evened out, they hitched again at the sight of a police officer standing in the entranceway of what used to be a garage bay. Full blues from the belt filled with gadgets (mace, knight stick, gun) to the shoes shining so bright that Mac thought he could've seen himself in them.

Was he caught out? Did Higgins turn on him and set him up? Take a human sacrifice from the Barnum projects, tie them down to a stretcher, and send the forces in to take the unhinged Mac Pulaski downtown to the station?

"Higgins here?" the officer said flatly. He wasn't there to take him in; he was in on the whole thing.

"Uh." Mac nearly choked on the syllable exiting his mouth. He was recovering from the scare. "Said he had some events with kids and a speech later. Don't really know. Told me to stay and watch this one." Mac gestured to the gentleman who was either in a deep state of sleep or among the dead. Either way, the plan would carry on.

"Oh. Okay," the officer said and walked back and plopped into the fully stickered police cruiser. *Bridgetown police. To protect and serve.* After this morning, that carried a whole different meaning.

"Wait," Mac said, a sissy pleading coming out.

The average-looking man with an average-looking fireman's mustache snapped his average brown eyes at him.

"Uh, I mean did you need anything?"

"I need Mayor Higgins," the officer said. As Mac stepped closer, he read the gold name tag on his right breast pocket. *Officer C. Morse.*

"Wh-what—"

Before Mac could stutter more words, the cruiser jetted backwards and took off up the alleyway back to the mean streets of Bridgetown, leaving Mac and the man on the stretcher all alone.

He whipped out his phone. Ten percent battery left, fuck. He tapped the screen a couple times, and Nat picked up on the first ring.

"Hey, Mac attack," Nat said in an upbeat voice.

"Need your help," Mac said.

"That's what I'm here for."

"Did you get the van home okay?"

"She's not in one piece, but in the garage like you said."

"Good. Any sign of Sadie?"

"Nope. The bitch is probably—sorry, Mac, I slipped up giving my own opinions."

"That's okay, baby girl. Is there anybody outside the home?"

"The MacMansion is in tip-top shape from head to toe, and nobody's getting through that front gate." Natalie was a good communicator, but she was too direct for her own good. When Mac found her half-dead underneath an Interstate 95 overpass with a dirty needle sticking out of her forearm, he wasn't ready for the personality that would come when she was nursed back to health. But she was obedient, and that was the way Mac deserved his women.

"But is there anybody on the driveway or in the street?" Mac asked.

"I can see the bottom where the street is, but I don't see anybody down there." Her sentences ended with an inflection like each statement was a question.

"Okay."

"Is that bad?" Nat asked.

"It is both good and bad. We need chaos but also need to make sure it's directed away from us. That's where you come in."

A giddy laugh was on the other end of the line. "I'll do anything!"

This was a plan Mac thought of as a last resort. It would change his life and end hers, but his desire to rule this city was above all else.

"Take the Lamborghini."

"Not Kerri," Nat said in horror.

"I'm afraid I need to bring out the big guns for this one."

"You want me take out the guns?" In her literal understanding, she predicted the next part of the plan.

"Yes. The AR in the safe. Keep it in the back seat, okay?"

"Mhmm."

"Take Kerri out of the garage, and when you get to the bottom, take a right. Right is correct."

"I remember."

"Good. Drive to the center of downtown. You know where the restaurants are and the baseball stadium?"

"I do!"

"Then get out of the car with the AR and pull that trigger, baby. Pull it back and don't let it go until it stops making sounds."

"What am I shooting?"

"Whatever you see. People trying to run away. Building with windows. You see it, you shoot it. You understand?"

"I do," Nat said, a bit shyer this time, like her mind was playing the devilish act over in her head. "But—what if—"

"What if you direct the city's attention to the downtown area and allow Mac to execute his plan without any flaws? Then you would be a hero, my dear," Mac said.

"Me, a hero?"

"Sure. And you can suck my dick as many times as you like."

"I do like doing that because it makes you happy."

"And making me happy is what you would be doing. I love you."

A gasp startled Mac. He never told the girls he brought home he loved them. They were his employees. The same with Higgins. He wasn't in charge of Mac, which was why he was going far from the original plan. Mac was a loner and always would be.

He didn't really love Nat, but it was the tipping point she needed to commit this act.

"Do you really? Love me?" She squealed in the phone, and Mac had to pull it away to avoid ear damage.

"Of course. Now this plan needs to happen at the perfect moment. I will send you a text when it's time to go. So have your phone ready."

"Okay. Okay. Okay. I love you. I love you. I love you."

Mac sure hoped so. From that point forward, nobody would love Mac Pulaski ever again.

CHAPTER 26

"You can tell me. Nobody will hurt you with me around. I'll make sure of it."

Ant knew he wouldn't be able to get Leo to speak again. In the years he made acquaintance with him and observed him from afar, Leo held his words to a small number of people. People he trusted. People he loved. If Leo was warning Ant of an impending danger, then he must've fallen into little Leo's trust circle. However, falling into the same category as Madeline or Brandon was something Ant knew was out of the realm of possibilities.

"Who told you about this danger?" Ant tried.

They were sitting in the city-owned unmarked vehicle with the car running and the headlights off. Ant parked in his own driveway. He wanted to get far from the Barnum apartments, and he wanted to get far from Bridgetown. If what Leo said was true, staying there could put Leo in danger as well. And he wasn't letting anything happen to him even if he had to give up his own life in return.

Leo fidgeted a bunch on the ride across the bridge to Ant's home. Pulling his legs to his chest. Making a fist with both hands and rubbing his knuckles together so much that Ant feared they would begin to smoke. He would grab one of his hands and pull his fingers so far in the wrong direction, they were close to touching the back of his hand. But the one that concerned Ant the most was he would take his pointer finger and claw at the point in his forehead where the two eyebrows separated. He already had a cut there with recently dried blood. Ant had seen that before. When some kids got anxious and didn't hold the mental fortitude to express their emotions, they would claw at their face, arms, and legs.

"Maybe a word or a name you can say?"

It was useless to keep the questions moving, but the clock ticked to 4 AM, and he couldn't exactly walk into the house while Mary slept and, when she woke, have a child sitting in the kitchen eating her Honey Nut Cheerios. There were a few police sanctioned events Mary attended, and she may recognize Leo, but he wanted to save her the morning heart attack. Poor Leo was without a family. His mother and brother were possibly killed right in front of him, and his father killed himself. He was a foster kid within the same twenty-four hours. No wonder he was having a debilitating meltdown in the passenger seat. Ant took a different approach.

"Are you hungry?"

The way the kid looked at him was as though he had never been asked such a thing. His eyes widened, and a wet shimmer grew in the corneas. The fidgeting and face scraping ceased, and now Ant knew how to get him to open up. Maybe.

***

Two pancakes, two eggs (scrambled), bacon, hash browns, toast (wheat), and a large glass of orange juice disappeared before Ant could get through half of his waffle. He was grateful for the Galaxy Diner being open twenty-four hours a day and even more grateful to be the only patrons inside. Which meant priority seating (by the front window) and silence as he attempted to pull even one word out of Leo.

"I guess you liked that," Ant said, nodding at the empty plate.

A slight nod was given in return. Progress.

"Did your mom ever bring you here?" Ant asked.

There was no head nod or shake. He was reverting back to anxious closure. Bringing up his dead mother wasn't the move. Ant was used to interrogating adult punks who wouldn't talk until you brought their mothers into the conversation. That tactic here made the kid sad.

"Let me tell you a little about what I'm working on," Ant said to take the kid's mind off his own family. "Would you like to hear about police work?"

A shrug of the shoulders. Or he was adjusting himself in the booth. Ant took it as a win either way.

What Ant was working on was trying to solve who killed that boy's mother, brother, and babysitter. And thinking of a way to get himself out of a situation where it was impossible to win. The entire department turned on him. He could leave and never come back to this town. But he was born here, and he would most likely die here. Those talks weren't for an eight-year-old to hear about. So, he skirted around the truth with some sprinkled in.

"There's this guy who stole from a grocery store. He did a bad thing, and he needs to face the consequences. But he got away when the officers arrived. What that guy doesn't know is that I know he did it or his friend did it. The only problem is when working with the law, there is something called probable cause that we need to put him in jail. But I know we will eventually get Mac and—"

Like a kid waking his mother from a dead sleep, a sound Ant never imagined would come from the kid sitting across from him exited his tiny lungs. A gasp like no other. Ant scrambled his brain for the next question. It needed to be timely before he lost him again.

"Do you know Mac?" Ant asked in a rush.

Leo had a red bump on his right upper lip. The kind kids got from time to time from bacteria buildup. Ant watched it. It twitched, and he could feel a word trying so hard to come out. This was big. This was game changing.

"Uh—"

"Are you two finished here?"

The waitress Ant hadn't heard approach threw Leo off. His attention diverted to her, then back to the tiled ground. Ant had lost the kid.

He nodded and asked for the check. It wasn't Jill. Jill knew to give Ant his time and not interrupt his discussions.

When they were back in the car and it started, Ant snuck a glance at Leo. Head down so far it should have been between his thighs. The radio was off, and the lull of the humming engine was all that could be heard. Gas burning off snuck in through the vents. Ant had his hand on the shifter when a faint whimper broke the idling purr.

"What was that, Leo?"

His eyes grew three sizes. His brown pupils looked cartoonish.

Leo leaned in over the center console, and Ant was ready with his listening ear. "I hear the man in my head. He's a bad, bad man."

CHAPTER 27

From the time Mac received that first phone call from the (former) police chief Kevin Stewart and meeting up with Mayor Higgins to sitting on the floor inside an abandoned factory staring up at the boxes holding the serum (the key) to his ruling of Bridgetown, he grew a hatred like no other for both men. He wasn't a political person. He didn't keep up with who was Mayor—other than what was shown on the local news channels—or the president of the United States. He just didn't give half a shit. And now, he was craving the next election to vote that bastard Higgins out of office. Everything he said was pretentious, and all his words were fabrications.

"You will be the ruler of this city," Higgins had said when he went over the plan. "Once this is completed, there will be nobody left except for me and you for so many years to come."

Lies upon lies upon lies. This entire plan was for his own political reelection campaign. Send in a person infected on the serum and rid the city of its poverty. Then rebuild with the rich in mind. It made him look like an economic hero. And Mac was the pawn the old mayor used to move around his chessboard until—checkmate—Mac was knocked off the face of the city never to be heard from again. His McMansion—which Higgins said would be the main attraction of Bridgetown—couldn't withstand the rebuild. McMansions would be built in place of the massive space the poor houses took up. His house up on the hill would be nothing but an eyesore compared to the new construction homes taking its place.

Were these delusions from the bump of coke Mac snorted while he waited for the time to pass? Or was this an all too real possibility? Was Mac being used as a tool to get what others wanted? Well, they would learn when his house maid wrecked the center of their precious downtown. Nat would be the enemy, and Mac would be the hero when he found her and ran her over with his Maserati. Oh, old Mac was just traveling through when he saw some crazy lady with an AR Swiss cheesing all that was in her line of sight, and the newspapers, social media, and the talk of the city would be hero Mac Pulaski.

His boner thoughts were interrupted by a buzz in his pocket. He removed it and saw Nat's name on the caller ID. She knew to never call him, but she hadn't listened in the past, so why would she listen now?

"What is it? I'm working."

"Um, Mac Daddy. I—I—I—"

"On with the words, Natalie."

"I think somebody broke inside."

"Broke inside what?" Mac's drug-fueled snarling made no qualms about his true feelings.

"The home. I heard broken glass, and I think there's somebody—"

"Where are you?"

"__"

"Natalie. Where the fuck are you in the house? I can hear you breathing and it's giving me a headache."

"In the bedroom closet. I'm playing hide and go seek with a killer," Nat whispered.

"Get to the armoire and get the gun, any gun, and fucking kill them. Why am I the one telling you this? You should know this already," Mac said.

"I can't. I'm about to be found. The footsteps—"

Mac stood and paced from one side of the old factory to the other. Its foul odor of mothball, spoiled gun powder, and oil from the van Mac crashed were a cacophony gathering in his olfactory, poking at the bile in his throat.

He had so many—too many—security devices that there was no way any one person could break into the home. Nat was his security guard, and she was fired. She was gone for good. Only somebody who knew—

"Nat." Mac's snarling ceased, and his even voice frightened himself.

"Yes?"

Bang.

The closet door was being kicked in. There was no secret passageway to the outside. His thoughts to place parts of his arsenal behind his clothed hangers had long passed. It was a weakness of the home. However, Mac figured he wouldn't need to hide inside the closet when part of his weaponry was in the armoire a few feet away.

Bang.

Sadie was kicking the door down. It was a simple pine wood door Mac heard splitting after two kicks. Sadie, whom he picked up at the homeless shelter. It was tough to convince her to go with him. But after she was raped by a man at the shelter and Mac beat him to a point where his testicles were no longer in use, she agreed. She followed his orders. She wasn't as submissive as Nat, but she did what she was told. The Madeline Cross job was her first. Before Mac sent his girls to do his dirty work, they were required to take a pill. Nat swallowed hers within seconds, and Sadie refused. This was fine with Mac since the pill dissolved nicely into Sadie's favorite drink. Sadie didn't do the killing. That was clear to him now. Nat did the slitting of the throats. Nat traced the letters into each of their bodies. Nat spilled the truth of the situation. Sadie had been unconscious at the bottom of the steps as the killings took place.

Bang.

Crack.

"Sadie is going to kill you in a few seconds."

"Why?" Nat reverted back to her childhood with the whiny inflection of the word.

"Because I pissed her off, but it's not your fault. Don't be afraid."

"I'm not."

She was. The shakiness in her voice was unmistakable.

Bang.

Crack.

"Where's Mac?" Sadie could be heard in the background of the call.

"I—I swear. I—I—"

"Doesn't matter. I'll find him," Sadie said and pulled the trigger twice.

Mac held the phone away from his ear to not hear the reports in the small space. The pops were undeniably the 9MM police-issued handgun. And Nat was undeniably dead.

The phone on the other end was jumbled for a brief moment before Sadie spoke.

"When I agreed to live with you in this home, I was just looking for a warm bed and three meals a day. Prison can give me all of those things. And I certainly wouldn't unknowingly get drugged. You're probably gonna cry since your precious Nat is dead now. Good. But you won't have tears for long. When I find you, you will be long gone by the time your body has a single thought. See you soon."

The phone call was ended, and Mac was back on the cold ground. His phone fell to the floor, and his palms were rubbing his forehead. He wasn't going to cry. He was going to fight back. He checked his phone battery: 8 percent remaining.

He didn't need an army to take down Sadie. He didn't need an army to take down Higgins. But he had an army. His followers were under his command.

A few screen taps later and Mac was live-streaming. As the viewer count climbed, so did his excitement.

Power was what he craved, but chaos was what drove him into madness.

CHAPTER 28

"Do you remember me?" Mary asked, sitting across from Leo.

"If he barely talked to me, then I'm sorry, honey, but he's not gonna talk to you," Ant said, pacing the living room.

"You never know. Sometimes kids open to people and surprise everyone."

Leo sat on the Rawlings' blue leather couch with a low-ball glass of water balancing on his thigh. His legs dangled over the couch's edge, and his ankles took turns alternately smacking the wood piece that connected its inner workings. The hypnotizing sound was grating on Ant's nerves, but this wasn't his turn for aggravation. This kid went through experiences in one day many—even on the police force—never went through in their entire lifetimes.

A heartwarming scene unfolded in front of Ant. There was one discussion about kids on his first date with Mary. It was the third phrase that left her mouth. They met at a coffee shop where Mary worked. When he joined the force, he became obsessed with the caramel macchiato with three shots of espresso. The graveyard shift wasn't kind to the human body, but caffeine made it tolerable. After a few months and daily visits to the local spot downtown called Kickstart Café, he was used to the shift, and his motivation for entering the shop turned abundantly clear that the woman selling it to him was the kickstart to his day.

Her long red hair flowed with perfect curls to the middle of her back when it wasn't tied into a tight bun plopped on her head. The 90-degree Italian nose was cut perfectly for the shape of her pale face and dreamy brown eyes. *Kickstart Café* was sewn to the breast of the apron draped across her front. Ant couldn't help but notice the two round humps when she turned around in those tight black leggings, but what made him fall in love was her personality. Her no-nonsense way of looking at the world and kicking its ass was a major turn-on.

Mary told it like it was, and their first date was no exception. Ant asked her out on a date after not uttering a single word other than the typical pleasantries. He had said when he pulled her from her work, "Do you have a second?"

"I've stopped making a coffee for a customer, so what do you think? What do you need, an extra napkin? They're at the end of the counter."

"Nope. Just a few extra seconds with you."

Out of respect, most women would storm off and roll their eyes. Mary performed the perfect eye roll for the entire shop to see. "That's the best you could come up with. Really?"

"I was going to ask something about cream for my caramel, but I thought that was overstepping."

Mary's eyes were stationary, and a twitch of a smile flicked in the corner of her mouth. "I get off at seven. Meet me at the table over there." Then she walked off and continued her work until the shop was locked up and her coworker left for the night.

They stared at each other in the darkened coffee shop, one light illuminated over them like the spotlight at a Broadway show. The store sat on a street corner of Main and the entrance to a public parking lot. Few cars passed during the hour they were inside.

Breaking the ice was easy with Mary. "My name is Mary. I have red hair—yes, it's my natural color, and I don't want any kids. If you do, then find someone who will harbor a human for nine months. It ain't gonna be me."

Ant had considered kids for a number of years, but forcing a woman who didn't want that destruction of their body, he would concede for those reasons.

The topic was never discussed again until one dropped on her living room couch.

"We need to keep him here until whatever's going on out there can be finished. He's been through so much. Don't put him in any danger," Mary said after pulling Ant into the kitchen to be out of earshot of the kid.

"I agree. If he knows I'm in danger, then we shouldn't be in the same space."

A knot turned in Mary's stomach. Ant could tell from the cute wince. "Where would you go?"

"I'll stay at the inn up the street, so in case you need anything or if the kid says even one word, no matter what it is, you call me."

She dropped her chin to her chest and hooked her arms around the back of his neck. "Please be safe."

"Ya know, you've become a little weakling in your old age," Ant said.

"Oh, don't you worry. I can still be a bitch when I need to be. And don't you think I won't think twice about whoopin' your ass," Mary said and smacked a kiss on his lips.

He went back into the living room and sat on the ottoman in front of Leo. The fireplace was silent. They hadn't used it in years. The television was on mute. The soundless news covered the Madeline Cross murders as they had been since it happened twenty-seven hours prior. Ant switched the screen off, hoping the kid hadn't seen his mother, brother, and babysitter in that condition. It would traumatize anyone, no matter how much censorship the networks used.

Ant took Leo's hand and said, "I'm going to be right down the street. Mary will take care of you. I've known her for a long time, and there's nobody I trust more than her. If you need anything, you tell her right away, okay?"

There was no response of any kind, but those hazel eyes spoke volumes of audio connection. Little Leo was listening.

And if he heard voices other than his own and Ant's speaking voice, the kid's head had to be spinning.

With a kiss to his wife and a check-in at the Grover Inn, a seedy-looking but nice stay for a night, ten minutes from home, Ant, who never felt tired from being constantly on the run, playing detective for over twenty years, was napping in his own drool as soon as his head hit the pillow.

***

From being on call for so many years on the job, Ant slept in three-hour intervals. He would get home from work, eat dinner, take a three-hour nap, wake up, watch TV, take a three-hour nap, and so on until the next workday, barring a call into the office or the scene of a crime. Mary bought him blackout curtains so even when the sun was out, he could get some rest, feeling like he was consumed by the darkness of the night.

When he snapped awake in the dark, his thoughts had dropped off, and he scanned the room to get his bearings and restore his brain to its previous day's settings. A console television sat on a nightstand stretching the length of the front wall opposite the bed. Two side tables flanked him. One had a clock radio showing 8:18. He wished for an AM or PM, as his brain was fried, his throat aching for a drop of water, and his eyes itching for moisture. Everyone should go by military time. No room for error.

On the opposite nightstand was his phone, and it flashed, illuminating the portion of the room showing him that the motel didn't carry blackout curtains, and full dark by the passage of time took care of that for him.

He returned to his phone and was blasted with a white light. When his sight adjusted, he had two missed texts from UNKNOWN NUMBER. As his memory caught up, he remembered the anonymous text telling him about the Barnum apartments. He regretted not going inside, but Leo needed to be safe. And his plan to go back after a nap was thwarted by the exhaustion of the previous twenty plus years.

The first text said, *Washington Carver—tonight—off the rails.* George Washington Carver apartments was another complex about five minutes from Barnum. He could get there before whatever was happening even got off the ground. Maybe evacuate the buildings to prevent catastrophe. Then he scanned the next text: *Check this out.* It was followed by a blue hyperlink. Without questioning the validity or safety of the link, he tapped it.

After jumping to a different app, a video loaded and began in the middle of Mac Pulaski talking. The bottom right showed a red flashing LIVE, indicating this was happening now. Mac didn't look good. His usual smooth skin was sagging under his eyes, and in the position he was sitting, his head was to his chest, showing some blubber under his chin. Veins thunderbolted his eyes, and his chapped lips were twitching as he muttered his nonsensical words.

"This is the day today. I need all of your help now. Fight to take back what was taken from you. Now. Go out and fight. Take back—"

Ant tuned him out to read the comments scrolling underneath Mac's face.

We will do whatever it takes.

Fight. Fight. Fight.

They can't take what is rightfully mine.

The background of the video was unrecognizable. It was a gray cement wall, but the video was so close, it was impossible to gather any possible location.

Anything else? Ant texted back to the number. It could be some punk playing a prank on him. But it gave him solid information so far. And Ant followed every lead he ever received until it was proven false.

While he waited for a response, he clipped his gun and badge to his belt and was checked out and in his car, unsure of where to go next. He could check on Mary and Leo, but she knew to call if there was an urgent matter.

As if on cue, his phone buzzed in the cupholder, rattling the plastic. Unknown number sent no words but another hyperlink. Ant took a second before tapping and recognized it as the local Channel 12 news website. He tapped and watched.

"Welcome to the Channel 12 news at 8:30. I am your host James Harfield," a goofy man with a military haircut and square head said. "We are seconds away from Charles Higgins, the mayor of Bridgetown, to address the people of the city." The host continued, "There is no word as to the context of the—hang on, here's Mayor Higgins now."

The screen flashed to Higgins sitting at an oak wood desk filled with a nameplate, books, a small American flag paired with the Connecticut state flag, and Higgins in a bright red chair. Ant flashed back to sitting across from that desk a little over a day ago when all went to shit. And Anthony Rawlings was left out to dry like a sheet with a broken dryer.

Higgins began, "To the citizens of Bridgetown and to all who may be watching. In the recent weeks and months, we have seen an uptick in horrible tragedies. We have a climbing number of deaths due to the Coronavirus each day. And it feels like the world is crumbling around you. I understand." Higgins held his hand to his chest as though he would be in solidarity with anyone. "While I can't fix all that happens in the country, what I can do is make Bridgetown a better place. That is why effective immediately, I am starting an initiative." Ant's heart jumped from his chest to his throat to his stomach. "It's called the 'Save Bridgetown initiative.' And what it will do is improve the city's economy while keeping everyone employed, and the best part is it won't cost any of you a dime." *Just your life*, Ant thought.

"You keep on living while knowing your way and cost of living will be better than ever in as short as a two-year period.

"In closing, I wanted to address the tragic loss of our leader within the police department. Chief Kevin Stewart tragically lost his life two nights ago, and as a personal friend to Kevin, I know the death of his son, Brandon, and his wife Madeline took such a toll on his mental well-being. We will miss his laughter and leadership. With that said, I am happy to announce twenty-three-year veteran detective Anthony Rawlings as the interim police chief of the Bridgetown Police Department. I know he will do a great job, and we here at Town Hall are very proud of him. God bless this country and God bless the people of Bridgetown. Thank you."

Ant failed to wait for the newscaster to continue the broadcast. The news of his advancement wasn't supposed to go public for weeks. His chest hurt. Was he having a heart attack? He couldn't take much more. He had heard enough between Mac and Higgins. Ant knew this was bad. But he didn't know why Higgins was releasing that plan. Now he knew it was for his own personal and political gain. He knew Higgins was a selfish piece of flesh, but telling the citizens of the city straight to their faces that he was going to execute you based on your economic status, in so many words, without giving away the main story, was psychopathic behavior. And what Anthony thought would be a bright future for himself turned into a living nightmare.

The phone he wanted to toss out the window and run over again and again buzzed in his hand. Mary's name showed on the screen, and he collected his troubled breaths. "Hey, hon, what's—"

"Anthony. Please help us. There was a brick thrown through our window," Mary said. Her words were coming out between breaths. She was on the move.

"I'll be right there. Go into our room. In the closet above my clothes is a shoebox. Take the gun out, load it, and lock yourself inside. I will call out when I get there. Don't let anyone inside except for me. Is Leo with you?"

"Yes."

"Good. Keep him safe. I'll be there in ten."

Ant hung up the phone as quickly as he could so he could release the cry he was holding inside. He could only compartmentalize so much. His line of work forced him to hold it together. Hold his emotions in check. But when it came to his family, the tears would flow for them each and every time.

CHAPTER 29

Mayor Higgins's message to the people of Bridgetown was the biggest piece of political bullshit Sherrie had ever seen in her life. Following the mayor's address was a twenty-second story on strange police activity at the PT Barnum apartments. The building was barricaded, and the police enclosed a perimeter, not allowing a single soul within two miles of the complex. It was a five-minute drive from them, so it sent a shiver of fear through Sherrie. But with no other details, the news moved on to the weekly weather forecast.

Walter said nothing when the news went to a commercial. But Sherrie felt this knot forming in her lower abdomen. There was something ominous about the mayor's words and the happenings at the apartments down the road. She couldn't quite place what it was, but she had the feeling that something big was around the corner. Sherrie pulled up Facebook, a big source for a scoop the news wouldn't care enough to cover. After ten minutes of friends' pages, a couple of whom lived at the Barnum complex, nothing seemed unusual, which only grew the wooziness in her gut.

Per their nightly routine, Walter watched TV for the next hour while Sherrie caught up on her magazines or stalked social media accounts—something she strictly forbade Shonda from doing, but that was the power of the parent. Shonda was a homebody. She never left her room unless she was going to school, coming home from school, or wandering the kitchen, pulling the refrigerator open until Sherrie got the hint to make dinner.

Friday night was pizza night, one of the foods her daughter liked because it wasn't outside the realm of child foods. Shonda's diet consisted of chicken fingers, tacos, hot dogs, freezer dinners, and a bagel with cream cheese for breakfast each morning. They lived in what the outsiders referred to as the projects, but between Walter and Sherrie, they made enough to feed their child grown-up foods. But she refused and stuck to her diet that hadn't caught up with her metabolism as of yet, though it soon would. Sherrie had been that same skin-and-bone kid, but in her teens was when the fat began to accumulate.

The tiff between Sherrie and Shonda the night before made Shonda miss the pizza. She wanted to hang out with her friends from school, but Sherrie wanted her to stay inside. Nobody held a grudge like a teen. Although pizza was often a great unifier, Shonda remained upset and locked away. That knot of worry was a mother's and woman's intuition that all was not well in the world. She attempted a compromise to do something tomorrow during the day, but being a teenager was their way or nothing. Sherrie understood that teen angst as well as anybody, which was why Shonda was staying safe in her room when nightfall came.

There was another back and forth when Sherrie told her to go to sleep and Shonda went on a tear. "It's Friday night. All my homework is done for the weekend. I can't hang out with my friends. What can I do, Mom? Like tell me. What?" Her gold "SS" charm bracelet they got her for Christmas last year jangled from her dainty wrist as she used hand motions to further convey her frustrations.

"I'm keeping you safe, and you will understand when you're older," Sherrie responded.

Shonda grunted and turned away in her bed, throwing the covers over herself. Sherrie felt bad. She was keeping their daughter from experiences one wouldn't have lying in their bed. Sherrie had those experiences, but they were always coupled with the death of her father at the hands of her then boyfriend. It was fear that held her back from setting her child free from her grip. And that grip wasn't loosening any time soon. Ms. Kara was right when she said, "Let her have a little fun. Explore. It's what life's all about." It was okay to agree with a statement and never act on it. At least that was what she told herself.

"Do you think I'm too harsh on Shonda?" Sherrie asked, lying in bed next to Walter just after midnight, who faced the opposite way, surely trying to get to sleep.

"I think—you are doin' what's best for her. But it wouldn't hurt to let her out on her own once in a while. She's getting older by the second. You don't want her to have a secluded life," Walter said, and it was a rare spark of knowledge from her mostly quiet husband.

"Yeah, I think you're right," Sherrie said, closing her eyes for some much-needed rest when the first of the screams for help came from within the George Washington Carver apartment complex.

CHAPTER 30

Cocaine was that one friend in the group who easily convinced everyone in their circle to commit the most heinous act they could think of. Cocaine infected your mind in so many different colors. In Mac Pulaski's case, that color was red.

He didn't need to tap the screen to end his live stream; the phone's screen going black accomplished that task for him. For someone who had it all, for someone who had most of his life handed to him on a gold platter filled with the most expensive hors d'oeuvres, he felt whittled down to nothing as his back slid down the cement structure to the floor. He melted into the linoleum, and all he saw was the cross-beamed ceiling, and when his head flopped to the right, the man on the stretcher. When he turned to his left, the woman whose body had been decaying for going on two days. The smell seeping through her pores was nothing he had ever experienced before. It was close to wet garbage and the one time one of his girls years ago had a rat obsession and hid thirty of the rodents in the basement until the smell caused Mac to go downstairs and discover the graveyard behind the washing machine.

Time escaped him. His Rolex was on its stand on the dresser just outside the closet where Nat's body was surely rotting with each passing second. He never wore that clunky, heavy slab of metal on his wrist regardless of the day. Outside was full dark, and considering the month being October and before daylight savings, it had to be at least after 9 PM. Which meant he had been mumbling nonsense for about an hour.

Higgins was off doing his political bullshit. Shaking hands and kissing babies. And Mac was stuck with babysitting duty. Why couldn't he just kill the guy on the stretcher and get anyone else in the stupid city to be the next victim on Bridgetown's shit brigade? What made that sleeping asshole right for the job? The serum would infect anybody's mind and make them act like they had a night of fun on crazy pills.

Mac wished he had more cocaine, and he was going to get some. He could probably go to any broken home a block over and slip a twenty to whoever opened the door for any drug they were slinging. The cocaine he bought from his dealer was a different blend from what they concocted in the basement of the poverty homes. Cocaine made him unhinged, but crack would make him tear the heart from his chest. He wanted to be high to escape, not to hold his mind hostage so his body could make its own rules.

Although he misremembered most of what he said in his live stream, the basic premise was asking his followers—of whom he had one million—to leave their homes, cross state lines, and make those who wronged them pay. They were empty words and empty threats. He was angry, and using his platform was his way of easing his frustrations. And it worked. Higgins disrespecting him, using him, was gone from his mind. He wanted him to return, and they could move on to the next project together. Using him and his girls to take down the police chief's family at the direction of the police chief was a brilliant plan. Then marking them with *PIG* and throwing the blame to those people, killing the chief's wife for making racist comments and making him pay for it. It would send the police lovers into a rage and therein trigger those people in retaliation. It was the perfect plan.

But it failed to draw riots and protests. There was nobody on the streets with handmade signs. Where were the looting assholes? Where were the fires to the establishments downtown? Where was the anger Mac created? Silence.

All the prepping and planning with his two henchwomen to strike at the perfect time and set the bodies up just like he was supposed to had triggered nothing. The chaos required for their plan was obsolete.

Even in his coke-fueled mind, he knew how to make them come out of their homes. He knew how to get them to take the streets.

Retaliation.

When his followers—many of whom he knew lived in the city—received his message and gathered up their pitchforks and tiki torches, it would upset the masses.

The world. The country they lived in today was one of opinion taking the lead. It didn't matter who you were. All that mattered was the opinion of the masses. In 2020, the decision of your fate was left to the judge, the jury, and the social media.

One picture, one video, one post of his followers marching, chanting, or protesting peacefully would result in the retaliation of the oppressed.

Those people had to have their voice be heard. Those people had to show their anger. Those people had to be better than everyone else. And why? Because their feelings were hurt?

This movement Mac created wasn't about skin color, class, or way of life. This was about taking back power. When entities were controlled by the man and people went about their daily lives, opinion was heard but not the decision maker. Regulation was control, and it needed to be taken back into the hands of the powers that be.

Excitement coursed through his body from his finger and toe tips and met up with his quickening heart. The impulses had returned to his psyche, and he was ready. He couldn't sit on the cold ground any longer.

Where the garage door sat mangled, a few bricks from the side wall aligned with the alley on the outside, lying helpless on the floor.

With this brick, I will start a war. With this brick, I can do more. With this brick, I will break down your door. With this brick, I will cause gore. And with this brick, blood will pour.

CHAPTER 31

When fear enveloped every cell coursing through your body, time was at a standstill. All Ant could think of were the fun, happy times with Mary. Their first date at the coffee shop, their love of movies and going to midnight showings, and their new love of cooking. Ant would cook his premier meal of boxed mac and cheese, and Mary would cook him perfect chicken Francese. Mary told Ant after teasing him for the hundredth time about his poor culinary skills that a good Italian father never let his daughter out of the kitchen until she knew how to cook.

Past Leo flashed into his mind as well. One particular memory of a Bridgetown department picnic thrown each year by former Chief Stewart. The last one before the pandemic took the world by its firm grasp was at the park near downtown. Picnic tables and coal grills littered the already crowded park over a grassy field for families to enjoy a summer day. The officers, sergeants, lieutenants, captains, and chief packed the park, filling every table there was to offer. Kids ran with kites, chased each other across the open space some had never been allowed by their strict parents' rules, and screamed with pure sounds of bliss.

Then there was Leo, who sat on one of the picnic benches the opposite way than its intended design, counting his ten fingers over and over as though one would be missing on a go-around. Ant excused himself from the table where he sat with his wife and the other detectives and their wives. He knelt to Leo's level and asked what he was doing. Leo shrugged and continued with his mindless count.

"Did you want a hot dog or hamburger?" Ant asked, pointing to the tray of grilled meats. Madeline looked over her shoulder with her oversized movie star sunglasses, blonde hair perfectly layered, and bangs cut so the upper arch of her eyebrows were obscured if she were not wearing the bug eyeglasses.

"He won't eat unless his brother eats, and his brother is never hungry. It's a household daily struggle," Madeline said taking a chomp out of a cheeseburger. Mustard and relish spilled out of the buns.

Ant scanned the greenish pale grass that met with the blue sky and minimal cloud coverage, spotting Brandon chasing another kid with a squirt gun. A stream pistoned out and sprayed the other kid in the back of the head. Then he turned his attention back to Leo. "You remind me of my brother, Stanley."

Madeline turned again. "I didn't know you had a brother," she said.

"I have two. Well, had two. One died when he was six. One doesn't talk to me."

"And which one does Leo remind you of?"

"Stanley. The dead one. We would sit at our round table in our small kitchen in our smaller apartment. My momma would be whipping up dinner after she returned home from her second job. Stanley, who would eat a bowl of cereal for breakfast, was seen napping during lunchtime at school, then refused to eat his late-night dinner. It drove our momma up a wall," Ant said, and Madeline turned away, seemingly uninterested in his story. "Momma would say things like, 'you are gonna be malnourished and the school's gonna call me and think I'm starving you or something.' Stanley would shrug his shoulders like it wasn't anything he could do about it. Watching this happen, I thought I could do something about it. Do you know what I did?"

The finger counting paused while Ant went on about his childhood. Leo shook his head, and it felt good to get that listening confirmation from the kid who didn't speak.

"I was the one who got him to eat. With distraction. When Momma placed the food on the Styrofoam plates, on this night it was rice and beans, I would tell Momma I would be right back, but really, I was looping through our den and back around into the kitchen behind Stanley, and when he wasn't looking, I would take his plate and eat a couple forkfuls. Momma was none the wiser when she turned back around and half of Stanley's food was missing. She was comforted, and it comforted Stanley to know I would do that for him. To this day, I don't know if it was guilt or thankfulness, but Stanley cleaned the rest of his plate."

During the story, unbeknownst to Leo and Madeline, Ant snapped Leo's bunned hot dog in half and hid one half behind his back while the other sat on his plate. When Leo turned, he was flabbergasted, as though the story had come to life in front of his very eyes. His brown bowl cut swished like a curtain with each head swivel from the plate and back to Ant. And the real win was the start of a smile on one half of Leo's sweet face.

Madeline noticed when Leo took a bite of his dog and said, "Leo. You're eating. Good job, bud." As though Ant failed to exist. But Leo knew, and that was enough for him.

As Ant approached his home where a frightened Mary and Leo were surely huddled in a closet, the memories flooded back of Stanley. And the tears flooded his cheeks. When Stanley was shot that night and emergency services refused to help in a timely manner, Ant felt anger and remorse for the longest time. He lashed out at his mother, at his remaining younger brother, at everyone. He did some things he regretted after getting mixed up with a bad crowd.

The worst night of his life coupled with what happened when he was thirteen changed his perspective and outlook on life forever.

***

"It hurts real bad, bubby."

Those were the final words Stanley ever said to Ant. Bubby was the word that came out of his youngest sibling when he tried the word "brother." Momma considered it to be the cutest thing

170

and, when they grew up, hoped Stanley would call him that even when they were in their eighties. But Stanley was gone, and so was his mother.

On the night of the drive-by shooting, they had late dinner, 9 PM, as they did every school night. Momma forced them to read a chapter of a middle grade book each. "Reading is learning, and learning will keep you outta the big house," Momma used to say. The big house was prison, and her worst fear was busting her own kids out for doing something stupid. Ant felt the nights were close enough to prison as Ma would set up with their respective blankets, ready to share the same queen-sized bed.

They would be settled from oldest to youngest. Anthony, the oldest, had his head aligned with the headboard. Roger, the middle child, would be faced the opposite way with his stinky socks in the face of his two siblings, and Stanley on the other end. Stanley was placed at the front end of the apartment facing East Main Street. If Ant had known the positioning would be an issue, if he recognized where Stanley was, he would have switched in a heartbeat.

Out of the three brothers, Anthony was the rule follower. When Ma took them on a rare trip to the aquarium a few towns over where kids under seven would get in for free, and when the ticket taker would ask how old the kids were, Ma would say they were all under seven years old. And, infuriating his mother, Anthony would say proudly that he had turned seven the other week. Ma would put on a performance and smack her head, going on about "how could she forget" when all she wanted to do was save a few bucks so her boys could have a fun day.

The gunshots woke Anthony out of a peaceful sleep, preparing to take on his work at Central Elementary School. He hadn't known one of the bullets struck the apartment. Gunshots weren't uncommon in the area where they lived, and Ma warned them to keep their head on a swivel when in the city and to always sleep with one eye open. Ant wished more than anything for Stanley to hold that talent.

The projectile left the semi-automatic pistol caused by the trigger pull from a man inside a Honda Civic. It placed a hole in the siding, burned through the pink insulation, tore a hole in the drywall, and pierced Stanley two inches below his rib cage. The doctor later explained the reason the round didn't exit the other side was it slowed down so much on its path, its remaining umph rattled around in his youngest brother's torso, ripping apart Stanley's intestines, liver, and lower ventricle before coming to a rest in his right lung. The sound of the tires squealing from the scene haunted Ant for years after. As did Ma slamming the bedroom door open, flipping on the light, and red liquid oozing onto the floor from Stanley's side. As he sat up, blood flushed out of his mouth. His little brother caught it in his hand as though getting it on the blanket would be the worst possible outcome. In Stanley's liquidy tone, he said those five words Ant would hear in his inner thoughts for the remainder of his life.

A young punk hanging on the front steps of the three brothers' childhood complex, who didn't live there, had sold the shooter some bad crack. The punk was unharmed in the incident, and the shooter couldn't be identified.

Ant was changed from that day forward. It began with his grades slipping when the school's bereavement period ended, and the adults expected him to focus on his schoolwork when all he could see when he closed his eyes was Stanley catching the waterfall of blood pouring out of his mouth.

When he hit his teenage years and was old enough to understand the inner workings of revenge, he set out for that purpose. That awful night, the police didn't show up until twenty minutes later. The medics followed closely behind. With no car and public transportation closed, Ma was holding her dead son in his sleeping blanket that had turned from white to a thick black color. Her tears weren't enough to resuscitate him.

One good thing came about experiencing the process of the detectives questioning all who were in the area, except for the punk who caused it. Even Ant and his brother were asked if they saw anybody or anything. It seemed important to Ant to keep all that was said inside his head and take a mental picture of the surroundings. Blue and red lights from every emergency vehicle in the city clogged East Main Street into the early morning hours. Most importantly, he listened to the conversations. The car was a silver Honda Civic that was seen by many witnesses fleeing the area. The shooter was in the passenger seat and was described as a Black male, in his teens, dreadlocks, skinny, wearing a wife beater.

Stored with that in his memory bank, he would look at every car that passed by the street. Every person that walked by on the sidewalk. All existing humans were persons of interest in Anthony's book. Skinny Black kids with dreadlocks were at every street corner on the east side of Bridgetown. And for a time after the shooting, Ant guessed the suspect would go into hiding.

At thirteen, Ant connected with a guy named Matteo. Matteo was a dealer who asked Ant one day if he wanted to buy weed. Ant's good boy persona in the first ten years of his life floated away with Stanley. Ant agreed to the drugs and would stop by after school on the days Ant ran low. They became good friends, along with Ant's remaining brother, Roger, and would hang out by the corner store on East Main and Lansing.

"You know we can rob this guy blind, right?" Matteo said one day outside of Franky's convenience.

"We're here every day. Why would we give ourselves away like that. The clerk says, 'what up, Matteo' every time you go inside."

"Dude, I'm just sayin'. We grab the cash from the drawer and bolt to another side of the city."

"That's a stupid plan. Even for you," Ant said as Roger moseyed over.

"What's goin' on?" Roger asked, giving them both dap.

"Matteo had the bright idea of robbing Franky's," Ant said.

"Yeah. That's stupid. Get away with a cool hundred and get arrested. Hard pass."

"Fuck both y'all. But I got an even better idea, if y'all are down," Matteo said.

"I'm listenin'," the brothers said in unison.

"This girl I've been fuckin' around with is stacked. Well, her pops is."

"And she lives around here?" Roger asked.

"At Barnum," Matteo said, pointing his chin at the apartments up the road.

"Then she or her pops are definitely not stacked," Ant said.

"No. Her pops got some inheritance, but something about this place is his childhood or some bullshit. He keeps cash in a safe."

"You're lyin'," Roger said.

"It's what she told me. If y'all don't want a cut, I'll take it all for myself," Matteo said.

The brothers looked at each other, and Ant said, "We're not killin' anybody. Just the money and run."

"No doubt. I'm tryin' to get rich and not die trying. Or end up in the electric chair," Matteo said.

The brothers hung back so Matteo could ruse his girl Sherrie into being the getaway driver. Once the escape plan was set up, Ant and Roger followed Matteo inside the Barnum apartments.

The plan was in action as they entered the front glass doors and took the stairs four flights.

"This is it," Matteo said, pulling a semi-automatic pistol from his waistband. Ant froze. He had handled and shot a gun at some bottles before, but seeing Matteo prepared to use it on another person freaked him. He could see on his brother's face that he was spooked by the weapon too. "I'm not gonna shoot him. Just a scare tactic. It's not even loaded." He didn't prove his statement, but Ant and Roger flattened themselves against the wall while Matteo knocked.

A thick voice came from the other side, asking who it was. Matteo altered his voice and said, "Neighbor from down the hall."

Before any of them had time to react, Matteo had the gun in the man's gut and the three were inside. The apartment was identical to the one they all lived in. Even Ant and Roger's apartment at George Washington Carver. A kitchen area and living area separated by two different floors and a bathroom and bedroom separated by thin wood walls.

"Where's the safe?" Matteo asked.

The man was heavy but looked like he was a body builder back in the day. He could take all three of them down no problem, but the gun in his gut glued his kicks to the floor.

"I-I, no. I don't have a safe," the frightened man said.

"Bullshit. I know you do." Matteo lifted the gun so it rested on the bridge of the man's nose. "In the bedroom now."

The man's shaking hands nearly missed the top frame of the bedroom door and he was shoved onto his own bed by the wielding gunman.

"I'm going to ask you one more time. Where is the money?" Matteo said.

Roger moved a couple steps toward Ant and did something he hadn't done since they lay in the same bed Stanley was shot in. He clasped his fingers, interlocking them with Ant's when he was scared. Ant was going to run. Take Roger and bolt for the door and not be involved in this crazy kid's plot.

A report rang out. Then another. The ringing in Ant's ear from the fear pulled the shots from the next room over and relocated them to blocks away. It wasn't real. The man went limp in his own bed. The place where a person was meant to feel as safe as possible. The same place where his youngest brother was killed for going to sleep for the night.

Roger and Ant came to an unspoken agreement. Get out of there and never look back. They did just that. There was no plan once they exited the complex, but Matteo had a car waiting. Ant felt the police were on the way, and he and Roger would be yanked into Matteo's crazy homicide. They agreed to the ride to get far, far away.

The darkness of the back seat was a reward so Sherrie couldn't see their faces. They did nothing wrong, but her eyes boring into them through the rearview mirror were eyes of confusion, of resentment, of loss of something; she hadn't yet recognized that she lost anything, let alone her father.

She drove them to the park near downtown where Matteo got out and dumped the gun and his bloodied shirt into the Long Island Sound.

When he was back in the vehicle, he forced Sherrie out, leaving her an orphan and alone at the park late in the night. Matteo, Ant, and Roger were silent as he drove back into the east side, dropping them at Washington Carver where their Ma waited to scold them for being home so late.

Some instances in a lifetime were turning points. The two brothers had two arcing turning points. The first was when their little brother died. This took them down the path of evil and revenge. The second was the killing of an innocent man they were partially involved in. This forced them to fork in the opposite direction. Roger became a lawyer, and Ant became a police officer.

Matteo was never punished for his crime, and it pained Ant to live with the memory as he stepped foot onto the hundreds of crime scenes throughout the years. He didn't know where he was. Ant hoped he was dead in a ditch.

As he pulled into the driveway of his home, his safety palace with the front picture window of glass shattered, he recognized this as his third turning point.

This was a road less traveled by many. This was a dark, desolate road, and the only sign you passed was a warning and a premonition.

It read: *One Way*.

CHAPTER 32

The George Washinton Carver apartments were built in 1956 as a way to house the homeless. Bridgetown in the 50s was a booming economic city with manufacturing holding the city as an upper middle-class destination, while homelessness ran rampant throughout the city. Sleeping bodies laid out against the front of the post office, people breaking into homes during the brutal winter months for an hour or two of warmth, bodies carried away after either hunger or heatstroke or frostbite took over.

The city had no resources for the growing number each day, those flocking to Bridgetown to seek refuge from towns where the cost of living was becoming above what they could afford. Mostly people of color would cross the bridge for the affordable housing Bridgetown was advertising.

It took 215 more dead bodies before the tower was constructed. Not a room was empty in the 122-room, five-story structure. Many homeless remained living on the sidewalks between those who refused the services and those who dragged their feet until there were no more vacancies. Free housing was a success for a few years until the deaths from the cold and heat became deaths by violent means.

Food was rationed evenly. Blankets and pillows were distributed one for each room, and the communal shower was large enough for groups at a time. When one didn't appreciate the length of shower time of the other, a man was stabbed through the heart and died instantly. Blood swirled down the drain. Another day, a dinner was stolen from a man. He stuck a plastic knife into the neck of the man who stole his food. He bled out and lay on the fourth floor for weeks before anyone notified the authorities. Similar stories to those happened every couple of weeks before city officials stepped in and began raising rent to stay in the apartments. All of the homeless were back on the streets with nothing but a meaningless past of full bellies and clean soaped showers. After years of small renovations and more monthly rising rates, it became the affordable living it was in 2020, and reading about its past inspired Sherrie to help as many of the homeless as possible with what little money she had to offer.

Currently, the Washington Carver apartments weren't much better than what they used to be. Ignored homicides, rapes, and drug deals were commonplace.

In the past, hearing screams for help was alarming at first, but Sherrie and Walter taught a frightened Shonda, who ran into their room after a call for help came from a floor above, to mind her own business and everyone else would do the same for you. It was an "every man for themselves" mentality Sherrie and Walter didn't find comfortable, but living in a hostile place, minding your own business was lifesaving. The sounds would stop, the police would show up, take an hour or so to investigate, remove the body, and no one would ever hear anything about it in the media. Even the residents of the building refused to speak about anything they heard the previous night.

On the night multiple screams woke Sherrie, it alarmed her. One was an attack happening in one of the many apartments, two was a coincidence, three was a problem. And when a fourth came minutes after the other three, Sherrie's chest tightened with fright.

"Walter, wake up," Sherrie said, smacking her husband on his hip.

"What the heck, Sher," Walter said, his eyes fluttering awake.

"I heard a scream."

"And we've discussed and agreed to let it be."

"Four in five minutes is not normal."

Another muffled yelp travelled up, dying at the moment Walter could catch it.

"That woke you?"

As a child, Sherrie was a heavy sleeper so much that a hurricane with 80 mph winds rattling her bedroom window failed to wake her. It took many shakes from her father to bring her back from sleep land. Since her father's passing, each small creak of the house snapped her awake.

"Yeah, I agree. Something is going down," Walter said, raising his head from the pillow.

In an instant, Sherrie was out of bed, peering out the window, looking down at the rear of the complex where orange lampposts shined little lights over the parking lot. Cars sat waiting for their owners to return so they could perform their duties of getting from point A to point B. There was no movement, and that scared her even more. Nobody heard the cries for help and was leaving.

"Where are you going?" Walter asked as his wife was out the door and into the living room.

He followed, softening his steps so as not to wake Shonda. His usual booming voice lowered to a whisper. "Don't you go out there," he scolded his wife like she was a little kid.

"I'm just looking," Sherrie said, unlatching the hook chain and snapping the dead bolt open. The door creaked as the perfectly timed scream was vocalized as clear as the Caribbean waters she dreamed of reaching one day.

The door was shut again, and the locks were placed back into the safety position. And Sherrie was left with the aching feeling, the feeling of dread, of hopelessness, of fear. Fear she failed to help others with in their time of need. The truth was each time somebody was struggling within the walls of the complex or outside, she was willing to empty her bank account, expend all her time to assist with what needed to be accomplished. And the next cry for help broke that wall of fear down. The cry was graveled and weak.

She reached for the door again.

"We need to stay inside. It's our safest option," Walter said.

"That was Ms. Kara. And I'm going to help her because that's what I signed up to do. Stay here with Shonda."

Sherrie was assertive, and it came across to strangers as mean, but Walter knew it came from a place of purpose and accomplishing tasks. Walter started to say something again and his jaw smacked shut. There was no convincing her to stay.

A nod of agreement and she was out the door. The locks clicked shut on the other side, and the nauseating twisting began with each step closer to the stairs.

Ms. Kara's apartment was one floor down and the third door on the left, just under theirs. At the second-floor landing, the knot in her gut was yanked tighter. Each beige wood door on either side of the yellowing wallpapered walls was busted inward. The first line of protective offense split down the middle. The hinges remained intact with half the door swinging loosely in the breeze of the year-round air conditioner blowing in the halls. The left side of the door lay feet inside just before the darkness blinded her from what she wasn't meant to see.

Some pep was in her step moving two apartments down to see Ms. Kara's entryway in the same damaged manner.

"Ms. Kara?" Sherrie called out. She took careful steps inside. If whoever or whatever broke through the door was still inside, Sherrie wasn't planning on sticking around. She was there to help her neighbor. The splintered remains of the front door were scattered within view of the light from the hall. The rest of the place was going to take some eye adjustment. She knew the layout, which would be her advantage. A couch on the right, the TV in that close corner, to the left was a kitchen where Ms. Kara and Shonda—begrudgingly—made some chocolate chip cookies one Thursday night, and a few steps ahead was Ms. Kara's reading chair. As the nothingness became silhouettes, the room came into view, as did their elderly neighbor.

Her head was nearly torn from her neck. It dangled like a Christmas ornament with a piece of neck flesh acting as the hanging attachment. Pools of dark liquid on the floor, the walls, the ceiling were overbearing, and Sherrie turned to run. Run anywhere but the apartment. Before she could think, Walter was bear-hugging her in the second most comforting place she could think of.

"She's—Ms. Kara is—"

"I know. I know. Let's—"

"Shonda. She's all by herself. Why—"

Arguments and blame would wait till later. Entering Ms. Kara's apartment was a figure of what used to be a man. He wore an oversized tee shirt, basketball shorts, and no shoes. His left shoe would be of no help, as his leg was bent in the opposite direction of its normal operating human motion and upward at a ninety-degree angle. He wasn't getting around well, but when he moved toward them, it was at a quicker pace than either of them imagined.

Walter quick-stepped to the right, and the man-thing lost its balance, crashing into the TV and the books Ms. Kara loved so much.

"We need to go now," Walter said as the thing rose again.

"Plez elp meh," the thing croaked. For the first time, Sherrie noticed the grotesque pepperoni holes burned into the thing's skin. Its eyes watered, and a blue tinted tear fell. It felt like a video game character who had control of their own thoughts and emotions but not of their actions. And as though a gamer with a controller pressed forward on the joystick, the thing leapt, but Walter was hand in hand with Sherrie and out the door.

"Go," Walter said, waving for Sherrie to go back upstairs.

"You must be outta your mind. I'm not leaving you."

"I can distract it. Make sure Shonda's okay."

After a brief pickle, she was up the stairs faster than she ever thought she could.

It was too late. The door was bashed inward, and she knew her baby girl was gone.

Once inside, the first stop was Shonda's room. There was a blind corner rounding the TV area to the hall housing her daughter's room and the master bed. Between the two rooms was a large man the size of a football linebacker. Shoulders wider than his hips and arms worked well in the weightlifting department.

"Where is my daughter?" Sherrie said.

"I am not here to harm you. I am here to help." The voice was soft and sounded like any White person Sherrie came across in the past.

"Where is my fucking daughter?"

"I don't know. But if you'll calm down, I think I know a way to—"

Sherrie wasn't in the mood for talking. She ran at him and threw every pound of the 160 she offered and was on the floor looking into a room with black curtains, posters of Shonda's favorite movies and TV shows, and a bed empty with the covers askew.

"Like I was saying—" The man's words were silenced with a sharp slap to the face. "My name is Roger and—" Another slap and Sherrie was being lifted like she was a little kid.

Arms constricted her airways, and the medium-length nails were not effective in the giant man's release.

As the world faded away, Sherrie thought of the first time Shonda laughed. She wasn't much of a giggly baby, but when she was ten months old, Walter came home from work with flowers and chocolates for Sherrie just because. When the two lovebirds were dating in college, each time he would do something sweet for her, she would place her lips on the side of his neck and blow a raspberry. Shonda was sitting in her baby yoga pose and giggled so much she teetered and fell over laughing some more. Growing up, Sherrie would do the same to Shonda until she was a pre-teen and didn't want her mom to show any affection. Shonda didn't laugh much anymore, but those rare times and the times still to come would fill a dark desolate room with her much needed light. A blurred Walter entered the apartment, relieving Sherrie that he was alright, but within seconds, Walter's, Sherrie's, and Shonda's worlds were extinguished.

CHAPTER 33

A brick crashing through Anthony Rawlings's front window was the beginning. In his drugged rage, Mac called on his people to step outside their homes and fight back against the system that was turning their back on them. The brick was a warning. A warning for the new chief of police to pack up his wife, his things, and get out of state. A message that said, *we weren't afraid to cross city lines, and we know where you live.*

Mac crossed the bridge back into Bridgetown, moved toward his house on the hill when he decided to take a stroll down East Main Street and make sure any traces of him in the old, abandoned gun factory were nonexistent. The mental thump after a worn-off cocaine bump crashed recent memories and awakened all his reality senses.

The woman Mac found living next to a dumpster in the rear of a Denny's with dirt and grime growing on her emaciated cheeks and a needle protruding from her arm had left and disrespected her savior. If she were found by a police officer, an EMT, a firefighter, or a random "good-natured" citizen, she would have been thrown like a rag doll through the system and locked in a room within a mental facility. Mac saved her life, fed her, bathed her, clothed her, and weened her off the heroin, breathing new life into a woman nobody else wanted to save.

Sadie spat in his face by killing Natalie. Sweet Natalie was never a druggie. She did drugs, but they were kinder to her than her sober brain was. On the day Mac found Natalie she had been booted from a homeless shelter for smacking another woman for touching her only meal for the day. She was a good listener and followed through with his orders. Out of all his helpers over the years, Natalie was the single one he wished he could hold on to forever. But things changed. Mac Pulaski came first. The world came second.

Now Sadie was after him. One good thing about the girl that would ultimately be Mac's downfall was she became unhinged when she was upset. Mac riled her up to get the Madeline Cross job done. Pushed her down, beat her down, drugged her until she complied. Whatever worked. The bad news was she now felt too pushed around, and from their brief phone conversation, she was at her life's tipping point. She would do anything to get to him.

The early morning breeze was cold. The Long Island Sound lapping on the piled boulders leading to the road to Bridgetown was a calming but eerie cacophony leading him into battle. With all his weapons in Mac Manor, where, if Mac had to guess, Sadie was lying in wait to place a hole in his forehead, he was shit out of luck, as they said.

The factory was his saving grace. His new home. He knew he couldn't stay long. Mayor Higgins's plan wasn't foolproof. There were agencies, there were leaks within the department that were sure to happen, there was Anthony Rawlings, who was tougher than Mac or Higgins would ever admit. Rellington arms gun factory could be easily traced back and raided by any law enforcement agency that would give in to corruption of another department. Police often turned a blind eye to the badness of other police, which was how the attack on the poverty building was lasting as long as it had.

Of course, along with the media not interested in the lives on the inside. Reporters were afraid to step foot near the east side of the city. Homicides were left to an old annoying White man wearing a fedora and a trench coat with a Facebook page, trying to make a name for himself. He reported on the odd police activity at and around the Barnum projects, but other than a few likes and comments, it was filtered away by the abundance of other posts attempting to ignore the real world. Or somebody within the police department was silencing all posts relating to the incident.

One step inside and a shiver climbed the vertebrae of his spine when the gurney and man strapped to it were gone. Mac had been gone for two hours, and Higgins returned, placed the man inside an ambulance, and released him.

Although, the woman who Mac stabbed a number of times whom he couldn't keep up with was gone as well. He was sure Higgins did this for his own benefit, but it assisted Mac all the same.

After a once-over to make sure there were no traces of the van he crashed through the garage door or any remnants of white powder, he also made sure the short rainstorm of the previous day washed the blood trail away, and any other pieces of his life of his short time in the small space. Then, he walked out of the back never to return again.

＊

Out of the four projects in the east side of Bridgetown, Mac had to admit the George Washington Carver was the nicest. Nice was a great overstatement. The brick structure was crawling with browned ivy scaling up the façade. The windowpanes were lacquered with a paint chipped white, making it look worse if they had kept it as its original color. The windows themselves were fogged glass with black bars reminiscent of prison cells. What were they trying to keep out? Or in?

Now, it was keeping the serum-injected creature from continuing to walk the halls of the property. Seeing firsthand how the green goo affected the persons injected, there wouldn't be much time to run or hide. They could sniff you out and take a chomp out of your flesh.

Screams, cries, and yelps couldn't deter Mac from watching. He missed the first go-around since Mayor Higgins was being his typical hard-ass self.

As he crested the cement hill entering the line of the property, a wooden sign welcomed him to the apartments. A one-way road in and a narrow path moving the opposite direction were the routes in and out. When the road ended at the large structure, a roundabout with one entrance and one exit sat out front. In the middle was a cracked fountain that was wet from the rain and little else.

A police cruiser was parked adjacent to the project, and a man leaned on the outside, smoking a cigarette. A steam of smoke lifted as he blew it through his mouth. Mac knew it was the asshole cop who shrugged Mac off back at the factory. He grew a resentment toward the cop, the EMT, the mayor, and everyone else in his way. But they were important players in his game. He couldn't win the game without them. His successes relied on others, and that was the worst of it all.

Watching from the outside in was fascinating to him. He found a small bush that concealed him from any of the nobodies looking out from inside the project and from anyone who decided to take a stroll or cruise, perusing the front driveway. The branches sticking in any place they could find on his body was uncomfortable, but he had the perfect view.

Before the hypothetical popcorn would be ready, an ambulance cruised up the drive and came to a stop behind the cop car. The officer nodded to the EMT, Rick, the same guy who dealt with the previous unfortunate contestant, as Rick removed the gurney from the back and entered the building through the front door as though he lived there. He was going in for a new victim.

As for the ones who did live there, they were vocal. Mac envisioned them resting three or four hours into their slumber, not a knowing care in the world except for the dreams that played in their heads, surely of a better life than they had now. Then waking to a creature in their home ready to feast. No time to react or think before permanent rest was granted to them. The "helps" and "ahhs" were getting through but cut short just as their lives were.

In what felt like seconds to Mac, Rick was back out with a new one strapped down. The two Mac assisted with were older. The druggie Mac drained the green goo inside had to be close to seventy. The second victim had to have been in his fifties. They were gradually getting younger, but the leap in age stung Mac. The feet were several inches from the bottom of the stretcher, as was the head. And skinnier than any normal human should be. A toothpick tied to a bed. If he had to wager a guess, he would say younger than a teenager who never ate her vegetables. The wriggling body was lifted into the back. Rick nodded to the cop, who gave a friendly wave in return, and the ambulance was gone. On to the next one. Just like that.

The time passed slowly, and Mac's ass was falling asleep in his waiting position. The project had to be well cleared out, when someone emerged. The cop wasn't expecting someone to exit. He was shaken and flicked his tenth cigarette to the floor. He stepped up onto the front walk toward the person, who was out of breath, hands on their knees.

"Help."

A cry for the officer, who met the adult man just as he collapsed from exhaustion. He had a basketball stomach and man boobs showing through the tee shirt he used exclusively as pajamas; no wonder he was out of breath from exiting a door.

The cop knelt and hovered over the collapsed man when they exchanged a few words. After what looked like acceptance on both parts, the cop stood up. This officer was what the kids online called an ACAB. The man had no time to react as the nightstick extended and cracked his skull. His head was between a hard place and a moving object. And that object moved again and again and again until pink brain particles spotted the officer's face and a trail of blood flowed toward the cruiser.

When the cop had enough fun, he returned to his work vehicle and popped the trunk. He reached inside and retrieved a rag, a bucket, and a white spray bottle. He placed the items next to the unrecognizable man and began the long drag of the limp body. A small echo made its way to Mac each time the cop used every ounce of his strength to scrape this man along the path he walked many times to enter his safe place. But it was the nature of the beast.

It took a couple of tries and was difficult, and Mac was embarrassed for the cop trying to get the man up from the ground and into his trunk. The task was accomplished, and the cleanup began. The spray attachment was not used, as the cop unscrewed it and poured the bubbling substance from the death spot and along the path of fat resistance. There was no scrubbing, but water poured from the bucket. He used the rag to clean the blood and human insides that remained on his face and hands. The dark stain on the ground was visible from where Mac sat, but the cop returned to leaning on the side of the cruiser facing the building, lit a cigarette, and waited for anyone else to exit.

By the time the cancer stick was down to its butt, it had grown silent. Any cars passing through had halted. Any persons on a late-night walk were nowhere to be found. The residents of the George Washington Carver projects were gone. This was the cop's cue to enter.

Minutes later, a single gunshot rang out. Minutes after that, the cop returned with a lifeless creature over his shoulder in a fireman's carry. The man Mac roomed with at the gun factory was reduced to a shriveled nothing. A visibly easier carry for the cop. The blood on the cop's dark blue uniform made it look as though the officer had lost a water balloon fight, but the man had mixed a bright green goo dripping from the gunshot wound that reminded Mac of a highlighter marker.

The already used creature was placed in the back of the car, and the shift ended for the officer. The rubber tires of the police cruiser under pebbles and moving along the blacktop were the final sound.

Another successful drain of the Bridgetown projects.

Until.

Until a burly, muscular man exited the door. He carried a man over his right shoulder and woman over his left. Both looked alive and slightly moving.

Where was he taking them? Who was he? And how did he survive the wrath of the serum monster?

There was one way to find out.

Mac emerged from his hidey bush and caught up with the man while keeping a safe distance.

The three of them were new players in the game. When he discovered their roles, then he could determine their end.

As for right now, Mac would do what he did best.

Watch on until the right moment.

CHAPTER 34

ICU.

"What does that mean?" Mary asked.

Ant and Mary swept up the broken glass and dumped it into the trash while Leo sat in their windowless bedroom with the television on, a plate of pancakes, encased by a locked door. Ant expected nothing to occur for the remainder of the night at least against him. But he wasn't taking any chances.

"It's a message and a threat all in one," Ant said, sinking into the couch.

"Who did this?" Mary said, joining him and placing a calming hand on his thigh.

"I know exactly who did this. And I'm about three seconds away from driving up to his mansion and throwing him in the back of my car in cuffs."

"Is he dangerous?" she asked.

"What happened to Madeline and those ki—"

Before he could finish, Mary understood and moved her soft hand to her chest, not wanting to hear more.

Mary was a tough cookie. Years back, she handled a criminal out on bond that found their home and broke inside, looking for his arresting officer so he could stick a knife inside him. Ant was on shift that night and as soon as he heard Mary's quick, whispery tone, he raced across the bridge, making it home in record time, but enough time for the man to enter Ant's own bedroom and ask Mary where he was. He was scared off when Mary hollered about having a gun and shooting him through the bathroom door. The single handgun they kept in the home was in a safe under the bed. Mary apologized profusely for forgetting to grab it before hiding. Ant never blamed her and was mad at her for blaming herself.

She was a police wife. She wasn't the one trained in those situations. She did everything perfectly right that night. As did the Brookfield Police Department when they located the perp a mile away in a wooded area of town. Ant moved the gun to a shoebox in the closet for quicker access.

So, a brick through the window, while terrifying, was something Ant believed Mary could handle with class even with the added anxiety of having a child to protect.

It was full dark by the time a sheet of wood left over from Ant's deck project was the new front décor until he could get to the hardware store for a new picture window. A project he felt would need to wait until whatever was going on in Bridgetown was resolved.

When the police force was stacked against him and the most powerful people had taken over, who else was going to remedy the situation? If not him, then—

His phone buzzed in his pocket.

Washington Carver—happening now—hurry

Another text from the anonymous source passing him information on the strange goings-on at the low-income housing on the east side.

Seeing George Washington Carver dropped his stomach. Memories of living with Mom, with Roger, with poor Stanley on the first-floor apartment. Good times. Good laughs. All desecrated by one awful night.

He knew Mary would be okay with Leo. She would protect him at all costs. But there was a twinge sitting within Ant. Leaving them alone when they must've felt they were under attack. How could he decide between the citizens of Bridgetown, a city he loved, and his wife and little Leo? The latter would win each time.

"Who is that?" Mary said, snapping Ant out of whatever trance he was trapped inside.

"Oh, I don't know. I've been getting these texts from a blocked number telling me where the next east side crime would take place."

"And you haven't done anything about it?"

The sharpness from his wife shocked him. She was tough, but he wasn't expecting such crass.

"Well, I did go to the Barnum apartments, but that's when Leo showed up, and I guess I…"

His thoughts trailed off into what the insides of the apartments would look like. The corrupt officers, detectives, and higher-ranking officials had gone to the housing and done their respective jobs. However, when Ant scoured the internet for news articles, local news stations, and social media, he found very little about it. The information he did find were news stories calling the mass killings of nearly all residents of the Barnum apartments as a freak accident. The most traction the incident garnered was through the victim's families' social media pages. They even collected a small group together and marched outside the Bridgetown city hall and down the road from the Barnum apartments, at least as close as they were able to get, hoping for answers. When the real answers were being withheld by those in power, the truth was impossible to break free.

"I guess you need to fix this. You have a life-or-death job that you signed up for. I understand that it comes with certain circumstances out of your control. If you think a little thing like a brick through a window is going to faze me, then you really don't know me."

Ant sat with Mary's words. Watched her pale face grow as red as her beautiful hair. Not out of embarrassment but from getting herself worked up. Her brown eyes like marbles shimmered with passion. Her pink lips quivered with anticipation of Ant's next words.

Instead of words, Ant kissed those lips and walked into their bedroom.

"Hey—"

Leo was curled in a child's ball on top of the blue comforter. A half-eaten pancake fell to the floor next to him, a river of dark syrup creating a sticky mess to clean up later. His inhales entered with a soft whistle, and his exhales left with a soft whimper. All explanations of where Ant was headed were out the window. They would see each other when he returned.

Ant exited with a soft cheek kiss for Leo and one for Mary.

As the door was closing, Mary called, "Kick some ass."

Ant was off with a hearty thumbs-up.

***

A moment of quiet.

Travelling across the only entrance point into Bridgetown, a path Ant took thousands of times before, felt different this time. The radio of his police vehicle he was granted access by the department to use as his personal mode of transportation was off. The past forty-eight hours from the moment he turned away from Mac in the diner and read the death of Chief Stewart, his head was spinning like never before. And he had an inkling that all talk would be surrounding protection of the secrets that lay behind the PT Barnum apartments and possibly the George Washington Carver apartments, happening now if his mysterious texts were correct.

Anthony Rawlings was the new chief of Bridgetown police. Anthony Rawlings was in charge. Only that wasn't entirely true.

This had been a plan set forth several years prior when Kevin pulled him aside and set him up. Place the one person, the scapegoat at the top of the food chain while Mayor Higgins swept the entire department from under Anthony's size 13 feet. He wasn't angry. At this present moment, reading the green sign with white lettering welcoming him to the city where he was born and raised, bone and flesh and blood and soul all ripped apart in an instant.

Anger was an emotion Ant had tucked away so long ago. A teenager wrapped up in the rage of his younger brother's death, searching for any outlet to express himself, death and violence the answer. The wrong answer. Matteo killing that man inside his own safety hole was the final day of Anthony's previous life. His brother's killer didn't matter anymore. His mother's death affected him very little. He learned when you were furious with the world, the world didn't give a shit back. So, he buried that past never to return. But the thing with dirt was, whatever lay underneath eventually tunneled its way back to life.

A cell phone that refused to stop its incessant buzzing was hushed. But Ant stared at the screen. With the world hushed by the car's insulation and his brain hushed by his talent of compartmentalizing, he held a thought to make a phone call. A ring to a higher power that would blow the mayor's and Mac Pulaski's little plan to smithereens. The FBI, DEA, Connecticut State Police, surrounding towns and municipal departments. Ant didn't care who of the authority alphabet showed their face; his plan was to stop this before anyone else was killed.

But, if the anonymous texts were correct, the next attack was too personal to call anybody else in. In the progression of eliminating anger from his repertoire, he gained a heaping dose of selfishness. When he was named the first and only Black detective in Bridgetown's history, he held an egotistical need to be the best detective, color of skin not applicable. And that's what he did for fifteen years. Each and every case solved. Same with his time serving the streets in a patrol vehicle. He treated every call as though he were being evaluated on the remainder of his career. He was proud of each call he answered and each homicide he solved.

The issue with selfishness was it came back and bit you on the ass. He voiced being the only Black officer in a department with 172 White officers didn't faze him. He was so caught up in the haze of that selfishness, he failed to see all the co-workers who surrounded him and called him a friend to his face turned on him when greed and money were on the table.

Fighting selfish with selfish was a recipe for disaster. The Washington Carver apartments were his childhood, and he would do anything to help them. He would be their savior when he couldn't in the past.

Ant chucked the phone at the dashboard, not caring what happened after impact. The device smacked the windshield, bounced in a perfect spinning motion off the dashboard, and slung past him into the rear passenger seats. As he crossed into the east side, ignoring the home on the hill, his head was spinning.

No. That wasn't right at all. The car was spinning. Barrel rolling once, twice, three times, and resting upright on the sidewalk. The crunching of the Ford's exterior base and the shattering windows filled his ears to replace the screaming in his own head. Vigilance he prided himself on, gone at a four-way intersection.

The intersection of King and East Main where four years prior he was called to a twelve-year old girl who had a single bullet wound to the forehead. She was exiting S&S Market after purchasing her favorite candy. Skittles. The rainbow candies surrounded her and the pale sidewalk. A drive-by shooting between two gang members. Both unharmed, but a little girl going to the store for candy shot dead in the afternoon sunlight.

The reverie shook him from his memories; a figure was approaching. White headlights Ant missed while selfishly inside his own head silhouetted the person, a man. He felt the need to reach for his gun, but the blood tainted his eyes, and the safety belt that kept him from dying was not releasing and being tangled with his service weapon on his hip caused the snap to not free him.

"You ought to watch where you're going, Chief Rawlings," a voice said, speaking through the now shattered passenger side window.

Ant wiped his eyes and cleared his vision enough to see the skinny-faced former Bridgetown chief of police.

"Kevin." That was all Ant could get out.

"Yeah. It's me. Don't worry. I'm not here to take your title away. That is yours to keep. But we are going to take a trip to my secret hideout since you wanna play Mr. Hero Cop."

There was no doubt Ant's right arm was broken in one or maybe two places.

He couldn't feel his legs.

Was that a good thing or a bad thing?

Kevin Stewart was alive and well.

The same question applied.

Chapter 35

The official time of death given for Sherrie's father was 12:24 AM, but the phone call to police to report the homicide wasn't made until 3:47 AM. This made Sherrie the number one suspect in the case. She was placed in handcuffs, dragged to the police station, fingerprinted, placed in a holding cell for seven hours with one cheeseburger and small fry to eat, then interrogated for the following two days. The only reason they had to hold her was the time between the death and phone call.

She repeated herself hundreds of times. To the responding officers, to the two detectives put in charge of the case, to the attorney provided to her, and regrettably to a news reporter who somehow gained her contact information. It was tiring and frustrating to provide a factual account of what happened and have not one person believe the story.

One aspect of the story she omitted was her activities prior to the murder. She was ninety-nine percent sure of who killed her father but refused to say so. Matteo wasn't a bad person, and he proved that many times by buying her gifts, being sweet by not allowing his masculinity to take over his mind and body. His family was never there for him, and his financial drug business was failing. She didn't feel bad for him, but growing up with a single father who, truthfully, worked two jobs to put together enough money to feed his only ungrateful bitch of a daughter, she felt *for* Matteo. And snitching on him would only get her and him into more trouble on the Bridgetown streets.

When she had a run-in with a former drug dealer friend at the Bridgetown foster home where she spent the next four years before she was kicked on out on her ass at eighteen, she was left alone for keeping her mouth shut. Though she had several spats with others at the home, she felt it toughened her when she lived on the streets for three years before she found a job sweeping floors and working her way up to a respectable position. Finding her father dead was not the end of her life as she once thought, but an experience that changed the mold of her existence.

The second aspect of the story was the truth. Seeing her father lying on his bed with blood still actively exiting his veins was an out-of-body experience for Sherrie. A dream that extended the length of her sixteen-year life, and she thought she would wake up, run into her father's room and squeeze him until he peered down, his scraggly dark beard with dots of gray scratching the top of her head. And in his authoritative tone, he would say, "What the hell's gotten into you, girl." And, "What the hell do you want? Money?" But when she came to hours later when she couldn't handle the gruesome scene, it was all the same. Above his bed, he showed off his two most prized possessions. His signed New York Giants Lawerence Taylor jersey framed and dusted each day to the right of his photo with Lawrence Taylor framed and dusted daily. It was what she saw when her fainting spell ended. Her first thought was, *Oh shit, he's gonna be pissed. There's blood all over his two favorite things.* The reality of the situation hit her, and that's when she picked up the house phone and dialed 911.

***

The disorientation of waking from a fainting spell was unlike any other feeling. *Is it AM or PM? What day of the week is it? What year is it?* All those questions now rushed through her head. The one at the forefront, the clearest one, was, *Where the fuck am I?*

There was a fireplace she dreamed of sitting in front of below a television she wasn't sure would even fit through her apartment doorway. She rested on a couch that would gain hours of nap time from Walter and occasionally herself. Leather, red, and cloudlike.

Walter's voice bounced off the too-high ceiling before she saw him. "Where the fuck is my daughter, you sick fuck."

Seeing that type of rage from her husband did not come easy. He was a soft, gentle, kind man, and Sherrie found it difficult to get him riled up about anything. But when it came to Shonda, they were in agreement that their daughter was top priority, and they would do anything to find her.

The initial weariness of losing consciousness had worn off, replaced by the memories of large arms octupussed around her neck, Ms. Kara's blood splattered across her apartment, the creature with the limp lunging at Walter.

A pang of sadness fell down her throat, but this wasn't the time. She was as angry as Walter, and her teenage anger was on the cusp of releasing all over this man in the suit chilling in a recliner.

Roger.

A name floated into her mind before he was out of his chair with Walter moments from cracking Roger's windpipe. Walter was built like an apple. All his muscle and fat were stored in his shoulders and arms, but he was slim in his torso and legs. Sherrie knew he could kill this man, and she knew she had to bring an end to the torture.

After a gentle hand on Walter's back, Roger adjusted his tie and fixed his suit jacket that looked like he would break through with his massive biceps, and then, they all had a chat.

"You have a daughter?" Roger asked, perplexed and worried.

"You know damn well we do. You broke down the door of my home and took my daughter. She's only a child, you freak." Walter was at a level that would take a major switch to bring his anger down. He was back on the couch, but he looked ready to pounce.

"Mr. Stevenson, I assure you, your door was like that when I arrived, and there were no occupants in your residence," Roger said.

"Bullshit."

"I am only doing this to help you, Mr. Steven—"

"If you call me that one more time, I'm gonna flip my shit."

"Walter, if you hear me out for a moment, rest assured, you will understand."

Sherrie was readying herself to pounce to prevent a death that would come at the hands of her husband. His blood rumbled beneath his skin. The rounded eyes and fists softly punching the couch were signs that he was seconds from an explosion.

"I may know who took your daughter," Roger said.

Shock and exhaustion came all at once for Walter. His shoulders drooped, the palms of his hands exposed, and his eyes softened. "Okay, I'm listening."

CHAPTER 36

The Bridgetown bridge being the only way in and the only escape out was a terrifying aspect for most citizens, but for Mac, he found it astonishing. It was one of the main reasons he made this city his home years ago.

Born and not so raised in Hartford, an hour's drive north of Bridgetown began as a harrowing experience and ended as an enlightening, life-changing one. His mother and father were born into drugs. They met at a detox center next to a Hartford hospital when they both happened to be between overdosing and emerging from detoxes with hopes of a better life ahead.

Mac's father's parents were killed in a car crash during an ice storm when he was ten years old. He was sent to live with his aunt, who bathed him in shit water and clothed him in shredded pants while she left him home alone many days of the week to go bar hopping. Most times, she didn't come home until days later, leaving Mac's father to fend for himself. The place to live was nice until he discovered cocaine and halfway houses where he could spend the night and get his drug of choice from other attendees.

Mac's mother was the opposite of her husband. She had loving parents who gave their all to their only child. But even everything they handed to her was not enough. Living through the mind-numbingly boring everyday life of school, home, school, home was not the life she chose. A friend's group invited her on a trip to a local beach at midnight where the teens skinny dipped and shot their arms with a shared needle. It made Mac's mother feel alive for the first time, and she never stopped again.

Heroin brought his parents together in a place of hope and change, but their love was an intermingled clash of addiction. Holding hands at night while they pressed the needle into each other's forearm crease. Their veins connected in a spiritual and physical lovemaking scene inside a poverty-stricken apartment.

A baby, Mac's mother knew in her heart, was growing inside her, but she made no conscious effort to break her dependence for the sake of a human. A baby born on the same bug ridden, heroin juice-soaked bed he was conceived. Mac was forced into a cruel world where he was meant to fend for himself in every aspect of life. His mother and father robbed jewelry stores and convenience stores to keep their fix up to date while he lay starving and helpless. A piece of fried chicken and a half-eaten apple core made it his way when his parents' cravings made it to the kitchen tile.

Eight years old was the age Mac was forced to get his own grub. Breaking into the rear door of restaurants and raiding walk-in freezers and pantries was the only choice he had. He was grateful for being caught and arrested four times, since he was given free meals and a place to rest—a cleaner, more spacious place to rest inside the juvenile detention center and, when he grew old enough and travelled to a new city, the Bridgetown penitentiary. Most importantly, it gave him time to think. The most powerful gift a man could be granted. And, associating with other inmates, he began his life rebuild.

His cellmate went on and on about his life of crime and murder. The guy bragged about in the end killing around twenty-seven people and living in a house so big he hadn't used every bathroom in the twenty years at the residence. Mac wasn't paying the guy any mind until he went on about using druggie girls as a way of making money off their dealers. It hatched a plan in Mac's dark mind then, a plan that would make him comfortable for the remainder of his life. And when he was released, he forged his new path to the life of royalty.

Hartford had been his home for fifteen years, and he knew too much, which in turn meant they knew too much about him. He needed a new destination. Not a place where the rich and famous played, but a place where the dead would be quickly forgotten. Where the victims' bank accounts weren't high but where he could build his wealth and sustain it for a long time. A place where he could take charge and rule over all. A place where control was easy to gain. And crossing that bridge into his new home put a big smile on his face.

***

The east side of the city repulsed Mac as he followed the bodybuilder man carrying a body on each shoulder. He kept a good distance from the man as to not alert him of anything unusual occurring until Mac wanted something to happen. He was a man out for a leisurely walk, albeit the darkness of night was not the best time to be under the cover of suspicion, but he had every right as an American and citizen of this town to do so. And with the protection from Mayor Higgins and the death of Chief Stewart, he felt the freedom consume his entire being. He was the man up on the hill that everyone feared and secretly wanted to embody.

Passing storefronts that were successful businesses at one point in the past were now wood boards with unclever graffiti markings by the bored youths with no structure at home. Mac was born with nothing and accomplished so much as of today. It was possible; however, this generation wanted the money and fame to land on their laps with none of the work.

It was interesting to follow this man, this Black man carrying two Black people whom he had rescued from certain death going in the opposite direction of the bridge. He was marching through the remainder of the east side and into downtown, which was where he decided the days spent at the gym with lack of cardio caught up with him. The hulking man placed the two bodies on the floor as though they were delicate china so he could take a breather. Mac found a cement enclave in front of a boarded-up failed business and across from a successful restaurant dark as can be this late at night.

He attempted to use his phone as a way to not stand out to any passersby on Main Street when he remembered using the final percentages to livestream his frustrations. As the cocaine bump wore off, a chime played in the back of his head, warning him how that would come back around and affect him later. His viewers listened to him, did what he told them to do, and he had no reason to believe his drug-fueled rant wouldn't encourage them to act upon his words.

Headlights of an approaching car snapped him back to the present: the rain that had begun to fall and the bodybuilder man he was tracking. He chanced a peek around the cement pillar that shielded him from the view of the hunted, and he was gone. The large man and the two living bodies he carried vanished.

Of course, Mac was caught up in his own thoughts again, losing track of his own head and in turn track of realities. The man was around the corner and farther into downtown, but the way he was dressed, a three-piece suit, Mac knew downtown was not his final destination. As with all cities, there were the bad parts and the better parts. The east side of Bridgetown was the worst of the worst, downtown was less bad, and Black Rock was the okay part of the city. Although if the residents of Black Rock were asked, they refused to admit they lived in Bridgetown. They had their own section of land where little crime took place and wanted no association with the awful city they were forced to travel through if they needed to exit. Mac considered Black Rock as his destination, but building a mansion on a hill overlooking the scum of this city was the most powerful act he could manage. A White man in control drove those in this city wild. That Mac understood well.

Coming from the bridge was the car, a sedan Mac would assume was also following the bodybuilder man if he had arrived at this moment in time. In a split-second decision, he decided to lift his dead phone to his face, eyes on the black mirror reflecting his cracked image. Painting a picture of what Mac was on the path towards.

"You're not fooling anyone, Mac," the voice from the car said.

He knew the voice; he never wanted to hear it again. "Mayor Higgins, what a horrible delight to see you. Fucker."

"Yeah, yeah, yeah. We can make up and make out later. Get in. I need your help."

A flicker of pride shot into Mac's body and warmed his cold heart. Being wanted was a delight, but being needed was a necessity.

"You left me without a word when we were in this fight together. You hit another project without me. Why would I help you with anything?"

"Because your home is in danger of being penetrated. Now stop acting like a fucking child and get in."

The drops of rain fell hard on Mac's bald head. He didn't weigh his options but acted and entered the passenger side of the Ford Crown Vic.

Higgins's mayor's slicked hair he had witnessed on video hours earlier had become a crazy mess of spindled strands sprouting every which way. Makeup for television purposes had cracked, revealing his aging lines that had deepened in a quicker fashion these past few days.

Before the door was shut, Higgins took off farther into downtown. "I thought we were going to my home," Mac said.

"You have a ten-foot-high electric fence on the perimeter of your property that sits three thousand feet above the rest of the city. Nobody is within yards of your home, I know, I just went by there. But I do need your help, and I know your dick gets hard by that phrase. Your house was the icing to get you in this seat."

Mac grumbled at himself because he passed by over an hour ago and said, "Fuck you. Okay, then what do you need?"

"You'll see. I've got somebody who's been dying to see you."

CHAPTER 37

The entire car ride to wherever Ant was being taken, neither of the former coworkers said a word to one another. Of course, Stewart's car was unscathed other than a missing front fender while Ant's was more than likely totaled.

Ant managed to be the scapegoat of Bridgetown for their destruction of the city. Operation Save Bridgetown in the head of Mayor Higgins and in the head of resurrected former (current?) Chief Stewart was a return to the old days. The days where factories and businesses ruled over apartments and housing. A time when money was at the top of the priority list for running a city, and the citizens were a second thought in the eyes of the politicians. Politics was the rich doing whatever possible to stay richer than the people below them.

When they arrived at the house, Ant recognized it as one he had been to before. There was no effort to blindfold or hinder Ant's eyesight on their ten-minute journey from the vehicle accident that was no accident. He knew Bridgetown better than he knew himself. Even blindfolded, Ant would have been in the ballpark of the location. But the use of his legs was keeping him from doing much of anything.

"Get out," Kevin said with a rash of anger behind his tone. As though Ant had been the one who t-boned his car at that intersection.

"You got some crutches I could use?" Ant said.

"Crawl for all I care."

Kevin was out of the car and into the broken home but left the barn-red front door ajar, so Ant knew he was still invited inside.

A scan of the neighborhood told him this was not a place to scream and yell for help. The early morning hour sheltered Kevin from nosy neighbors witnessing a man commando crawling up the snaking walkway and lifting himself up two steps and through the screen door. And even if an early riser saw that, this was a place where people kept to their damn selves. Especially if they recognized him or Stewart as cops.

A flashback to living in the Washington Carver apartments. Seeing, hearing, and smelling murder was nobody else's business but between them and the deceased. And on the rare occasion the police were sniffing out a crime committed there, you didn't know nothing. As a child, his momma taught him that well, but after his brother's murder, everything changed. Ant turned into the one asking questions and growing frustrated by the lack of answers. They wanted the crime solved when it was their family member, but strangers could waste away with the rest of them. Ant understanding and empathizing with both sides was difficult to operate around.

Sweat and rainfall dribbling from his high forehead, lacerations scabbing open on his elbows and legs, and an intruding hunger rumbling in his gut couldn't stop him from falling embarrassingly inside the foyer that split the kitchen and TV room. Kevin was behind the door and shut the hunk of wood before Ant was fully past.

"Oh, so sorry, Anthony," Kevin cooed in a mocking tone.

The pain was present, but Ant had been through worse situations. He was trained for much worse than a door closing on his undoubtedly broken tibias and/or fibulas.

"Question for you, Chief." The final word had some spice on his tongue.

"You are in no position to be the one asking questions."

Kevin peering down in a blue and white striped polo tucked into a pair of blue jeans with no belt forced some bile to rumble in Ant's throat. Kevin was the skinniest guy he had ever seen but still had fat rolls on his obliques, under his neck, and the beginnings of a beer belly. Ignoring Kevin's words, Ant continued.

"You created a car accident in the middle of a fairly busy intersection and expect nobody to walk by, snap pictures, post them on the internet, and expect the incident to just disappear."

A huff was all Ant was expecting until Kevin said, "I have an entire department in the palm of my hands. I can make anything disappear. I've made a career out of doing that very thing. Especially photos on the internet. And in case you haven't noticed, this isn't the same city you remember from days past. We are in a new era of Bridgetown."

"What about me? I'm not some sad sack with no family to go home to. And I'm the fucking chief of police by your own doing." Ant's burst of anger surprised himself, and by the swivel of Kevin's head, it surprised him as well.

Whatever Kevin was cooking up in the kitchen could wait until he said his piece. It was a tick Ant knew he had. Kevin couldn't be wrong, about anything. And he would argue for hours until the other party was too tired or didn't give enough of a shit to carry on. A dish towel landed on the molded countertops that were white in a different century before he appeared in the entryway again.

"I know more about you than you know about yourself," Kevin said and began counting off on his skinny fingers. "Your momma died when you were a teen, one of your brothers was shot and killed in a drive-by when you were a young thing, your dad never wanted any part of you, your other brother is still living in this godforsaken city but hasn't talked to you in twenty-five years, and your wife is next on our list to take out." Ant tried to stay strong through this ordeal, but the mention of harm to Mary while in a helpless position caused a visible jolt Stewart failed to recognize or care to acknowledge. "Any fucking questions?"

There was no pause for a rebuttal as he disappeared back into the kitchen. The undeniable sound of boiling water followed the whoosh of pasta dumped out of a cardboard box was the only remaining sound. Ant's head pounded as it lay against the off-white linoleum floor. This entire place was like a torture room for the criminally insane. A test before he put Kevin inside the real one forever.

The quips about his life were largely true but too broad in nature. Ant knew his brother lived in Bridgetown, but neither made the effort to reach out. Ant didn't even have a clue what he looked like nowadays. But in a familial thread that connected them for eternity, he would recognize him as soon as he laid eyes on his face.

Mary was easy enough to locate, but she was the toughest person he knew. He believed wholeheartedly that she would protect Leo with all the will she had in her body. And knowing what he knew about little Leo, he could hold his own as well. But a deeper, darker thought lingered in the caves of his mind that if the department, if Kevin wanted her dead, she would have been six feet under already. Which Ant understood as Mary being used as leverage. Momentarily paralyzing Ant, dragging him to this house and killing him was not the end of the story. They wanted him for something else. What that was, he didn't know but feared he would soon find out.

Headlights flooded the front half of the home, and like a paranoid freak, Kevin ran to the window, pulled back the blinds, and, relieved by what he saw, returned to his stove.

"Not the neighborhood I would have picked for you," Ant said while continuing his commando crawl farther into the TV room. A carpet blew a puff of dust into his lungs, and he had to stifle a cough with more words. "You're kinda like the single peanut in a Hershey's bar in this hood, if you know what I'm sayin'." No couch and a single console TV sitting on the ground not plugged in. "Wanted to see how the lives of the human beings you're massacring lived before you were thrown in the big house, huh?"

He knew these words would dig under his skin a burrow there but remained silent as he opened the front door for his guests.

"No fucking way. You piece of shit. You faked your own death to make it more difficult for—" Mac Pulaski paused as he looked over at the sad hump of a human unable to stand. "Oh, Anthony. I didn't know you were joining us."

Mayor Higgins shoved Mac farther inside and slammed the door. "Do you ever fucking shut your mouth?"

"Only when the mayor's dick is—"

Another shove ended Kevin's quip and with Mac at Ant's level. The only difference was that Mac could stand again. Mac was part of their plan. Of course he was. Evil always found evil.

"You got the stuff?" Kevin asked.

"And I can't believe you were in on it. Are you trying to make me—"

"Shut the fuck up, Mac," Kevin said, receiving the plastic shopping bag from Higgins.

All the thoughts and digs Ant was feeling and wanting to say came to an end when Kevin removed a syringe and vial filled with a green liquid.

Ant was not going to be the scapegoat.

Ant was going to be the blame for the entire fucking thing.

CHAPTER 38

Seeing new police Chief Anthony Rawlings and the old police chief, presumed to be dead, by what the fucker of a mayor told Mac, caused his head to spin. The neighborhood Mac promised himself he'd rather be dead than pass through mixed with Kevin Stewart cooking in the asbestos-filled, mold-ridden, cracked floors of what barely functioned as a home nearly sent him to be level with Rawlings.

"You fucking liar," Mac said to Higgins, the words spilling out in close to a child's whine.

"We needed you to be out of the loop because it was important word didn't get—"

"I was not fucking talking to you. You fucking ghost," Mac said, cutting Kevin's words short, pointing an accusatory finger his way.

"You need to get over this so we can move on. But since you are so insistent—God, you're a fucking child—I have the same answer as Kev. You have fucked us so many times during this process that you had to be on the outside of the staged death. You would have preached it to your online freaks. We didn't think you would drive a hole through our well thought out plan and start without us. But the past is the past," Higgins said, passing the syringe from one hand to the other as though it were on fire.

The new information sat heavy in the silent home and inside Mac's mind for a beat. He understood he wasn't a man sent from Jesus who was to spread good to all the citizens of this godforsaken city, but he wasn't the imbecile they thought he was.

Minutes passed before Mac trudged across the rotting wood floor and through the threshold of the cracked tile kitchen, extending his arm toward Kevin. It was taken into a firm handshake, and the smiles that broke between the two business partners was a release Mac required to move on.

"Maybe y'all can touch dicks too," Anthony said, lying on his back, his words floating to the ceiling.

Anthony sprawled out on the floor helpless with two legs refusing to function was a wet dream coming to reality for Mac. The khaki pants that were coming up on day three were stretched by an overwhelming sensation of his penis growing three sizes.

"Even when we worked together, Ant always used wit and comedy to distract from the bad happening around him," Stewart said.

"Oh, please, Anthony, continue. You know when we had our little chat at the diner a few days back, you thought you were in control of the conversation and the whole situation with Kevin's bitch of a wife." Mac paused, glaring at Kevin. Kevin appeared out of touch with reality.

When Mac was inches from the immovable object on the floor, he squatted and looked Anthony in the eyes. "I'm in control now, motherfucker." With a wave of his hand, Higgins approached with the syringe at the ready. Its green juices bubbled in the barrel.

"Don't worry. The pain you feel in your legs will disappear once this stuff is in your veins," Higgins said, standing shoulder to shoulder with Mac.

There were many discussions with the former police chief and the mayor about "Operation Save Bridgetown." The brilliant plan of sending unsuspecting infected people in to clear out the projects, leaving all three of their hands clean of any wrongdoing. And building Bridgetown to its once great economic status. However, infecting Anthony with the serum and letting him run wild was not part of any talks he was involved in. But he wasn't mad about that. It was a brilliant turn of events Mac was pleased to witness firsthand. At the tail end of the last project clearing, he witnessed a little girl tied to the stretcher presumed to be the next of the infected, so Anthony seemed to be the best for last. The three escapees he followed until Higgins picked him up and all that happened before this moment was in the past. This was all he cared about from now until the end.

A light tap on the front door caused a simultaneous head whip to the entryway. Even Anthony, lying there accepting his fate and probably praying to God, lifted his head at the unexpected sound.

"See who it is," Mac saw Higgins mouth silently to Stewart, who was watching this unfold from the kitchen. As though if he were far enough away, he wouldn't need to claim responsibility.

They watched as Kevin moved the baby blue curtains littered with cigarette burns, which he most certainly did not choose himself, and pressed his face against the window to view the front porch. As quickly as his face lay on the window, he pulled away with his palm cupping his mouth.

"Who is it?" Higgins mouthed again as they waited in anticipation for a response. But Kevin was backing away, exiting stage left into the only bedroom.

The faintest tap at the door came again.

"Go see," Higgins instructed Mac.

Mac grumbled under his breath, unlatched the dead bolt, and opened the door ajar.

"Don't open the fucki—"

All was silent again as Mac's body took over his mind and stepped back into the house as though a gun were being held to his stomach.

Leo stepped inside. Kevin's missing son. The boy Mac was feet away from killing at the park.

Call it instinct or curiosity, but Mac took a peek back at Anthony, who had pulled himself into a sitting position featuring a smile that touched each ear, showing off his perfect white teeth.

CHAPTER 39

Ant had no idea little Leo would show up on the doorstep of the home where his presumed dead father was hiding out. But seeing his rosy, red cheeks, oval head, and calm demeanor plastered a feel-good smile on his face. There was a panic still in the back of his head, thinking of how fear-stricken Mary would be once she opened the bedroom door to find the bed they shared, rented out for the night to Leo, empty.

Questions flooded his head, as he's sure they did for the two men standing before him and the dad who scampered into the bedroom, doing everything he could to not be a father. How did Leo get here? How did Leo know where to find them? How did Leo have such impeccable timing?

Little Leo sauntered through the door, passing by the opened mouth, reddened faces of Mac Pulaski and Mayor Higgins to stand in front of Ant with his little arms crossed over his chest. Evil men with a death serum ready for injection, scared to move forward because an eight-year-old kid blocked their path.

"How did you know we were here?" Higgins said, kneeling to become level with Leo as though he felt he had any connection to the kid.

The response he received was one Ant knew all too well: silence. In a triumphant return of Ant's wit in terrible situations, he thought this kid would make a great CIA agent. *Loose lips sink ships.*

"Yeah, what the fuck you doin' here, kid?" Mac said, taking a couple steps back.

Silence again, but movement this time. Leo took small steps back in his untied, muddied, formerly white sneakers. Guilt racked Ant for not offering him a bath or washing his clothes at the very least. Leo's eyes burned through the two goons as he stood beside Ant, whose elbow was hurting from carrying his top-half body weight and his presumably fractured forearm.

Hot breath and words wafted into Ant's ear canal. "Dad. Here."

He knew. He knew his dad was alive and just in the other room. Little Leo didn't care what these two were up to. He was here to see his dad. His dad who wanted him killed for his own personal gain. His dad who abandoned him for another woman. His dad who shouldn't hold that title any longer. He wanted to see him.

"What did he say? What does he know?" Higgins said, holding the syringe like he was preparing for a sword fight.

"Kevin." The name felt strange on Ant's lips. Chief Stewart was his boss for the majority of his career, and calling him by his first name was never an option. But considering the last few days, all respect he held was gone. "You can come out. The kid knows you're here."

A click and a creak echoed through the unfurnished space, each step more prominent than the last. The top of Kevin's balding head appeared, then the rest of his hair curtained around his oval head, followed by his uncomfortably disproportioned body.

"Hey, buddy," Kevin said.

The rush of anger that flooded through Ant was going to spill from his mouth until Leo spoke for himself. Not with words, but with actions. He sat on the floor, a floor Ant had been on for close to an hour and wouldn't recommend to his worst enemy, but Leo placed one hand on Ant's back and the other on his chest. A small gesture that changed the air in the room. The squeeze of little Leo's embrace shot Ant back to the night before his brother's death. A hug he had never received before. One final touch before he couldn't talk with him or play with him for as long as Ant lived. It felt the same now. A flash of doing whatever possible to protect this kid pulsated his entire body, including his useless legs.

"That is a bad man, Leo. Come with me," Kevin said and held out his hand.

Leo squeezed Ant tighter.

"Fuck the kid, Kevin. We got shit to do," Mac said, moving toward Higgins.

Within seconds, the syringe exchanged hands, and the silver point was headed for Ant's chest.

"No," Ant heard from one of the two in the back.

What followed was a piercing, continuous sound. Ant thought an alarm was triggered inside the home but quickly realized this was not the kind of home with a burglary prevention system.

It was Leo. His eyes had glazed over, and his mouth hung open like he was going for the world record longest yawn in history. Ant's head was spinning along with the room when he noticed he and Leo were the last two standing. The front door was open, and the three men stumbled into the east side neighborhood where none of them belonged.

"Sorry," was the last word he heard before Ant fell into darkness.

CHAPTER 40

"I don't trust him," Sherrie said, looking out at the single-floor home with the front pane glass window showing off the living room where Walter and she were brought after a tumultuous event at their apartment complex. Roger's home was a place where Sherrie never imagined owning or even stepping foot inside.

"He's our only way to finding Shonda, so we have no choice but to…trust," Walter said, his words tripping at the end. As they sat in a second car Roger was letting them borrow for the next steps, Sherrie was trembling with rage. Rage at being controlled. Rage at the unknown.

It was a tough situation to be in when every aching bone in Sherrie's body was screaming to go back to the complex and search every square foot for her baby. Roger warned against going, especially considering he expected the police to have a mile-long perimeter preventing any person not associated with the police from getting close.

Walter was right, of course, but she remained uneasy about a guy who knocked them out, carried them to his home, and strongly suggested they stick around with him.

After the smoke cleared between the two men, there was a somewhat healthy conversation that took place. Roger introduced himself and explained that he worked for a law firm in downtown Bridgetown. He received many phone calls from family members of the residents of the Barnum apartment complex who got alarming phone calls from loved ones, trembling with fear as death climbed closer, then the call went dead.

When the family members attempted to access the apartments, the police had the place cordoned off miles from the entrance and were not allowing anyone on the property. It was a suspicion Roger took seriously, even going and checking out the scene for himself. Knowing the area of the Barnum tower well enough, he was able to get a view of the front by accessing a building of an associate a couple of streets over. He could see the front door boarded up and a ton of police activity, although the cops seemed to be enjoying themselves with a laugh and a meal.

Feeling a close connection to Bridgetown and having grown up in the George Washington Carver apartments, he decided to take matters into his own hands. Maybe getting ahead of a possible next hit of whatever was happening could be lifesaving. He camped out the next night before any activity began when a police cruiser pulled up outside. He said it seemed eerie because they didn't look like they were responding to any sort of emergency. Behind the cop car was an ambulance. A stretcher was unloaded with a person or what remained of a person strapped down. An officer retreated from his vehicle and stood by as the EMT rolled the gurney inside the complex.

Knowing the apartments, he snuck in through a side emergency door. He searched for the EMT or the person/thing on the gurney, but all he could hear were the sounds of splintering wood and the short screams for help, then silence. The cycle continued for what Roger said felt like forever. Since it seemed the destruction was moving upward, he sprinted up the stairs to the third floor where it was quiet, so far. He didn't want to move into any apartments, so he just waited for the bad to come to him. Something he said he regretted.

He saw Sherrie, then Walter exit their apartment and hurry down the stairs. Minutes later, sitting on the floor at the end of the corridor, the person, more of a monster with a limp, penguin-walked its way to each door, using its head to demolish the safety net of each living space with one smash. The thing never noticed Roger. It was out for blood and would go one by one until the end.

As the thing was causing its mayhem, the elevator dinged and the EMT was there with an empty stretcher. This part of the story caused Walter to pounce on Roger again and give him a few good hits for not taking action, which Roger said he deserved. The EMT checked a few apartments ahead of the monster until he found an unlocked door. Sherrie and Walter's. Seconds later, a teen girl was strapped down, bucking and begging for release, and she was on the elevator and gone before Roger could move.

As the monster thing smashed the door and cleared their apartment, Roger snuck inside Walter and Sherrie's as the thing was snacking on someone else's flesh. And that was when he created the plan to take them out of the complex when all was quiet again.

"Why didn't you just call somebody?" Sherrie had asked.

"Who would I call? The police were the ones who looked to have initiated the entire event."

"I don't know. The FBI, the CIA, the president of the United States?"

"You need to trust me when I say stopping this on our own is going to be the only way to put this to rest."

Now, Walter drove them to set up at one of the two remaining housing apartments in Bridgetown where the presumed next hit would take place, and Roger would be at the other, three blocks away.

Sherrie would never put herself in this type of situation, but for Shonda, she would die for that girl.

CHAPTER 41

Mac woke facing the sky. White clouds smoked the blue and he guessed by feel that it was mid-morning. Where had the time gone? One second, he was running from the awful noise coming from the mouth of that child, and now it was several hours later and he was laid out on a sidewalk like weekly trash pickup. In the foreground, faces stared down upon him. Three faces. Three Black faces. Eyes white as the clouds surrounded by a thick dark skin and no other features.

"Mac?" The teeth of one of them showed yellow as he spoke. How had one of them known his name? He didn't associate with their kind because they didn't like him for his beliefs. Mac was always outcasted.

"I told you it was him," another of the faces said.

"We're here to help, Mac," the third said.

Help? Mac didn't need help. But just then, a memory of being in that old factory babysitting one of the run-ins. Hearing Natalie, sweet Natalie, murdered inside Mac's closet by that bitch, Sadie. A repressed recollection that remained controlled for a little over twenty-four hours. A cocaine bump and using the remaining of his cell phone battery to livestream, asking his followers for…help.

A look around told him he was across the way from the dump of a home Chief, or former Chief Stewart hid from the world while the city of Bridgetown mourned the loss of a great man. Except that was the furthest from the truth. An honorable man didn't screw another man trying to help save his ass.

Now it felt like a dream, these faces, fans, followers, who had come from wherever to help take Bridgetown back to what it used to be. They were late. But better late than never.

"What do you need us to do?" the first of the speaking faces asked.

This was the east side of the city where no rich, White man should be caught dead. Mac was dragged by Mayor Higgins against his own free will. The three faces, while he wasn't sure of their financial status, would be dead if anybody exited one of these abandoned-looking homes and spotted his helpers. However, if Mac was lying on this front lawn of fried grass for hours, he figured at least the homes in this particular area were vacant. Which was why Stewart chose that place. Run-down, quiet, and undetected from the city.

"Get—" Mac tried but was met with a coughing fit. "Get out of here. Go downtown and make some noise."

"Noise? What do you mean by—"

"I mean do anything to get the attention of everybody. Cause mayhem. Burn shit down. Make fucking noise."

The three heads nodded in understanding in unison and were gone in seconds.

Scoping the area again, Mac was now looking for Kevin and Higgins, who had inevitably disappeared. Logic, though there was none to the situation, told him they should be lying passed out in the same place. There was nobody. The door to the temporary residence of Stewart was wide open, waiting upon the next squatter to call home. The surrounding homes—if they could be referred to as such—lined the road far beyond an eyesore, leaving Mac wondering why these shacks of brokenness weren't included in "Operation Save Bridgetown." Then the silence answered his ponder. Not even the broken scum of this city would live in these sorry excuses for a dwelling. But Mac knew some were around.

Dizziness and pain ravaged his head as he sat up. Once he found his bearings and was steady on his legs, he approached the home he was chased from hours ago. One cautious step inside told him it was as empty as expected. Anthony gone. The kid gone. Where could a fat cop with two broken legs have gone? After checking the bedroom to be on the safe side, Mac closed the door, locked the dead bolt, and plopped onto the floor. He knew his followers had received his message. There were more than the three he met outside. And even with three guys starting the ravage downtown, Mac was back.

As he scanned the small space and located the intact syringe, Mac was back in control. In control of the city. In control of the mayor and chief. And once the chaos commenced, Mac would walk through downtown assessing his work and return to his home to take his place as the king of Bridgetown.

But for now, he was safe in the least safe part of the city.

Squatters' rights, bitches.

CHAPTER 42

The smell hit Ant before his eyes opened. Bleach mixed with floor cleaner mixed with the chalkiness of medication so strong it stung the upper part of his nose as his vision came into focus. A woman in blue scrubs stood at his bedside, hanging an IV bag of clear liquid and saying, "Hello there, Mr. Rawlings."

Remembrances of being in the house in the east side of Bridgetown with Kevin, Higgins, and Mac sprang into his thoughts. On instinct, he attempted to get out of the bed, but before he could lift his upper half, the wire from his finger ox reader, the nasal cannula impeding his nostrils, and the nurse placing a gentle hand on his chest lowered him to the bed again.

Ant had been to Bridgetown Hospital many times. Once as a kid, a year after his brother's death—Stanley had been taken from George Washington Carver apartments to the coroner's office, to the morgue, and soon after the smallest coffin Ant had seen. Ant had become much more reckless in those years and decided to ride his bike, one he found lying in the front grass of the apartments, into East Main Street.

He would watch as a car came around the sharp curve and pedal as fast as he could until he reached the other side. Most cars flew around the bend at twenty over the speed limit, and it was a thrill to hear the squealing of the car's tires as they tried to avoid the kid on the bicycle. Words Ant had heard his mother repeatedly say in frustration only to say, "never say that word," were spit at him each time, as the close call with death continued toward downtown. A full -sized pickup truck with a driver distracted by his dog in the passenger seat made no attempt to slow as the others did.

When the expected sound of squealing tires was absent and the truck barreled across the yellow line dividing east and west travel routes, he hit both handle brakes and wanted to swing around, facing the direction he came. He wished he could be back home in his room, forgetting the world outside and forgetting this stupid game, but the bike's front wheel jerked to the left and locked in that position, throwing Ant to the pavement. He landed on the edge of the road where all the weight on his left shoulder shattered it on impact.

The lie he told his mother was that he tripped on the curb running to the grass area that split the front sidewalk and parking lot, a Momma-approved spot, and to this day, he wasn't sure she believed him. After six days of complaining, she finally took him to the emergency room where the doctor berated Momma for not taking Ant earlier. A sling for a few weeks fixed his arm just right.

As an adult, Ant was in Bridgetown Hospital too many times to keep track of due to his job. Following up with doctors and nurses on arrests he made that landed criminals in the hospital. Being dispatched to the hospital when a patient became irate. And each time some mentally unstable person made an empty threat to cause harm to hospital staff. Each time, those automatic front doors opened to an emergency department filled with citizens who were hurting, looking for a drug push, or simply for a day off from work. Even with all the bodily fluids painted on the walls, the smell remained the same.

"Oh, Anthony," a familiar voice called before Mary's face appeared over him and smacked a wet kiss on his forehead. "I'm so sorry."

It was unclear what she was apologizing for. A sympathetic one for his two broken legs or letting Leo out of her sight?

"Leo," Ant said in a choked gasp. His throat was a cascade of bee stings as he fought to swallow any ounce of saliva he could locate. What had happened between the time Leo turned into a siren and where he lay now?

"He's right here, honey," Mary said. "And I know he got out of the house and I'm sorry. I hope you can trust me again."

"He's here. That's all that matters," Ant said with all the smile he could muster.

A twist of his neck spotted Leo on the green chair with chin resting on his knees, staring at Ant. Leo had saved him. It was unclear what the syringe of liquid would have done, but based on what he knew about "Operation Save Bridgetown," he knew Leo had saved his life.

"What time is it?" Of all the questions shuffling through Ant's slot machine of thoughts, Mary's reaction told him it was the last words she expected from his mouth.

Either way, she looked at her watch and said, "Six thirty-seven PM."

"Good. I still have time," Ant said out loud but more to himself.

Mary knew that look that crossed Ant's face, Determination. The aim for completion. Not stopping until the job was done. "You are not leaving this bed. You just got out of surgery."

The temperature dropped in Ant's body. The passage of time had been clouded by him finishing off his three enemies. Surgery. His legs were under a knitted blanket, and if not for the fear of sending his nurse into a panic, running into the room, he would have screamed so every patient, nurse, doctor, and even the chaplain could hear. He muffled his voice with further thoughts, thoughts of how much pain medication he had to intake for no feeling at all to be in his lower half. The thoughts of how he was the only one who knew how to stop Stewart, Higgins, and Mac, and he couldn't do that from a hospital bed. The thoughts of being bedridden for possibly months. The thoughts of failing the city of Bridgetown.

"They say your femur broke on your right leg and came inches away from severing your femoral artery. On your left leg, your femur is fine, but your shin bone snapped in half. You were possibly bleeding internally, and I signed off for surgery." Mary's mouth was moving, and he heard her words, but all he could think about was finishing the job. "I had no other choice," Mary continued, tears tracing the same path where earlier ones had travelled. "I was so scared I would lose you." She plopped her whole body on top of him, and even though her weight was crushing his rib cage, any pain, especially from love, was what he needed at that moment.

What he hadn't realized was Leo had gotten up from the chair and placed a small hand on Ant's right leg. Even love that could not be felt was impactful all the same.

CHAPTER 43

The plan was simple, but Sherrie still didn't trust Roger with any part of her being. Growing up in the projects changed and would change anyone else's perception of people and life. Neighbors were the ones you had to rely on because they were in the same living situation, holding a full-time job that paid well but still forced them to live in an apartment complex in a section of the city where the political leaders refused to better the east side complexes and instead spent millions of dollars to put a baseball stadium in the already booming downtown.

The comradery with those feeling and experiencing the same issues and struggles was like no other. And when a rich man, Black or not, waited in your apartment to knock you unconscious and carry you three miles to his home, no matter the reasoning, he was untrustworthy in the eyes of Sherrie. He reminded her of politicians. The rich passing laws to make them and their friends richer.

Now she and Walter sat in their car with the engine running and the headlights off at eleven at night down the street from one of the two apartment complexes that hadn't been hit yet. And if anybody else had to endure what Ms. Kara and all the other residents of the George Washington Carver apartments had to face, Sherrie hoped she could save them from any trauma or death, along with finding and saving her only daughter.

The waiting was the worst part of this ordeal. Walter sat next to Sherrie, drifting in and out of sleep, waiting like goofballs parked on a side street a block from Trumbull Gardens apartments, a college dorm set up for those less fortunate. Roger was waiting at Greenfield Hills complex. With time to think, the thoughts Sherrie could spring up in her mind were all three of them were sitting ducks, waiting for a hawk to swoop in and destroy them for looking suspicious. And the icing on the cake was not knowing if this would occur or not.

From what Roger told her, this incident that they lived through was not the first. The Barnum apartments were hit, apparently clearing out the entire complex. Then George Washington Carver was the same. If she hadn't seen the creature limping towards Walter, and then Ms. Kara torn open, there was no way she would believe any of it.

There had to be hundreds of fatalities, which meant there had to be hundreds of family members of the deceased wondering what happened to their loved ones. There should be a fight for information. There should be a fight for justice. But if what Roger had said was true, police corruption led to an easy cover-up. Deem the building a hazardous place and nobody could enter or be within a mile or two of the apartment, then make the bodies disappear. Authority was control, and citizens were under that control.

Walter's phone ripped Sherrie from her thoughts, and he answered immediately after being woken from what he called "resting his eyes."

After a back-and-forth that Sherrie could hear one side of, Walter said, "Shit" and flung his phone, nearly striking Sherrie in the knee with the dead phone.

"What do we do now?" Sherrie asked.

"Get there ASAP," Walter said, flinging the transmission into drive and taking off with what looked like not a thought behind those brown eyes.

Within minutes, they were parked under a sodium light that flickered the sedan in and out of the low-lit neighborhood existence. The exterior of this complex was a different set-up than Washington or even Barnum. Instead of a driveway leading to the entrance of a front circle separated from the city life, this complex was mixed with long abandoned businesses of Bridgetown past. A much more difficult, in Sherrie's opinion, place to pull this off unnoticed.

"You stay here, and I'll see if Roger needs help," Walter said, reaching for the door handle.

He was keeping Sherrie out of the rescue of their daughter, and she wouldn't take that erasure without a fight.

"No. I'm going with you. If I have a chance to save my own daughter, I'm taking it. Even if it takes my own life." Before Walter could protest, she was out of the car, already crouched, sneaking alongside the dilapidated building.

Walter followed while she remained in the shadows, which was easy enough, and saw the police cruiser sitting out front. It was a relief to witness herself as it meant Roger wasn't a total bullshit artist.

Walter was doing his best to keep Sherrie out of the light, as she was far too focused on getting inside the apartment but glad to be yanked out of sight of the police officer leaning on the cruiser staring up at the building enjoying a cigarette.

Approaching from behind the cop was Roger doing a duck walk that caused Sherrie's lip to twitch upward, and almost as a response, Roger held his index finger to his lips to indicate silence and control of the situation.

"What the fuck," the cop said when Roger smacked the side of the cruiser as a distraction, then snuck up and wrapped his large bicep around the cop's neck, putting him out in the same amount of time Sherrie had lasted in the same stranglehold.

Within seconds of Roger dragging the unconscious officer across the street and into the alleyway, he emerged, an ambulance pulled in behind the police cruiser, and as the EMT exited and assessed the area with pinched eyebrows, he said "hm" and continued to the rear of the ambulance. He pulled a gurney from the back and rushed inside with a body bucking at the straps that helped the thing down. The creature. Sherrie realized that this was happening.

A whispered call brought Walter and Sherrie to Roger across the way where the cop lay motionless.

"Okay, at least we took out the one with the weapon. However, he will become conscious momentarily. I will remain with him and do some interrogating while you two attempt to stop the threat." Sherrie knelt and pulled the service revolver from the officer's belt.

"Let's go," she said, darting toward the apartment complex without permission from either of the men that had brought her to this place in her life. And if Shonda was inside, she needed to be the first to know.

The EMT was nowhere within the first few steps, but the first of the screams sounded, the same tone and crippling fear behind each one that were still ingrained in her head from her own apartment that had been part of this tragedy.

The first floor was nothing more than a desk that was used for a concierge person years prior, an elevator the EMT had surely taken, and zigzagging steps leading them to this devastation.

"We need to follow the screams," Sherrie said.

"We need to get ahead of them," Walter said and bolted up two steps at a time with Sherrie close in tow.

They touched the top of the three flights of stairs where the silence was eerie, knowing what was to come to these folks.

"No," Walter said, keeping Sherrie at bay when she ran for the stairs. He understood where she was going. She wanted to put an end to it as the cries grew louder and the splintering of wood sent gooseflesh through her entire skin.

The creature was as grotesque as she remembered, only this one was different. Shorter, younger, skinnier. The skin peeling away left the person they used to be unrecognizable. Sherrie readied the gun to take the thing out in the hallway, putting an end to this once and for all. But when it came ready for her to pull the trigger, something prevented her finger from bending.

Flashes of Matteo and the two guys in her car and finding her father dead in his bedroom created a mental block that she would soon understand. She couldn't do it.

The creature ignored the two of them huddled in the hall and reared back, destroying the door, rendering the piece of wood keeping the bad out useless within seconds.

"I'll take care of this," Walter said, snatching the gun from Sherrie's hand and running for the apartment. Sherrie followed but couldn't watch. She hunkered down in a small kitchen while the creature snacked on the apartment owner's neck tendon. She had experienced too much pain and destruction in her lifetime, and more was not on her to-do list.

There was no hesitation when Walter pulled the trigger. The thing's head exploded like a pin to a water balloon. Its gooey green contents painted the walls into a beautiful silence and an end to the violence. Another shot in the back that was not needed but was what Walter needed.

"No, no, no," Walter cried out, and it was the most distressed Sherrie had heard her husband. She couldn't see from her position on the floor, so she approached with cautious steps.

"What?" Sherrie said, but she saw what had brought Walter to tears. A gold bracelet with the initials "SS" dangled from the dainty wrist of the creature now reduced to a puddle of nothing.

After what felt like a lifetime of disbelief inside the small living space, they forced themselves to move forward. This wasn't about protecting a city she knew so well and loved with her entire heart any longer; now, this was about revenge.

Their steps were quick from floor three to the ground floor where the EMT crossed their path with a new victim strapped to the gurney, a syringe of green goo in the middle-aged man's broken arm plunged halfway. The twenty-something EMT was as surprised to see them as they were to see him.

There were no words exchanged. A single gunshot in the center of the EMT's forehead was all the conversation that needed to happen. Sherrie unstrapped the man on the gurney, and he thanked her and ran off. It was a decision that may come back to haunt her later, but she was done with the death and the sadness of her people.

"What happened in there? I heard gunfire." Roger sounded panicked when they reached him. But the look on their faces explained the situation to him without saying a word. "Sorry. I did get some information out of him, though," Roger said, pointing to the police officer, who had bruising forming around both eyes.

"What?" Walter sounded defeated.

"Well, it turns out that this isn't something the police force and medics have set up. This is coming from a higher authority." Roger paused, then said, "Mayor Higgins."

Walter and Sherrie shared puzzled looks. "How can you be sure?" Sherrie asked. She could feel the tears staining her cheeks.

"With this." Roger pulled an iPhone from his pocket. "I had Officer Morse here unlock his phone, and I called the contact under 'Boss.' Higgins answered the phone. He seemed to be expecting a call because he asked if the job was done. I tried to interrogate him, but once he recognized it wasn't his cop friend, he hung up."

"So, what do we do now?" she asked. "Go after him?"

Roger looked at the bloodied, unconscious cop, then back at Walter and Sherrie. "I'm going to guarantee they will be coming to us." On cue, a fury of sirens blared and echoed from a few blocks away.

"But what were they doing? What is their end goal?" Walter asked.

"Targeting low-income housing and eliminating everyone inside. That sounds like common sense to me. C'mon, we should go."

They exited the alleyway when Walter stopped. "No."

"What do mean, no?" Roger asked.

"We can't let them get away with this."

"They have an entire police force with a multitude of weaponry, and we have a pistol with maybe two rounds. We lose that fight every time," Roger said.

"Then I go down defending my brothers and sisters."

"This is suicide, Walter. Please come with us. We'll get them back for this. It's guaranteed, but right now we need to go," Sherrie said.

Walter extended his arms to the mouth of the alley with the gun barrel at the end. Sherrie knew Walter well enough that before today, he had not a bone in his body that could kill, but he had a determined look in his eyes, a mission of killing every cop he saw like he did the EMT. But right now, he dropped his arms to his side and conceded. They needed more firepower and more people.

Walter stuffed the gun into his rear waistband, and they exited the alleyway.

The three of them would not give up. The strength of community was stronger than any police force could ever know.

CHAPTER 44

Mac lasted three hours in the deplorable, wretched shack of a living space before he walked out the door never to return. The clouds that he saw earlier receded, and the sky to the west was preparing for night by painting the Bridgetown skyline, not the few skyscrapers that stood out, mixing with the baseball stadium and backdropped by an ugly industrial plant topped off by a smoke stack barber pole of red and white, but the opposite way featuring all this city needed, Mac's McMansion in full view, in a magenta and turquoise stunning visual.

To the east was downtown. It was where Natalie would have been causing mayhem for a diversion from the mayhem he was part of causing in the projects. The plan was to go again tonight at the Greenfield Hills complex, but Mac had enough of the mayor and former police chief. Mac's internet followers were there in place of Natalie, and he was walking away from the chaos, because once again Mac was innocent while those around him suffered from his actions.

With the sun setting over the past two days, Mac was ready for his own bed again. There was a possibility of Sadie sitting on his very bed waiting with Mac's entire arsenal spread on the hardwood floor shared with Natalie's blood that surely had flowed her life juice like a river from the closet into the space that Mac looked forward to at the end of his hard-fought days. Up on the hill, protected by the electric fence, and his girls trained to end anybody who tripped the security system. Now, Mac's biggest threat was one of those girls he trained well enough to execute Mac before he entered his own property.

Sitting on the hill above those who would never have a place like his was Mac's warm and fuzzy feeling. He worked his ass off to get what he deserved. Some guy working sixteen hours every day, providing food for his family, was praised for his dedication. Working himself to death so his wife and kids could live comfortably. Mac was doing the same but received none of the glory. Finding the correct victim for his crimes, methodically planning out each step, and removing the body without a trace of evidence leading back to him was more work than some 9-to-5 desk job. He knew because he was that guy for years.

At ten years old, Mac's parents had their final needle entry. He waited and wished for that day to arrive. He would wake in the morning and his mom would be in the kitchen, rubber band still tied to her upper bicep, needle hanging over the side of the chipped wood round table where Mac ate his meals, and a coffee mug in hand while she stared at the empty walls bleeding rust in the drug-infused state that disregarded her only child. Dad preferred the bedroom and after his shot he would lay supine and study the growing yellow stains on the white ceiling. When they escaped their separate drug worlds, they would become angry and lash out at the first human they saw, which was Mac each time.

That morning routine came to an end when Mac completed the typical two-mile walk from the local elementary school back home on a Tuesday in February. His fingers were reddened and had gone through the changes of the brutal cold from normal, to painful, to numb. Before the feeling in his joints could return, the rest of his jacket- and pants-covered body joined in when his mother was lying on her side, eyes unflinching and pupils a size he would never forget. His father, who preached hard work to Mac, in the bedroom lay on his back with dried maroon vomit covering his face and his chest at its final resting place. Most kids his age would be upset at the loss of both of their parents at the same time, but Mac welcomed the weight being lifted: of a mom who rarely remembered she had a son and a dad who remembered he had a son but between work and drugs never performed the basic fatherly duties.

Weeks after the bodies were stretchered away and the determination was made that Mac had no extended family that wanted to take responsibility for the son of two druggies, he was placed into a foster home. His first day in the home was the first time after his parents' deaths that he wished for that life back.

He was mostly on his own, making his own decisions, providing his own meals and getting used to being independent. The home took those freedoms away from him because of his age.

"Don't do this, don't do that," was constantly thrown at him by adults who felt they were in charge of his life. Mac was there for two and a half weeks before he had enough and snuck out one night, not telling anyone where he was going, not even the kid he bonded with in his short stint. More importantly, he had no idea where he was going himself. He had no parents, no family, no friends, and no place to rest his head at night.

As the days of wandering the state passed, he found his way to the outskirts of Bridgetown. A bridge that led into and out of the city, the only way in and out, was a fact Mac loved. He knew he would call this place home one way or another.

Hunger was what first landed Mac in juvenile detention. There was a fancy five-star restaurant downtown three blocks from the run-down projects. A spot of sunlight in a sea of darkness was Mac's meal ticket. The rear door leading into the kitchen had a busted lock after Mac took a hammer to the weak hold. Inside were long silver tables flanked by cook tops, and hovering over all were pots and pans. But where Mac could be found was the walk-in refrigerator. Vegetables, drinks, snacks, meats at his disposal. He knew, even at a young age, that it would be short-lived. He would go back through the same back door every night after the final chef left for the night. The owner became wise to his routine and had one of the Bridgetown officers stake out the place. Mac was halfway through a full cheesecake when an officer flung the fridge door open and placed the barrel of his gun on Mac, who laughed as they slapped handcuffs on him and drove him to the detention center.

The first time Mac was placed in the detention center, he was twelve years old, and the final time he was thrown in big boy jail, he was twenty-one years old. The system failed the teenage foster kid who had nowhere to go, and he was ready for the constant cycle of prison and freedom to take up the remainder of his life. Petty theft and soft burglaries were his ways of making money. He held a few jobs, but if the entry-level position didn't come with a supervisory role, he refused to take orders from anyone superior to him.

His final prison stint matched him with Frank. Frank was Mac's cellmate who was in for a double homicide.

"I don't regret shit," Frank said the first time Mac asked the most asked question in the big house.

"Why?"

"If you think the double was the only thing I did, you would be far from the truth. I got twenty-seven kills in my arsenal. I was raised by myself after my parents died in a car accident. No money, no home, no nothin' at twelve years young. Years after being depressed, I hatched the perfect plan. Find a girl who nobody will ever miss. A druggie who lives under an overpass, a nobody who uses a tarp for a blanket, shit like that. See, I had no interest in drugs, but they know the stuff and they know who deals the stuff. So, you treat her real nice, like a nice loving boyfriend. Give her gifts, rub her back, and fuck her if ya like. Eventually you meet her dealer, and she buys her usual fixation. Say you'll do it with her and before she can even open the baggie, *blam*, she's dead, and now you can sell to the other useless humans, especially in this godforsaken city. Lather, rinse, repeat. Don't get caught is the obvious take away from all of this."

"How did you get caught?"

Frank leapt up from his bed and clamped his palm around Mac's scrawny neck and wouldn't let go until Mac's face was a shade of purple. "What a stupid motherfuckin' question."

"I mean—" Mac coughed out, regaining his voice. "So I don't make the same mistake."

"I like you, Matt. That's why I didn't kill you just now. Remember that," Frank said. Correcting his name was the furthest thing from Mac's mind. "I took on too much at once,"

Frank continued. "After a couple consecutive connections with dealers, I was raking in some serious cash. I still have some hidden in the city. Although, life in prison means it will sit there for the rest of eternity. Anyway, I thought I could take on two girls at once, you know double the cash, but one was a fucking rat, and I fired two shots from my pistol with sirens down the road. Both girls dead and a cop at my fucking front door. When a cop is a witness, you are royally fucked in the ass."

Mac was released a month later, and his plan was going to be put into action.

But Gloria put all of that on hold. She stood at the corner of Main and Capitol where prisoners were tossed back into the streets with the unwashed clothes they were booked with on their back. All thoughts and gripes Mac had were flushed away by the beauty of Gloria.

His eyes began at her toned calves accentuated by blood-red stiletto heels, climbing to her perfect thighs barely covered by a tight pencil skirt. A white blouse not afraid to show off a red lace bra held humps Mac salivated over. Her face, though, was the most perfect piece of her. Bug-eyed sunglass were perched on her adorable nose just above red lips Mac could already taste. But what really caught Mac's eye was her shimmering bald head.

"This is the last time. I swear I am done giving you chances," Gloria said into the phone she held to her ear. Her accent was South American or European. A gorgeous sound Mac wanted playing in his mind on repeat.

She ended the call and turned to see Mac's jaw unhinged from the top of his mouth. "If you're going to stare, at least give me a compliment," she said.

"My-my uh, I-I-I." Mac was speechless for the first time in his life.

"This is a great compliment," she said. "I tell you what, my dimwitted boyfriend has lied to me three times about when he will be released, he keeps getting into fights and pushing his sentencing date. But you, you are a free man. So, take me on a date."

"I—yes—okay—yes," Mac sputtered.

"I came to this country ten years ago and am fluent in this place's language. But it seems you have been here longer and cannot complete a sentence. Maybe on our date, I can teach you some English, okay?"

Mac nodded, and she grabbed his hand with her manicured fingers and dragged him across the street to the five-star restaurant where Mac was first thrown in the juvenile detention center.

After a steak meal for each of them with sides of mashed potatoes, green beans, French fries, and au jus, Gloria had a ribeye bone and red steak liquid remaining while Mac could only fit half a filet and a bite or two of sides.

"We will have dessert, yes?" Gloria asked.

The bill would be well into the hundreds without any extra, and Mac was hoping she would open her purse and slap a credit card down, as his pockets were full of lint.

"I would love dessert," Mac said. Those brown eyes were in a constant state of seduction that had Mac hypnotized.

"Peach cobbler," Gloria said when it came time to order dessert.

"The same," Mac said.

A plate scraped clean for Gloria and two bites for Mac later, the check was placed between them.

"I figure you got this covered," Gloria said, getting up from her seat and throwing her purse over her shoulder. But before leaving, she winked at Mac, and he knew what to do.

He didn't run, and he didn't panic; he calmly walked out of the restaurant. Even the maître d' wished him a good night, and they had escaped a $456 check.

"That was so exciting," Gloria said, waiting for him at the edge of the building, hiding like a kid playing tag. "Let's keep the excitement going." She dragged him by the arm, running through traffic, leaping fences in random backyards. Mac had no idea if there was a destination, but he didn't care. He felt weightless with Gloria leading the way, and with her by his side, he let go of all of his previous issues. This was his life now.

They ended two miles from the restaurant at a Cape style home, and before Mac could blink, Gloria's clothes were off and he was inside her. Her screams of pleasure were enough to allow Mac to last for twenty seconds. No woman had ever done that to him before.

Nine months later, Mac sat in a hospital room while doctors and nurses surrounded Gloria while she used every ounce of her remaining energy to push out their baby. The past months had turned Mac's life around. Not doing anything illegal where he was looking over his shoulder at every patrol car that cruised by was a refreshing feeling. The day Gloria opened the bathroom door, peed, and ripped the shower curtain open, waving the positive pregnancy test in his face was the day he vowed to himself to be everything his father was not. Everything both his parents were not. His dedication for this child dropped him inside a classroom where he completed his GED, then into trade school, learning all there was to know about plumbing. Gloria paid for the schooling, and Mac helped with anything she requested.

"I'm craving some cookie dough ice cream." Got it.

"I need a foot rub." Every single day.

"Drive me to the hospital now, she's coming."

Gloria insisted it was a girl even though they were waiting until the baby came into this world. And of course she was correct. Witnessing childbirth was an out-of-body experience like no other. The pain and sweat she went through and refusing medication proved that childbirth was a miracle and women were the toughest mammals on the planet.

"We should name her Peach," Gloria said after the nurses cleared and allowed the new parents to become acquainted with their new human. She wore a smile, and Mac wasn't sure if she was joking or not.

"Isn't that a stripper name?" Mac asked.

"Perception is granted by those who do the perceiving."

And without any further back-and-forth, Peach Rose Pulaski was in her crib inside the room Mac built and Gloria decorated, resting until she would relentlessly bother her mom and dad for the remainder of their lives.

Until one day.

One day, four years into Peach's life, she was two feet tall and eighty pounds. Mac loved watching his baby girl grow each day. Every morning, he leaped from his bed and into the room that quickly transformed from a crib, changing table, and border along the crown molding with pink elephant's trunk to tail, to a twin-sized bed with princess sheets, posters she saw at the store and shouted "pretty" with a finger that direction, and a chest filled to the brim with stuffed animals. Peach got all she wanted, and Gloria got all the loving. Mac was a month away from becoming a licensed plumber and was creating his own business with clients already lined up for his services. There was nothing that could alter the perfect life he was living.

Until one day.

The three of them were driving home from downtown after leaving a baseball game at Harbor Yard. It was a decent-sized stadium for a minor league affiliation. None of them, Gloria especially, were into the sport, but the Bridgetown Bluefish put on a fun show for the whole family. Activities for the kids, in between inning fun, and a mascot to keep the energy of the crowd moving. On this day, it was a night game, so the sun was removing the light, and the beautiful sky darkened the ugly city. But the interior of the vehicle was where the ugliness of this night lived. Gloria hadn't spoken a word to Mac for the entire day, and the only spoken words were to Peach. Sitting in the blue seats while the game dragged on and her silently eating hot dogs and popcorn was eating away at him.

"If you told me what I did, then I could fix it. You know I would do anything for you," Mac said, placing a hand on her denim thigh, which she abruptly shoved off.

"Could we have ice cream at home?" Peach asked from the back. She asked the same question over and over, and Mac thought that Gloria had had enough, though Gloria answered each question with the excitement of their four-year-old.

Mac took this one. "Sure we can, darling."

Peach cheered and continued to gaze out the window at the part of downtown that was nothing but scattered vacant homes and open fields with dead grass for miles.

"Do you remember when we talked about your past and how with Peach around, you were to never go back there?" Most of the words were lost on Mac, as he wasn't aware she was speaking to him.

"Yes, of course," Mac said with caution in each word.

"Then why the fuck were you at a drug house last night?"

His eyes were in the rearview mirror, focused on Peach. She didn't deserve to hear such words or her mom and dad in a fight. He was most angry about the timing of the discussion.

The truth was, Mac got a phone call a few days ago from an old friend. He was a dealer on the east side of the city. He spoke with him briefly, and the old friend said there was a ton of money involved. Mac knew he wasn't bluffing, and the past four years killed him, knowing he was not the provider. Mac had zero dollars to his name, and the income he made during that time was fixing a leaking faucet for the owner of the corner store they frequented. Gloria paying for everything wasn't fair, so taking the deal would take some of the money pressure off her wallet.

"I was—"

"I don't care what excuses or truths you will throw my way. This is an agreement we had, and I told you over and over that it is a deal breaker."

"So that's it? You are tearing our family apart because I am doing what I can to provide—"

"Provide? I have paid for your schooling so you can start a job and we can be comfortable for the rest of our lives. That is what I want you to provide."

"Now you're gonna use that against me? I'm a man and it's emasculating to—"

"Daddy."

The voice from the back seat snapped Mac's eyes to the road he had taken his focus from for the past minute. The perimeter wall of Veterans Park was growing ever closer, and with the last-second jerk of the wheel, he was able to maneuver the car to avoid an accident, but the speeds were too great that they drove under the wrought iron sign, and instead of following the cement path, the car was rolling down the embankment. A grassy hill Mac rolled down during good breaks in his horrible childhood. When Mac's foot hovered over the brake to stop before the car reached the bottom and entered the Long Island Sound, Gloria's words ripped at his psyche. He was returning to the old Mac. Selfish and knew he could count on nobody.

Moments before impact, he opened the driver's side door, then glanced in the rearview mirror at the chubby, rosy-cheeked creation he was so proud to bring into the world. Tears filled those precious cheeks and a look of worry that crossed her face for the first time in her short four years. Mac had forgotten about his daughter in that split second of Gloria's words striking his ego. But he made the leap anyway. The car rolled off the embankment and sank until it couldn't be seen any longer. He would need to check again in the morning, but looking around in the dark, nobody saw the accident, and other than the healthy grass pressed down where the tires traveled, he would be the only one who knew about the car in the Long Island Sound. Ever since they began dating, they kept a low profile and bonded together about the lack of friends and remaining family. And returning to the old Mac could easily cover any traces of Peach or Gloria. As though they never existed.

As Mac approached his McMansion, the reminiscence of the past came crashing and burning around him. As he wiped the tears from his face, he heard the unmistakable sound of destruction and death coming from the miles' distance of downtown Bridgetown.

Sadness to smiles. *Burn this city to the fucking ground.*

CHAPTER 45

Sherrie, Walter, and Roger were thirty steps from the officer they left in the alleyway and the apartment complex their daughter would never leave again when the ground beneath them shook and something similar to a sonic boom pierced their eardrums, causing them to fall to their knees.

"Ah, what the fuck was that?" Walter said. Sherrie had rarely seen her husband in true physical pain. When he sprained his ankle years ago playing football with his friends, she recognized the winces and sharp inhales he tried his best to conceal. She appreciated him toughing it out in front of her, though she knew it was for Shonda.

"It definitely came from downtown," Roger said. She felt Roger, although she had only known him for hours, would conceal his pain, but what she felt deep in herself was his childhood forced him to tuck away any negativity and replace it with resolution. It was a tactic that held strong until the compartmentalized events broke down the crumbling barrier.

"What should we do?" Sherrie asked.

The sirens were growing closer. If the Bridgetown Police Department was running this system of murdering the less well off, then they would do all they could to keep it contained within the city. If the information got out to federal officials or as simple as breaking a major news story nationally, then the plan would go up in smoke and the three of them could save some lives. If they exited the third hit, then the events were well isolated. Although, with the cop running the show unconscious, the EMT shot dead, and a majority of the apartment complex untouched by the devastation, it was time for the secret to be exposed.

"There's no more waiting around for the next attack. We know where this one will be. Trumbull Gardens. We go there now and evacuate all the residents," Roger said.

They had stopped moving for a moment, so Sherrie had time to peer over the not-too-tall structures toward downtown where a thick gray smoke billowed into the sky. "What about downtown?" she said, knowing what rebuttal she would get before the words left her mouth.

"Our people need us," Walter said. The man who would take his jacket off his back for anybody of any race, creed, religion, color, gender, or sexual orientation was sticking to his own. But Sherrie felt for any citizen of this city who might have been going for a walk through the green, an area of downtown with trees, benches, and a people-watching mecca, blown to bits by an explosive device.

"We need to finish what we started," Roger said and began the three blocks to the final remaining complex. It wasn't a choice she was dealt; it was a decision already made for her. She remained stoic and still as her husband and their helper rounded the cracked sidewalk, listening to the wails and cries of those that were deemed helpers before corruption and murder became their priority.

The last time Sherrie ran this much was after her father was killed and the hours of police interrogations concluded she had nothing to do with the murder. To help with the anxieties and grief she felt in her core, she would run as far as she could until her lungs seized and her sides cramped. Typically, the resting spot was Veterans Park, which was a five-mile run from the Barnum apartments. Then she would run back. The sick irony afterward was being taken in by her aunt and uncle who lived two floors down in the same complex where she found her dead father.

The running cleared her head and was a large part of focusing on growing toward the next positive goal of her life. It helped her with further education where she met Walter and with Shonda soon after her life settled into George Washington Carver, a place where she was okay with remaining until God decided it was her time.

Trumbull Gardens was a name the city picked—as they did for all the complexes—to make it sound like a sophisticated area without using any money to fix the issues and help families with two full-time jobs barely able to afford to survive. All the while city funding spent one million dollars to install a fountain, along with a filtration system, in front of the baseball stadium that was losing money each year.

Sherrie realized as she stood on the edge of Trumbull Gardens that she had never been there in the lifetime she spent in this city. This complex was a vast difference from the previous three. This one had a multitude of small single floor multi-family homes. All ten with a similar white siding and red shingles, a step up to a single door entrance, two families split by a railing but closer than if they knew each other intimately.

"We need to start now," Roger said.

And they did.

Roger ran to the first home closest to the road and used his giant fist to rattle the screen door to both families and continued to the next. Walter wasn't a runner, but he hustled to the left to do the same as Roger. At the first house Sherrie came upon, two Black kids sat on the stoop smoking a joint that the one kid hid behind his back as smoke poured from his mouth and nose.

"You know what's goin' on downtown?" the kid hiding the doobie said. They were around Shonda's age, and Sherrie felt the urge to lecture them, but this wasn't about that.

"You two need to go now," Sherrie said, heavy breathing lingering from her run. Her nerves of what she experienced at the last complex, combined with what the police would do when they arrived there within the next couple minutes, triggered furrowed brows in return. One of the kids cracked a smile.

"This is my home, lady, I don't—"

And whether it was the tears that welled in her eye's inner corners or the shaking of her limbs she couldn't control, it caused the kid to stop his speech, and worry fell over him.

"This is not a joke or a game. You and everyone here are going to die if you don't leave." Sherrie's words were cold. The same ice she feared they would hear from their own mother if she caught them smoking. And they didn't move until Sherrie added, "Now."

They were inside their respective homes, and she hoped they were collecting necessities to leave the area. It was tough telling residents to leave where they lay their heads each night on a comfortable bed and feeling safe with family. But lives were at stake, and those were more precious than any purchase a person could make.

Walter and Roger were fifty feet away, crossing the grassy piece of land where the city had lazily, thoughtlessly placed these homes not much bigger than a dorm room at a respectable college. The citizens that fell into said homes were the same as the three apartment towers where nobody remained due to a power that did what it wanted with no consequences.

That power was in view now, red and blue lights Sherrie once saw as a relief. A human who held an occupation whose duty it was to protect from the bad guys. But when the good guys became bad, then who was left to help the hopeless?

"Run. Run as far as you can," Walter shouted when he recognized time had ended for the evacuation process. Walter never yelled; it alarmed her.

"Go across the bridge. Leave the city," Roger yelled louder than her husband.

And almost as though the residents of Trumbull Gardens heeded the warning of the two random Black men, Sherrie could have sworn every door of each individual home swung open simultaneously. Though none of them ran. Women, men, children, teens who, living in such close proximity had surely met many times before, stood together as one.

One community. One entity.

Some had weapons, ranging from handguns pointed at the ground, to knives at the ready, to one man on his front stoop with an old-school rifle.

Sherrie felt useless standing in the middle of the tension empty-handed and no fighting skills in her arsenal. Her history was made up of either avoiding her problems or running from them. She had planned the rear parking lot of Trumbull Gardens, then over the short chain-link fence and running west to the bridge. But now she was bolted to the ground. She felt a sense of comfort with a group of about fifty people who had her back. She was a stranger to them, yet they were fighting for the same cause.

The thunk of the police car doors, then the subsequent opening of the trunks of each of the eight respective cruisers parked haphazardly in the middle of Pembroke Street caused Sherrie's head to stir. They were going for their larger weapons, and with all that she knew and the police of Bridgetown covering their death, destruction, and corruption, she feared they would be trigger happy.

Even in her head that was spinning between the folks of Trumbull Gardens apartments with no fear in their eyes, she found Walter striding toward her. Her first instinct was to shout and tell him to stop moving, not to give the police one more reason to fire and kill. But in that moment, she found herself moving to meet her husband in the middle. Whether it was seeing Roger, a person she had great distrust for, making his way to the apartment's property line and into the face of danger, or if losing her daughter, her only child, placed her in this mindset of taking risks for all she had left: Walter and Bridgetown were who she would remain beside until either of them turned on her.

"This is not what this city is about," Roger said, becoming the spokesperson with his residents behind him ready for a fight.

A man recognizable to Sherrie and everyone in this city stepped forward, an automatic weapon grasped with both hands, as all of his personal cop protectors held. He seemingly intended to be the spokesperson for rebuttal in favor of the Bridgetown police. He said, "You were the ones holding AKs before we even pulled up."

"You started this war, Mr. Mayor," Roger said. Sherrie had to admit that in this situation, given he could be eliminated at any moment, Roger held a chill demeanor.

Mayor Higgins chortled a laugh and said, "This right here, right now is the only war I see. So," Higgins boomed his voice for all to hear. "Place your weapons back inside your homes and rest your eyes, as I'm sure you were woken from a deep sleep."

"Fuck you," a voice floated from the back of the group of apartments.

"You are corrupt, and so is your entire police department," another voice said.

Sherrie scanned Trumbull Gardens as she squeezed Walter's hand that was surely in pain, but he gave not even a facial wince in response. None of the residents moved from their stoops, and none of them relinquished their weapons.

"Very well," Mayor Higgins continued, his loud tone growing more aggressive with each word. "Then I will have my officers here go to each individual home and seize your illegal weapons." His smirk at his own words enraged Sherrie, and she was sure each resident felt the same way.

At the mayor's command, the officers armed with assault rifles began their approach to follow orders, allowing their livelihoods, a simple occupation, control the entirety of their existence. They did not hesitate when delivered a task that was unconstitutional. Though the constitution held no substance when those going against it had no pushback.

"What do we do?" Sherrie asked Walter as she felt the walls of safety close around her. She was shaking, and her hand was soaked from the sweat her husband was pouring.

There was no answer from Walter, only a shake of his head. A big man who fought off a monster in their building, who made it his mission in life to protect Sherrie and Shonda, who was the only man who didn't think Sherrie was broken and crazy when she went into great detail about her father's death, silenced with fear.

Broken. The police halted their approach. Though it was not because of Roger, who held firm at the front, using his body and outstretched arms to slow the blue line; he was braver than she ever thought possible. What broke the cops and diverted attention of all involved was an approaching vehicle.

A silver sedan that came from downtown stopped, and the rear passenger side door swung open. A child hopped out. Must've been seven or eight years old. From the driver's side, a red-headed woman in blue jeans and a white tank top hopped out and opened the passenger's side where a man was helped to his feet. Both of his legs were braced, and the woman helped by providing crutches.

Mayor Higgins went sheet white at the sight of the man. The child had no fear when he stood beside Roger, taking a stance against the police. "How the fuck, Anthony," Mayor Higgins said.

Roger snapped his head to the man he hadn't given attention to until his name was mentioned.

"No fucking way," Roger said loud enough for the ones farthest in the back to hear.

The man on crutches used any momentum he could muster and landed with a wince at each advancement. Sherrie watched as Roger ran to the man and hugged him. Sobs could be heard across the bridge from the man who Sherrie thought couldn't show emotion.

CHAPTER 46

Anthony knew it was his brother before the embrace came. Even after twenty-eight years of not seeing a single glance of whom he remembered as the little boy who slept beside him each night on the single mattress that was soaked in his now dead other brother's blood. The trouble he and Roger got into after Stanley's death. The murder of the man in the Washington Carver apartments. Matteo pulled the trigger, but he and Roger were guilty accomplices. That was the last day he saw Roger. Ant knew he was a lawyer within Bridgetown, and he assumed Roger knew he was a police detective, but they never crossed paths until now.

Roger had the same face shape, round with pudgy cheeks. The same eyes, wider than almond. The same mouth, big lips and white teeth. The same ears, too big for his big head. Everything the same, but he had become a grown human being doing well for himself. And the same voice, only a bit deeper. "I'm sorry." Those were his first words to his brother in twenty-eight years. There was no context, and none was needed.

Ant replied, "I'm sorry, too."

"Maybe we can all hug and have one big orgy," Higgins said. "Anthony, if you're done, you've interrupted some important police business."

"In case you've forgotten," Ant said, taking crutched hops with malice towards Higgins. "I am the chief of police of this city, and you are harassing these people. And you are under arrest for the operation of the murder of an undisclosed number of Bridgetown residents."

The laugh Higgins released was the clearest *HAHA* Ant had ever heard. "You are arresting me? Now you should be writing TV sitcoms because in case *you've* forgotten, I am your boss. I can have you out of this city within the hour. And with the added luxury of two broken legs done by your predecessor, plus the entire department in the palm of my hands, give me fifteen minutes."

"You just confessed to a crime in front of an entire group of citizens who make this city what it is," Ant said. "Makes me proud to be the chief of this city. I can't fix the destruction you caused, but we can prevent it further."

When Ant turned toward the landscape that was Trumbull Gardens, he failed to notice the homeowners leave their respective doorsteps and create an orb of protection around Ant and Roger. It was near one hundred angry citizens up against eight cops and a mayor. No matter the extensive and rigorous training the police went through to hold their occupation, surviving on the streets was a far more supportive test.

"You're fired," Higgins said. And now it was Ant's turn to let out a laugh of his own.

"And who would you say is your new chief of police?" Ant asked.

"Me," Higgins said with a smirk Ant was seconds away from smacking off.

"When I first got the job as a police officer, I was so proud to further the lives of everyone in this city. Now you've made us the laughingstock of not just the state but the entire country. However, there is nothing funny about murdering the residents of the George Washington Carver apartments." Ant raised his voice so all behind him could hear. "All the residents of—"

Ant was silenced by Higgins revealing a weapon much more powerful than a gun. Ant had not fully experienced what the green liquid did when injected into a person's body, but he had almost experienced it firsthand and more abruptly saw the fear and tears fall upon his brother's face at the sight of the syringe. Ant recognized it as the device that controlled what happened in those apartments, and he couldn't let that happen here.

"You have a lot of witnesses that would escape your plan," Ant said.

In the haze of protecting Trumbull Gardens and seeing his brother again, one of the cops slipped away and returned with his wife in a headlock.

"Let me go, you fucking shit," Mary shouted with blows to the officer's stomach, though he was unaffected due to the Kevlar vest.

Ant instinctively reached for his sidearm only to find an empty shorts pocket. But the unmistakable clack of readying weapons grew from behind. The Trumbull Gardens residents raised their firearms, daring Higgins to stick the needle in Mary's skin.

"Seems like you're outnumbered, Mr. Mayor," Ant said, trying to keep the shake out of his words. The person he loved most in the world was one jab away from not being her wonderful self any longer, but Ant had to do what he did best, keep calm and compartmentalize.

The officers raised their weapons to create a standoff, waiting for one person, daring one person to pull the trigger to set off a deadly event.

Higgins paused for a minute and chuckled to himself before moving toward Mary. "Well, if nobody is going to start the party, why don't I do the honors."

Ant peered away, not able to watch his tough, takes-no-shit wife lose to the system. The system Ant was a part of building. One he was unknowingly coerced into, the endgame being the opposite of why he took the job in the first place: to stop the violence, to which he never admitted to being an accomplice. Now Bridgetown was the violence.

In his glance to the right, he saw little Leo crouched with his jaw resting on his knees, staring into the dirt. Then he reached his hand to the ground, holding his palm to the dirt-covered cement road, his eyebrows tense. Leo sensed something was coming. Ant wished he would use his alarm vocals again to stop this. To throw the mayor and the cops into the sides of the long-abandoned buildings so Ant could get his wife back and live comfortably. But Leo's mind was elsewhere. He heard voices, and Ant was curious about what he heard now.

It didn't take long to get the answer.

On the way to Trumbull Gardens, the remaining untouched apartments in Bridgetown, an explosion shook the ground underneath, three minutes after leaving the hospital against medical advice. Four minutes later, they walked into the Trumbull Gardens standoff.

This second boom caused Ant and all those in the vicinity to lose their footing for a moment. The explosion was loud, but the aftermath was louder. Earsplitting metal scraping against metal pierced the air. Ant's first thought was the apartments that were emptied by the mayor and Mac Pulaski took the destruction one step further and collapsed the towers from top to bottom one floor at a time. But over the surrounding skyscrapers, the tops of George Washington Carver and Barnum circular structures could be seen from where he stood. Then the sound ended with a barrage of slaps into a body of water. Large objects falling into the Long Island Sound.

"Oh shit," Ant murmured to himself. The realization hit him at the same time as his wife escaped from the distracted grip of the officer.

"Hey, get back here. We're not finished," Higgins called as Ant nodded for Roger to follow, and without question, the Trumbull Gardens folks were in tow, their weapons forcing the mayor, once in control, to take a step back and allow the real heroes of Bridgetown to pass by and do what Ant set out to do from the beginning: stop the hate and stop the violence once and for all.

Before Ant rounded the corner, a shadow rounded the buildings that downtown Bridgetown was thriving from. Large corporate businesses at the top and fancy restaurants at the bottom created a rise of money for the city. The shadow was coming up fast on Higgins, who looked so far from his speeches sitting at his desk at City Hall. His hair typically swooshed back in a gel-infused neatness now stuck up like uncared-for grass, his button-down he wore to yesterday's speech busted at the top. Ant thought he appeared drunk, and he may have been. His plan he envisioned was coming to fruition, and Ant theorized he went too far.

"Donny," one of the cops shouted. It took Ant a second to process to whom this was being directed. Then it clicked. Donny Higgins. He never referred to him by his first name and out of respect called him mayor. That ended today.

The shadow was a creature with skin peeling in circles and its mouth separating from its upper jaw. Its remaining teeth clamped down on Donny Higgins's neck and tore it off. His head lolled to one as its support was promptly removed.

Ant refused to stay for the bloodbath and continued toward the downtown area and farther on to the bridge that was no more. Mary, along with the fight that was Bridgetown residents, ran past Ant with Leo in her arms. The gunfire assured Ant the creature was dead, and the silence of the former mayor of Bridgetown assured Ant that he was dead as well.

CHAPTER 47

"Holy shit," Mac said, a grin growing at the corners of his mouth, butterflies fluttering in his gut, his fingers and toes tingling with excitement. The time had come. The start was from former chief Stewart asking Mac to get his girls to murder his family, to create chaos that would divert all attention away from the projects of Bridgetown so that they, with the assistance of Mayor Higgins, could make this city great again.

He was halfway up his winding drive when the Bridgetown bridge collapsed. He often would stand at his easterly window after the sun was well away and take in the steel beam crisscrossing each side while blue light illuminated from its undercarriage for the few cars that crossed into and out of the city. Mac loved that to enter Bridgetown, you must witness what was the big house on the hill. And with that came humans acting like animals attempting to gain access to his dwelling.

One kid dying from the electric perimeter fence was enough to keep anyone else from trying. When they took the fried kid away, they tried to arrest Mac, which was the beginning of what already started as his disdain for the authority in this city and all over the world. But when the chief of police and the mayor had a proposition, it was impossible to turn down. Mac's acceptance wasn't to help them; it was getting the end of the first part of their plan, only Mac never wanted what they wanted. Mac's plan all along was to not just tear down the ugly project towers; it was to burn the entire city to the ground while he watched from high above. And the only entry and exit into this city was gone within seconds. This was the beginning of the end for Bridgetown.

Mac's joy and positive visions of the future were halted when he reached the top of his driveway and the fence that ran on a generator with a code, the singular way to access his property, wide open. How long had this been open? Who opened it? Who gained access to his personal space? *Fuck.*

He knew that bitch Sadie broke inside and murdered his sweet Natalie. She knew the code to the gate and how to access each entry point of the home. Mac was cursing himself for giving these girls too much information. But his typical routine of pulling girls from the streets, using them, then killing them and dumping their bodies into Long Island Sound had become keeping then around for months at a time.

His first thought was to acquire weapons from his arsenal, but they were inside the armoire, inside his bedroom. If anybody was waiting for him to ambush, he could be dead before he stepped inside the front door. In the dark of the night, the interior lights were off, which wasn't unusual, but the exterior lights being off was alarming.

After stepping through the gates' entrance, keeping a keen eye on the windows for any shadows, movement, or gun barrels, he wrapped his fingers around the bars of the entrance fencing and tugged, squeezing his large bicep muscles, knowing they would accomplish his needs, but they failed. The generator that ran the gate, separate from the home's electricity, was powered off. The low hum that rumbled from the back was silenced.

Since it felt safe enough, Mac followed the cable from the gate motor and looped around the right side and into the back. He barely spent time in his backyard. There was an inground pool surrounded by a patio with an unused grill and seating area. The generator was there, and as he suspected, it was turned off. He took another glance at the windows; the ones at the top were his bedroom he missed climbing into and having a relaxing snooze, but once this city was under his control, he would sleep well for the rest of his life.

With nothing in sight, he grasped the pull start and yanked. A rumble answered in response, but nothing happened. Another yank and another dull rumble before the machine died out again.

"Fuck," Mac murmured, then another look at the house in case somebody, anybody was watching him. That was how he felt. After a third failed attempt, he unscrewed the cap, and the moon did not reflect any gasoline inside. He filled it to the top four days ago, knowing he could be away for a few days when a full tank would last weeks. Something was wrong, and Mac, with the shirt he was going on day three of wearing and pants soaked with sweat, other people's blood, and his own piss were going to need to be his defenses for whoever or whatever was surely in his home.

The back door was unlocked, another indicator he wasn't alone, and he crept through his kitchen on his toes, listening for rustling or creaks. It was dark, but the moon was enough light to maneuver through the place he had mapped out for a construction company to build in five months. He could close his eyes and know where his next step would lead.

A brief brush sound paused his movements outside his den with a padlock hanging in the locked position. The room had no windows and no other way in, and if the authorities gained access, there was enough evidence against him to put him first in line for the electric chair. He listened while his eyes were trained on the television, turned off. The red light on the bottom of the screen indicated to him that the power inside the house was running. The sound came from upstairs, and his skin jolted thinking of the phone call from Sadie after the murder of his beautiful Natalie. Her body must still lie inside the closet of his bedroom.

Sadie. That's who must've been hiding and waiting. She had any and all killing devices at her disposal. Mac recently took interest in explosive devices and found a grenade that would blow his house to rubble in seconds.

"Sadie," Mac called out. It could be the last word he ever said. The name of the woman he saved and the name of the woman who murdered him. But there was no answer, so he continued up the stairs, listening after each step.

A groaning creak as he reached the top landing and footfalls growing louder sent Mac into fight or flight, but he could do neither. The woman who stood before him was not Sadie. This woman had long, dark hair sticking up in different directions as though Mac had awakened her from a sleep in his bed. A silk pajama shirt one button away from exposing herself and matching shorts long enough to not qualify as underwear.

Before Mac could speak, another set of footfalls rushed to the woman's side. A girl, aged ten or eleven with the same dark hair, straight and down to her waist. The woman was bald the last time he saw her, but she had the same small mouth, bent ears, and deep brown eyes Mac looked into for so many loving years.

"Glo—" The words wouldn't come out. The name he hadn't thought about in eight years. The faces of the two most important people in his life gone after one night when he had chosen to focus on himself and not others. "Gloria, what the fuck," he said with breath leaving his lungs. A weakness he hadn't felt since he last saw them. "Peach. What are you—"

He went to hug his daughter, but her mother stood strong. An arm provided distance between the two bodies.

"What's the matter, Mac," Gloria said. "Looks like you seen a ghost. Actually, you are the ghost. All the color in your face is gone."

Her lips that had Mac kissed so many times, multiple times a day, were moving, but his eyes could not leave his daughter. When he last saw her, she was—

"You're not gonna say anything, Mac? You left me and your daughter for dead and all you do when we come back is stare. That's not like you, in fact, since I've been talking to that chief—"

"You talked to Kevin?" Mac asked, his breathing as though he had recently finished a marathon.

"No, Anthony something or other."

"Rawlings. Why were you—" Then the sit-down at the diner where Anthony was eating the peach cobbler came roaring back.

"After you left us in a car floating to the bottom of the ocean, luckily the window was open, and my daddy forced me to take swimming lessons when I was five, I had to give Peach C-P-fucking-R, Mac. We never looked back. I had to send Peach to therapy at five years old because of the trauma she experienced of her own daddy trying to kill her."

"I—" Mac was silenced by Gloria, although he had no words in mind.

"She was waking up in the middle of the night screaming her lungs dry because of fucking you, Mac. Our happy little girl can't go an hour without feeling that trauma."

"She seems okay right now," Mac choked out, staring at the girl hugging her mom from behind.

"Because we worked through the trauma. She is getting good grades, a star pupil, her teacher said. She is playing softball and is doing so good at it. You would be so proud of her, Mac. So motherfucking proud."

Mac's throat was closing, emotions flooding him, rising to his eyes. "I am pr—"

The syllables died where he left Gloria and Peach, unfinished and lifeless. Or so he thought.

"We never wanted to come back," Gloria said. "And I know you're gonna ask what we're doin' standing in your bedroom right now. That chief, Anthony, told me what you were doing. Killing people. Getting away with it. Turning the whole police force against one man. I didn't believe him. Other than leaving us for dead, I told him, 'That can't be my Mac. My Mac is a charming, rehabilitated man that would help people before hurting them.' I told him that, and do you know what he said?"

The tears couldn't hold any longer. This woman and that child were his ultimate weakness.

"He laughed," she said. "He fucking laughed right in my ear. Then he told me all the horrific things you've done to people. And I could not believe it."

"What are you doing here?" Mac asked, wiping at his tears like an untamed tiger.

"Anthony said he didn't know how else to stop you," Gloria said. "But we are too late, I see."

Over Gloria's shoulder was a perfect view of where the bridge once stood. Without any investigations or questioning, Mac knew his followers were responsible for the explosion downtown and the destruction of the bridge. He was so happy that the people of this city were contained in one place. It meant he held the control, but Peach didn't deserve this. Gloria didn't deserve this.

"I can get you both out of here," Mac said.

"Throw us back in the water and swim across?" Gloria asked.

Any other time or person, Mac would not have allowed them to speak to him in that manner, but those brown eyes were hypnotizing.

"I can get you a boat," Mac said. His voice was hurried, and his mind was racing. His phone. It was dead. He pulled it from his pocket and raced past Gloria and Peach, who didn't stop him, to the phone charger, waiting for it to turn on.

"Where are you getting us a boat?" Gloria asked.

"I just need to make a phone ca—" Mac was frozen. At the position on his bed, the closet door was cracked and red painted his suit jackets, rows of dress shoes, ties, and diamond encrusted cuff links. "Did you go inside my closet?" Mac asked and shot up, slamming the door shut. The carpet soaked up the blood Natalie lost, and the incident was contained to the room.

"No," Gloria said, falling to her knees and holding Peach, rubbing her back in circular motions. "Why, Mac? Who is in there?"

"Nobody, er, nothing. Look, there's a lot of shit you don't know." Mac hadn't recognized his voice climbing until after each word, he watched Peach's frown lines grow deeper, and then her tears started.

Mac's phone came to life, and he ran back to the bed. He unlocked his spiderwebbed screen and tapped on Kevin Stewart's number. He hadn't seen Kevin since they were at his hideout in the shit part of the city along with Higgins and Anthony. When Kevin's kid let out an inhuman scream that knocked Mac on his ass for hours, he didn't know where Higgins or Kevin Stewart went, but now he needed the former chief's help.

"Fuck," Mac said when the call went to voicemail. "No, don't." The lump that sat in his throat prior to the tears was back, but for all the wrong terrifying reasons.

Peach opened the closet door.

"That wasn't m—"

The wails from his daughter were so aggressive he braced for impact for another unconscious period, and when none came, he opened his eyes to the cries fading away. Gloria snatched his daughter, and they were down the stairs and out the front door. If they were trying to escape the singular body inside the closet, then stepping out into Bridgetown would send Peach and Gloria back to therapy for life, if they both escaped this deteriorating city with their lives.

The plan of hiding away in his castle for the people of this city to destroy one another, at least until the helicopters and boats from other towns and the state came roaring in following the bridge collapse, was a long-forgotten dream. Making sure the two loves of his life were safe was his new number one priority.

Mac was out of his partially safe home and into the streets with danger at every corner. A higher danger than this city had ever seen in its century-long history. A danger of his own creation.

CHAPTER 48

That was the one.

The one Sherrie and Walter released from the Greenfield Hills apartment complex where the shell of her daughter's body still lay, fresh green blood still wet to the touch as the scenario played over and over in her head. The one with the EMT strapped to the gurney must've been the one they were planning on using for Trumbull Gardens, and he showed at the perfect time to tear the neck flesh from Mayor Higgins. In the rear of Sherrie's thoughts, there was a doubt that releasing the human turning to creature would negatively affect the good people, and she was relieved the bad person got what he deserved.

"What's your name?" Sherrie asked the man on the crutches, who she could feel would want to be at the front of the pack of Trumbull Garden residents. Sherrie ran to him when he struggled to keep his balance exiting the madness the street corner standoff had become. Multiple shots exploded as she assisted him uphill and along the crumbling sidewalk. Melanie's Salon was at the safe corner, and the large bay window and chairs lining the mirrored walls with a washing station in the rear nearly suggested sitting him down while the rest of them headed for downtown. But she could see the fight in this man, and not solely fight: Sherrie saw recognition.

"Anthony," he said, and she could see his struggle, anger with the use of his legs gone.

"How do you know Roger? You two seemed close," Sherrie asked, not sure if Anthony was in the proper headspace to respond.

"My brother," he said flatly. "And you? Good friends?"

"He saved my life."

This appeared to shock Anthony, as though his own brother couldn't be capable of such heroics.

"But we've met before," Sherrie continued.

"You and my brother?"

"You and your brother."

Anthony stopped his momentum at a four-way intersection, the flashing yellow traffic light reflecting off the approaching skyscrapers of their destination and the pupils she was positive she had stared into through a rearview mirror.

Without warning or any other words, Sherrie slapped him across the face. Palm to cheek. Walter and Roger were a block ahead, keeping pace with the group. Tears stung her eyes at the memory of that day. Matteo in the passenger seat covered in blood. Two boys in the back, scared for their lives. Finding her massacred father an hour later. Meeting up with Matteo to—

"I know you didn't do it," Sherrie said as Anthony rubbed his cheek that was reddening his dark complexion. "Neither did Roger. I know that, and I want you to know that."

"That day ruined our lives. Today was the first day I've seen him since—"

The cops Sherrie saw with Mayor Higgins were hardened and trained for anything. Emotions for them were packed away and on a permanent vacation. But Anthony was different. Tears were flowing without a care in the world.

"That was the worst day of my life," Sherrie said. "Until today. That day with my father was a string of bad things with a bad person. As much as I'm sure you blame yourself, I think about the argument I had with him, the final words I spoke to him. Choosing a boy three years older than me over a father that raised me by himself. It was my decision to leave the apartment that day, not anyone else's."

"You can't blame—"

"I can and I have for so fucking long. But this is my redemption day. I left my daughter in our apartment alone, and these horrible men snatched her up and turned her into—I am not blaming myself this time. This time I am ending it where it never should have started."

He nodded and finally wiped a tear from his cheek. "Just for the record, I'm sor—"

Sherrie placed a hand where her slap landed and rubbed his cheek. "Keep your sorries. You'll need them for the coming years." He returned with a tight-lipped smile and hobbled on his crutches to catch up.

The smell hit Sherrie before the smoke and fire. In the center of downtown, a green where the homeless slept on steel benches and everyone else cut across for a quicker route to the bus station was not green any longer. A reddish brown flattened the life from the area. The old bank and trust building, an unused white structure hosted by four pillars and a gorgeous marble façade, was actively burning. The playhouse featuring local comedians and stage productions was at the end stages of the burning. The downtown public library appeared to be ground zero of the first explosion heard round the city. The brick edifice was down to three layers and hollowed out from the inside. Charred pages floated down, stories used for an escape from the bad of the world now creating a snow shower worse than any winter could ever conjure.

The Trumbull Gardens group, most of whom were holding a weapon that could take out their enemy in seconds, were looking up at the ashes that seemed to be never-ending. Looking at a downtown where, when Sherrie, Walter, and Shonda were free of work and school, they would venture to the playhouse for a show, or the library, or a restaurant.

Tony's Bar & Grill was five hundred feet down Main Street along with an Irish pub, a dry cleaner, and eventually to Harbor Yard, the baseball stadium. There were so many small places that made the people in this city happy for a short time, and most was gone.

Whoever was behind this made themselves God and felt they could control the world when the devil was flowing through them their entire life.

Aside from simmering embers and popping from the heat of the flames making contact with air pockets and furthering the hell that had become this part of the city, there was an uncomfortable silence. As though the world wasn't sure how to proceed from its altered state.

"Sherrie." Her name snapped her out of the haze she found herself trapped inside. Walter and Roger were running through the smoke. "We sent the group to split up, Roger's idea, and see if they can find who did this."

At Roger's name, Sherrie snapped her eyes at him. He and Anthony could be twins. Same wide-set nose, same head shaped like an umbrella, same look of bewilderment. But Roger was younger, mature beyond his years, though clearly younger than Anthony. She considered having the same conversation with Roger that she had with Anthony, but this was neither the time nor place. And most importantly, she was living in the future. A time when the city was restored and exceeding what it was in the past.

"Find them and bring them to the police station," Anthony said.

The looks he received from Roger, Walter, and Sherrie must've sent him thinking his words turned him into the enemy. Sherrie felt the prickle of a laugh rising in her throat.

"Ant," Roger said. "Look around. There is no order. These people are not going to listen to order."

"I know. But we are not executioners. Our violence in response to their violence is going to further death, going to further destruction. Nobody else is going to die on my watch. Even if it's only me in this godforsaken police department, I'm going to do what I feel will resolve this matter."

"I get it. I do," Walter said, and Sherrie was surprised by his eagerness to join the conversation. "But honestly, fuck who did this. They've already initiated the violence, and that gives us permission to fight back."

"Yeah, brother," Roger said. "I agree. This is something that needs to end as soon as possible."

Anthony looked between the three inadvertently circled around him and said, "Then I'll do it myself." He reached into the rear of his waistband and removed a handgun.

"You're on crutches," Walter said. "Let us—"

"I said I've fucking got it," Anthony said, grasping the crutch handle between the gun and making his way into the fight.

Walter, Roger, and Sherrie watched him hop away, but before they came to an unspoken agreement to help, gunfire rang out in the distance. One pop, two pops, three, four, five, six pops in rapid secession.

The stillness of the group became full sprints down Main Street, formerly filled with a constant flow of traffic, even in the early morning, now an abandoned road with a visibility of zero.

Sherrie was not going to shut down. She was wrong in thinking this was revenge, for her daughter or her father; this was standing up for the wrongs being done by those with power. She was walking into the smoke of danger. She was going to fight back.

CHAPTER 49

When Ant was seven years old, his mother called him and his two brothers into the living room and explained that she got a bonus check from her job and was going to take her three boys on a camping trip. It was a campground three towns over and along the Long Island Sound. This was the first time Ant or his brothers left Bridgetown, and, on the drive, there were no words spoken. Stanley, who knew very few words at the time, said, "pretty" in response to the trees and pavement ahead, entering into the dirt driveway under the sign: *PINEWOOD CAMPGROUND.*

Ant was mesmerized by the campers as they drove along and used the crank handle to roll the window down. Each campsite had its own water and electric hook-ups and a stone-enclosed ring where fires blazed, and white smoke swirled in the wind. He inhaled the burning pine and closed his eyes, imagining the remainder of the day running around with Roger and Stanley, playing tag, chasing each other around a baseball field they passed on the way in, and Ma said there would be games like bingo and an arcade. The day was perfect, a rare perfect day for his family. When Stanley was dead a couple years later, perfect never showed its face again.

But that smell never left him, a sweet and savory scent that was unforgettable, one of good memories, now dashed by the present of the city he was placed to protect burning to the ground. The smell, though mixed with burning oil and toxins he shouldn't be breathing, was all the same. A new memory he would live with in a negative light.

Like a fog one could choke on, Ant pushed farther down Main Street. He was running towards danger because that was what he felt he was meant to do. This right here was for his dead little brother, and that was who every resident of this city became.

"Anthony, hon," a voice said and placed a warm palm on his back.

Ant had forgotten his wife was with them. His focus was on Sherrie, Sherrie's husband, little Leo, his own brother, and all of Trumbull Gardens. Mary wrapped her other arm on his shoulders and squeezed. Mary, whom he knew from day one to be this rough and tough woman who would back down from nothing and proving that by begrudgingly helping him out of the hospital bed, driving into danger with a child that was thrown on her lap, marching into a war Ant felt guilty he should have stopped days ago, and nearly being stuck with a needle full of what would turn her to a monster. But he could see the fear in her eyes, a sheen quivering behind those beautiful brown irises. She hid her anxiety so well that Ant took her to be a superhero. And seeing that break as she pulled away from her embrace shattered his heart into a million pieces.

"I don't want you doing this," she said.

"I need—"

"I know you well," she said. "I know that you will say everything and anything to hobble down the road and do whatever you can to help because that's who you've always been. But, babe, there is a whole group of people fighting for you. Please," Mary said, grasping his hand while using the other to steady his crutch. "Stay with me."

Ant understood she wasn't asking him to stand with her in the middle of Main Street; she was urging him to stay alive because with two broken legs and a bandaged arm, he never stood a chance.

"When I first took this job," Ant began, watching Sherrie, her husband, and Roger disappear into the thick smoke. Leo crouched a few feet away from Mary and Ant, tracing his finger along the ash that was created by destruction. "I told you this job would be my life, and I would need to risk it no matter if I was on or off duty."

274

"And what if the whole department left you to fend for yourself? Then does that mean you need to do anything for this city?" Mary's words were harsh, and her tears cut through him.

"It's not for the department. It's for whom the department let down. These people who fight and claw every day of their life to exist in a world that doesn't want them to. That's who I fight for. I am better off than them because I have this job, but that doesn't mean I'm better *than* them."

Gunshots filled the air around them, and the echo of the rounds was in surround sound, booming from beyond where they could no longer see. A view that hours ago would give them a beautiful view of the sunrise moving along the baseball stadium.

"Then I can't watch. And I can't go with you," Mary said. Her hand had been in his for the past few minutes, and it released. "I will take Leo to the other side of the city where it's safe until something can be done to get across the sound. To get home."

It pained Ant to see her go, and he knew she was giving him an option in that moment. Without asking, she was asking if he would go with her and let the helpers they gathered fight for him. The gunfire in the haze gave an apocalyptic feel. A movie come to life in the city he never left. Scenario after scenario that should have forced him out long ago. Then, he was presented with the most important scenario of his life. Go to safety with his pleading wife or do what he could to help the others.

Without a word, Ant turned on his heels, an about-face perfected in the police academy, and marched into the danger as he had so many times before. He could feel Mary staring at the back of his head as the silence pocked each crutch advancement into the air, telling those around him that he had the biggest target on his back. Of course, Ant knew his wife was correct: his death was imminent, and he only had himself to blame.

Most of his travels to the east were uneventful. The gunshots ceased, and the filtering of unknown voices dissipated, as did the smoke as he approached the sound and Harbor Yard. The stadium was in view along with the ticket boxes that ran along the bottom of the structure where during the summer, fans lined the windows to collect their tickets and climb the stairs to see the minor league baseball team.

Ant's heart stuttered as the familiar sound of a round from a semi-automatic rifle exploded and the tink of the bullet smacking against something metal in his immediate vicinity caused his hobbling to move in a westerly direction. A moment of reflection as the bridge into the city was previously a perfect view. A sight when he would do traffic details for the games. Dead and gone.

Two hundred feet ahead, Ant found a cement planter holding a tree with green leaves waving in the light breeze. A small sign of life that comforted him. Though he knew the planter and its contents would not stand a chance against the whizzing projectiles hoping to land in his skull.

Where had they all gone? About a hundred residents armed with weapons, Sherrie, her husband, his brother. There were no dead bodies he could see, but he was being shot at, he could assume from above at stadium level.

Then he glanced at the next planter sixty feet apart where a man was holding his gaze on Ant, a rifle in his grasp and a single finger instructing Ant to remain quiet. Then back into the parking lot where few cars were enclosed by a chain-link fence. The undercarriage gave away the spots of more bodies. Living bodies set up around the stadium created an unspoken plan to eliminate the threat together.

The way the stadium was placed, the front where the crowds would funnel up the stairs to the turnstiles for entry faced west. East was fenced in private parking for the players or any VIP guests gaining entry through the rear of the stadium. South was the open air outfield where the train tracks ran and home run balls would land from the big hitters and farther into the Long Island Sound, backdropped by a beautiful industrial plant stuck between a red and white smokestack, the most recognizable landmark of the city. North faced back toward the Black Rock section of the city where the residents of that area didn't associate themselves with Bridgetown. With the threat being inside the stadium and not knowing how many there were to be concerned about wandering the mezzanine with a clear view outside, they were easy targets.

As Ant's crutches lay beside him and his elbow grew uncomfortable in the grassy region across from the danger, a vibration hummed into his hip bone. The last thing on his mind was his cell phone, but the reminder forced his hand into his tight pocket to see Mary on the caller ID. The eeriness around him screamed to not make a noise, so he ended the call and powered his phone off, slipping it back inside his pants. Their final conversation hadn't ended in an argument or any resentment towards one another, but there was an understanding that Ant's decision was the final chapter in their lives together. So why had she called?

The man taking cover behind the next planter, the only one whom Ant had in his full view, motioned his index and middle fingers with the fingertips glancing his eyes, then he followed the man's pointer finger to the upper level of the stadium. Ant had surmised on his own that the shots were coming from there, so what was the man telling him? To pay attention?

With some broken pride of a guy he never met before telling a veteran police officer to be aware of his surroundings, especially when the shots were aimed in his direction, he moved his eyes to the brick wall, twisting the bowl shape of the structure where someone with a weapon was sliding their back along its shape. Then another body followed in the same manner, then another, and another. The Trumbull Garden residents had devised a plan that was steps ahead of Ant's thoughts at the moment.

A never-ending line of the group kept any line of sight from the potential gunman to make their way inside and eliminate the threat. Ant began a crawl with his little 9MM handgun issued by the department that placed him in this position. And that thought, along with no use of his legs forcing him into an army crawl that would get him killed within seconds, planted him to where the safety was and allowed others to be that hero dreamed of lying on the same mattress at night next to his two brothers. A memory dashed by the rattle of an automatic weapon sputtering rounds at a large rate.

Two sides were firing at one another. During his years as a police officer, there were numerous times he unholstered his weapon when searching a building or when up against an armed enemy but had only fired three times while on duty. And during one of those, a fire fight broke out between him and a man who had a mental breakdown and killed his family, who refused to go to prison so he fired upon the sole officer who arrived on scene, Anthony Rawlings. That sound never left his mind, of two or more humans using a deadly device to end each other's lives. It was a cacophony that drove the memory of that day to the forefront of his mind.

Once the firing started, the rush began. Tens, twenties, thirties of people filed inside up the stadium steps that so many had taken before with joy and excitement for a family-friendly day of entertainment. But these were angry, revenge-fueled humans that had enough of the violence and hatred for simply existing in the city, trying their best at life like everyone else, all dependent on who birthed them.

For once in a long while, Ant was comfortable. In the most uncomfortable he ever felt in his body, lying and not able to stand, his mind was placed at ease listening to a problem being solved by others.

Staring up at the dissipating smoke and the pre-sunrise light making the shadows more focused, a face looked down at him. It was almost a dreamlike feel with the chilly bite of the air mixed with the cloudless sky and a man hovering above taking up most of Ant's vision. But when Ant recognized the man, he used all that was left of his abdominal energy to at the very least sit up. It did not happen.

"Anthony, so lucky for me to find you here," Mac said, squatting to his haunches.

"You did this. You did all of this," Ant said, his breath hitching.

"Well, I'm going to plead the fifth, as I'm speaking to the chief of police, but what I really need right now is communication with my wife and child. I know you've been talking to them."

Without a second thought or warning, Mac grabbed a fistful of Ant's shirt and dragged him like a firefighter saving an unconscious lump from a burning building. But Ant could feel every inch of movement through the grass and out into the double yellow line of Main Street. He could look up and hope any gunfire from before was ended by the Trumbull Gardens crew.

Mac was searching Ant's pockets, and removed his phone. He powered it on and said, "Unlock it. Now."

With those words, Ant understood that this wasn't the same Mac he spoke with three days ago at the Galaxy Diner or the last time at the house where former chief Stewart was hiding. This Mac had lost that arrogance and swagger that dripped with every word he spoke. His usual assured face poked with grayed facial hair along with his typical bald head. His calm, cool eyes were flicking left and right. His lips quivered, and his eyes shimmered, ready to release tears down his cheeks. He was pretending nothing was wrong, but something had changed in him, a change that was bad for him but good for everyone else.

"Unlock your fucking phone, Anthony," Mac said, his voice with a lilt of shake.

"She doesn't want to talk to you. Neither of them does," Ant said with precision shooting through each word.

Stars and darkness drifted as Mac's fist landed between his eyes and on the bridge of his nose. Pain that had previously left his legs now settled in his head and travelled back to his broken left femur and shattered right fibula and tibia. Mac was panicking, and Ant knew why.

"She doesn't love you," Ant said and chuckled in the face of danger. "Gloria and Peach." Ant could get no further words out before hands were around his neck and breaths were becoming hard to come by. Ant had so many more words to say, but with his head already swimming and his legs useless, there wasn't much time left for him.

When the blackout came, his vision wasn't there, but he could hear the sounds around him. Footfalls of many growing ever closer. Shouts of panic and anger. Ant could feel the hands release from his windpipe. Ant could taste blood and bile roiling deep in his esophagus. Ant could touch hands, good hands, rubbing his face. Then his sight returned. Faces, so many faces looking down at him.

"Kill him."

"Fucking do it."

"This is Mac Pulaski. A bad motherfucker."

Words swirled, and Ant had one of his own, but it wouldn't come out. "N—" Prevention of speech made it impossible. "S—" Communication was not coming. Ant placed his palm out at the kids staring at him. Teenagers that should have been home getting ready for school instead out fighting for their lives because of where this fucked up society chose for them to live.

"Hang on," one of the teens standing over Ant said. The group listened because the chatter dulled to an uneasy silence.

"Stop," Ant said. The word came out like static. "Help me up," he asked the kids.

With one on his right arm and one on his left arm and a third at his back, Ant was on his feet again. It was an unsteady wavering stance, and all the feeling was gone, but he was standing, and Mac was down. They had bloodied his face, and some had their weapons drawn on him.

"Mac Pulaski, you are under arrest for the murder of Madeline Cross, Brandon Cross, and Sarah Plax."

"Fuck that."

"This guy needs to be dead, not arrested."

The chatter surrounded Ant, and he knew it would come. He had heard it throughout his career. Officers who were beaten to a pulp by a murderer ready to fire a round into the perp's skull and Ant stopping them and advocating for the justice system instead. He heard all the excuses and reasonings. Some he even agreed with, but it wasn't his job to play executioner, and neither was it the job of the citizens.

The silence was broken by the fluttering of helicopter blades in the distance. The collapse of the bridge was going to be a major event, and the surrounding towns would send their resources across the sound to assist with the aid of Bridgetown. *Three days too late*, Ant thought to himself. There was mounting guilt of not easily reaching out to a single officer from the surrounding towns to garner some traction into stopping the death and destruction by the authority in this city. But, like many times before, Ant's pride got in the way.

Laughter cut through Ant's thoughts. Mac was curled in a fetal position, reduced to how his life began, and his raucous laughter moved through the streets. "Under arrest? Anthony, it's so sad how you could never see how this city and its department were turning on you for years. Stewart told me all about your good guy persona and how you reported any corruption, refusing to take part in it. Of course they all turned on you, you gullible fuck."

In the heat of Mac's words, his laughs transitioned to sobs. He was a broken man.

"Just let me talk to them one more time," Mac cried. "One more fucking time. Fucking time. Time."

"I'm killing this motherfucker," a teen with an assault rifle said.

"I agree," another said.

And within seconds, the group surrounded Mac, ready to end his life.

"No, this is not the way to handle things," Ant shouted, but it was drowned in the chaos. "I am the chief of police and—"

The final word before the cutoff was enhanced when there was quiet. Ant was still being held up and did a zombie walk on his two leg braces to the middle of the formed semi-circle. Leo stood inches away from Mac.

"Leo?" Ant said.

Little Leo turned and smiled.

"What are you doing here, buddy?" Ant said, and this would be the time when he would squat to his level.

"Helping you," Leo said, and Ant was stunned. The words were out in a clear, concise manner.

"This is a dangerous situation for—"

"I'm sorry, Anthony." Mary was running toward the group, and her auburn hair, perfect as ever, swept across her perfect face. His wife was perfect in every way, and he never wanted to choose this city over her.

As Ant peered down at Leo grasping his leg, he had flashes of Stanley sitting next to him while Ant put in a movie he stole from Blockbuster. A horror movie Momma would never let them watch. Roger to his left and Stanley to his right. Stanley couldn't look at the screen as an alien burst from the main guy's chest. His face was buried in Ant's shoulder, and his hand was on Ant's knee. Ant always thought the hand was to comfort Ant during the movie. He wasn't scared, but Stanley was always the comforter. While he lay next to Ant at night, sometimes in the heat of his sleep, his hand would rest on Ant's chest and even when Ant was wide awake unable to get to sleep, it would be morning, and Ant would be fully rested before he even knew what happened.

And even through the leg brace, Ant could feel that comfort hand from Leo.

"Death and destruction, brother," Roger said, appearing at his side. "He started this, and we need to end it. Quick."

"We are then promoting more death and destruction," Ant said. "Him rotting in a jail cell thinking of his wife and daughter he will never see again is going to be more impactful than death. Death would be the easy way out for him. It's what he wants."

"It's what he deserves," Sherrie said, blending in with the group.

"Agreed," Walter said, his hand laced in Sherrie's.

"I know death well," Sherrie said. "I know it too damn well, and if this man was part of my daughter's death, then I'm sorry, but I'm not gonna stand around and debate his existence like I have in the past."

Barks and howls of agreement riled up the group again.

"This city needed change," Mac said. The man whose life was on the line spoke into the cement. "There was already death. There was already violence, and none of you gave a shit. Your own kind killing each other in the streets and you see it as normal. There needed to be a big change because none of you would do anything about it. If you—"

"Enough," Ant boomed. "Enough. Your definition of change is not anyone else's. You live in a big mansion above the city, above everyone else. The way you see us is not how the world should see us. I am, was the only Black police officer on a force of 172. An entire fleet of police against me. My White co-workers were proud to stand next to me because we both wore blue. The Black citizens of this city looking down on me because I wear the blue. I was born in Bridgetown Hospital. I lived in the George Washington Carver apartments. I experienced some horrible shit. I have been involved in some horrible shit." Ant paused to glance at Sherrie, whose eyes were locked onto his, and she nodded. "But through all that, I stayed here and did all I could to protect it. Taking the bad off the streets so the kids here could go outside and play in the streets without fear and wouldn't need to suffer like I did. I didn't take part in the corruption because the corruption at City Hall is what is preventing this city from being better. So, this change you said you made by murdering innocent people is not a change at all. You and the mayor and former chief Stewart all had a hand in furthering what this city is and has always been, a corrupt city that held the money for useless spending and to pay you."

Mac sniffled and wiped his nose drippings with his hand and sat up. "You all can do whatever you want to me. But please just call Peach so I can tell her how sorry I am. Please, Anthony, before I'm dead."

Ant couldn't help but smile. "When I bring you into the station, I'll allow one phone call."

Ant turned and received his crutches from a random stranger. He hopped with his back to Mac. "Follow me to the station and we can begin the process."

As he was around the corner and up the burning street with Leo, Mary, Roger, Sherrie, and Walter by his side, he heard the final cries of Mac Pulaski as the city descended upon him. The smile never left Anthony Rawlings's face.

ONE YEAR LATER

"I stand here on the rebuilt Bridgetown Memorial Bridge with my wife," Ant said, gesturing to his rear and acknowledging Mary. "My adopted son, Leo. And my brother, Roger. A small family that was once divided and brought together by the most despicable acts not even the worst minds could imagine. But, just like my small family, this city has come together and laid bricks of the downtown library. They have created groups to help those struggling with mental issues from surviving quite possibly the most difficult time of their lives. And to the families of those who lost loved ones one year ago, it is okay to be angry, it is okay to be sad, it is okay to take action against those who made your life hell for simply existing, but know I am fighting for every single one of you to ensure there is compensation and grief counseling for all who require the service. In closing, please remember that if you live in this city, you are all of equal value. We are all the same and we should be treated as such. Thank you."

Ant stepped away from the podium and, joined by Mary, Leo, and Roger, grasped a pair of oversized scissors and cut the blue ribbon, allowing cars into and out of Bridgetown once again. A chorus of cheers from the gathering crowds of citizens continued as Ant passed through them, stopping to be sure to shake each individual person's hand on his way to the waiting car.

"Any stops along the way to City Hall, Mr. Mayor?" the driver asked when they piled inside the car.

"No thanks, Paul," Ant said, and the car was on its way.

"That was a great speech, honey," Mary said, kissing him on the cheek.

"Yeah, and this city is looking better every day," Roger said.

"What did you think, Leo?" Mary asked, fixing his bowl cut in the places the wind had moved some pieces.

"It was good, Daddy," he said. Ant wasn't used to the word *Daddy* yet, and the pit in his stomach riled and made him choke up each time he heard that term. It was a word Ant never got to use when he was little, so it was more special in his mind.

"Thanks, buddy," Ant said, ruffling his hair and messing it up again.

As the car left the crest of the bridge, Ant looked up at what was Mac's mansion. Now, it was a mess of wood and iron fencing sitting in a large pile, as the demolition was completed yesterday.

After Mac was found alone, clinging to life outside of the baseball stadium by the incoming helicopter, he was rushed to Bridgetown Hospital where he lay now in a medically induced coma. Ant tried all he could to get the cord cut, but as Mac had no family, there was nobody to make the proper call. Ant lamented as he didn't become mayor to push any agenda or do what he wanted, he wanted to end all the corruption and build Bridgetown from the ground up in a new light. Not as it was in the past but as it should be for the future. If Mac ever emerged from the coma, Ant had no plan of what he would do in that moment, but most days he didn't think about that outcome. Mac was a horrible person whether his crimes could ever be proven or not; his mindset was dangerous, and he had not a care in the world for human life. Unless it was his wife and daughter he thought were long dead.

After the Madeline Cross, Brandon Cross, Sarah Plax murders, Ant was convinced Mac had something to do with it, and he knew he rarely committed his crimes himself. Hours after the investigation, Ant had received a call on his work desk phone he checked close to once a month but had decided to check his messages on that day. He had upwards of two hundred messages, but one stood out to him.

"Hi, my name is Gloria, and I dated Mac Pulaski for four years. I saw on the news about the disgusting murder of that poor family, and while Mac was a kind, gentle human being for most of that time, I have a strange feeling he has something to do with it. Please call me back." So, Ant called Gloria, and they talked for hours. She talked about Peach and how he attempted to murder them one night. Ant was grateful she used his personal desk phone because if she called anywhere else in the department, corruption would have eaten it up.

So, he tried to mock Mac with the information and play with his head, but as the days went on and the murders of the apartments continued, he needed to have them here in person.

They found Ant after Mac was placed into the coma, and they were grateful for his help and wished they could have confirmation on Mac's death before they left but more so could not stand to be in Bridgetown for another second. Ant called and checked up on them on a regular basis. Peach recently promoted to the fourth grade with straight A's, and Gloria was hired at a law firm fighting for women in domestic abuse relationships.

"You alright?" Mary asked, placing her red manicured hand on his.

He squeezed hers and said, "I am now."

Minutes later, they were passing the George Washington Carver apartments, and Ant looked from the bottom to the top.

"Could you stop here, Paul?" Ant asked the driver, and he pulled in through the driveway and to the front.

There were so many memories of this place from childhood to adulthood, and since reopening three months ago, there were major changes made. Every space was upgraded with proper safety features and technological advances, as well as new bedding and comfortable modern design. And the price would be the same as it always was. An actual affordable place where those who lived could be proud to call this place home. While the cylinder structure remained the same shape, the façade had a major upgrade with new brick layering and a working fountain out front. The city's money that should have been going toward building up what needed the change was being evenly distributed amongst all the citizens. While the unchangeable ghosts of the past remained in the space, the apartments were filling fast, and from what Ant heard, the people were happy with the space.

Sherrie and Walter Stevenson still lived in the same apartment from before. With all that happened with her father and their daughter, Ant made it his mission to offer them a home free of charge miles away from the place that gave them the worst memories of their lives. They refused. They accepted the upgrades and to continue to pay the monthly rent but refused to move. Sherrie said, "As fucked as it was for us, it is our home and always will be. It feels rebellious to stay. As much as they try to kick us out, we will be back forever." While Sherrie's memories were attached to both PT Barnum apartments where she grew up, this city as a whole and all the apartments were a part of her that was impossible to let go, and Ant understood as he stared up at the same place where he lost his little brother. He understood completely.

"Lots of memories, huh?" Roger said as Ant took his seat back in the car.

"When you think about the good ones and block the bad ones, ya know, with Stanley and Mom, then it is a great place."

"Remember when one of the moms got a sprinkler for the front lawn one summer and you, Stanley, and me put on our gym shorts and ran through for hours without Mom knowing?"

Ant chuckled and said, "Stanley was so afraid we were going to get caught, and you convinced him, and me, that Mom would be reading her book and not notice we were gone."

"She was so mad standing with her arms crossed at the front door. I will never forget that look she gave us. What do you think Stan would be doing right now?"

That choked up feeling returned as the question caught Ant off guard. He thought about Stanley every day but never considered where he would be if he was alive. "Hmm, probably the fucking president." Ant peered at Leo, who was smiling at the curse word, and Mary, who was scolding him for using it. "He was smart even at four years old and so in tune with the world around him."

"Couldn't agree more," Roger said. "You could get to the White House for him, Mr. Mayor."

"No, no, no. You're going to need to physically remove me from this city."

Mary was smiling now. "It is so nice seeing you two together. The way it should be."

Ant and Roger nodded at the same time in agreement, and Ant returned to the window as they entered downtown. The library was back up and running after thousands of book donations and wonderful citizens helped build it back up.

The small businesses were booming with lines around the corner at a clothes shop, a record store, a bookstore, and a deli on the corner before the baseball stadium.

Ant heard from the FBI that they found four dead bodies inside the stadium. Four White guys with brown paint plastered on their faces who crossed city lines with intent to cause mayhem. Three AR-15s and four explosive devices, not including the two used to take out part of downtown and the bridge. The investigation concluded that Mac's cries on social media brought them here to cause destruction. And if Mac did return from the coma, he would be immediately arrested and charged with a laundry list of crimes. Ant would make it his mission to see that Mac never saw the light of day or the death penalty. He deserved the punishment that fit the crime.

The stadium was set to be demolished in the next few months with no plans on what would take up the space. Ant suggested an elementary school, and his constituents were fighting for an outdoor music venue. He may lose that battle but was planning on fighting till the end.

It was a cultural and jarring shift going from the chief of police, a political position but one he felt held no power over decisions of the city, to the mayor where he could control what happened inside the city and make a difference. After former Mayor Higgins was found dead five weeks before the election, the position that nobody wanted was open. Ant stepped down as chief, ran unopposed, and was elected mayor. In the past year, he had an entire department to build back up immediately. Every officer, lieutenant, captain, and chief was handpicked by Ant himself while he attempted to charge every former Bridgewater officer criminally. They all took part in the murder of 156 human beings. The largest mass murder in the history of the United States. And every person needed to be held responsible.

As far as what those outside of Bridgetown knew about what happened, there would be stories floating in and out about monsters that invaded the city along with stories of evil politicians and the rich man on the hill, but the whole truth seemed to remain stagnant in outside circles. And that was how Ant would like it to be forever. When somebody died, there didn't need to be a full gossip column with every detail. There needed to be words about the great things the dead did to make the world a better place, because without contributions from those who once lived, then change would never be possible.

And if there was nobody to fight for a change for the better, then the world would fall into disaster.

As Ant looked out upon the city that had given him so much pain and suffering, he used change to turn utter destruction and catastrophe into strength and weaponry. And looking at his family, change was what brought them together forever.

EPILOGUE: LITTLE LEO'S FINAL ADVENTURE

Leo loved his new home with his new mom and new dad. There were times when he would lie in his new bed surrounded by posters of superheroes and a new gaming system and a bigger television than he had ever seen, and his old mom would pop into his mind. She was so comforting to talk to. She was the only one he felt safe enough to whisper to until his new dad saved him and caught the bad guy who killed his old mom and brother and babysitter. Then he felt he could whisper to who became his new dad when he understood the voices in his head.

The voices never stopped. They were constant, and he rarely talked to others because he had to listen to multiple people talking, and he never understood who to trust.

It was dark now, and his old mom was in his head. Not talking, but when he closed his eyes, she was there like a floating head and a smile that made him happy. Brandon didn't really go into his head, but he missed when he would barge into Leo's room with his PlayStation in hand and hook it up to Leo's smaller television so they could play together. Leo didn't want to play but would eventually pick up the controller and play a wrestling game he didn't understand. Brandon would get mad when he lost and take the gaming system back to his room. He wished Brandon would come into his room now and play video games.

Sarah Plax would sometimes be around more than old mom was around. Anytime she was there to wake them up and get them to school, Leo would hide in his room as much as possible, especially on the weekends when she would be there all the time. She showed Brandon and Leo this old movie called *The Indian in the Cupboard* that was on this old rectangle tape. She must've forgotten she showed them because they watched it every weekend. Though Sarah did say it was her favorite movie of all time. Leo did love that she tried with all her energy to get Leo to go out to the mall or do something that he enjoyed. It was a kind gesture Leo couldn't comprehend a year ago.

His old life was sometimes better.

Now, he sat up from his new bed and slipped into his no-tie sneakers. It was chilly, so he shrugged on his coat and was out the front door. New Dad used to be a police officer, that's when Leo first met him. At a party old Dad put on because he was the old chief of the police. They were friends but not after Bridgetown turned to a dark place. New Dad was the mayor now, so Leo couldn't be seen by anyone because he didn't want to get new Dad in trouble.

New Mom and new Dad lived in a new house from the last one across the bridge in a different town. Now they lived in Bridgetown three streets from where Leo used to live. They asked Leo if it was okay that they lived so close to his old house where the bad thing happened. Leo said it was okay, but he still wasn't sure if he was telling the truth or not.

He learned over the last year how to ignore the voices and listen to those in front of him that were talking, especially adults. But last night he heard a voice that was familiar. A voice that he heard when he was at a restaurant with a different woman than old Mom. Old Mom told old Dad to move out of the house. Brandon was more upset than Leo. Brandon loved old Dad and thought it was cool that he was in charge of the police; old Dad never talked to Leo. And he never felt connected to him.

But the connection now was his voice. He was with the man in the cave. The man in the cave was a magic Leo never understood. Although the man told Leo he was magic from the day he was born, Leo didn't believe him. But the man gave him the power of a supersonic scream that saved his life in the car with old Mom and Brandon. And saved new Dad's life in the old house where old Dad was living. The man in the cave told Leo that his dad was there, even though he lied about him being dead before.

The walk was long, but he knew where to go, so it felt short. It was different than before. Before he felt he had to hide from so many people out in the too early morning hours, but now there wasn't anybody out, and there were less sirens ringing in the air.

The same rusted sign welcomed Leo into Veterans Memorial Park, and the dark of the morning welcomed Leo's tummy to twist in fear. There were two lights that guided his path to the cave, but the entrance was impossible to see at this time.

"Leonardo, I have your daddy in here," the man in the cave said.

"I don't believe you," Leo said.

"Leonardo, if you didn't believe me, you wouldn't be standing outside of my home."

A man exited into the light provided by the minimal lamps and moonlight. It looked like his dad, but different. His face was skinny like a skeleton, and his bones were showing through his skin. His hair was long in the back but gone on top, and it looked like horses' food. His clothes were torn, and he had socks with holes around his big toes.

"Your dad has been with me for a long time. He came here to hide, but this is my house, Leonardo."

Leo had no clue what the man meant, but this was a different version of the dad he knew.

"You got—" his dad spoke, but the critters in his throat caused him to cough. "So big."

"You don't know what I am or who I am," Leo said. "You left Mom and Brandon because you found a different person that you liked better."

"And he ordered for you to be killed, don't forget, Leonardo," the man in the cave said.

"I—" his dad tripped on his words. "I'm so sorry, son. I never meant for any of that to happen. I made a mistake. You can forgive a mistake, can't you?"

"No. I have a new mom and new dad that take care of me. I don't need you in my life." Leo's words stung his old dad as tears were bumping over his facial wrinkles.

"Pl-please. I have nothing. Nobody."

"Everybody makes mistakes, but some are bigger than other ones. Your mistake is too big. It hurt a lot of people and not only three. I walked all the way over here to say I don't need you anymore."

Leo walked farther into the cave without a second thought or any fear and said, "I am ready to get rid of my power."

"Leonardo, you have saved lives. You used it for good. Not everyone does. You are able to keep it and help others. Are you sure?"

"I have myself and my own voice, and that is strong enough."

A hand the same width of a tree branch reached into his focus and squeezed Leo's shoulder. A pinch of pain shot through his nerves, and he released a screech that was louder than any of the other times he had before. When the pain subsided and Leo's eyes shot back open, he was outside of the cave, listening to the water on the sound crash into the side of the rocky edge of the grassy hill. He watched cars' headlights pass over the bridge into and out of the city. His mind was quiet. He waited for a voice, but none came.

"I can hear your voice, but I want to see your face," Leo said to the man in the cave.

Old Dad was on the ground and looked to be sleeping or dead.

"Leonardo, come inside," the man in the cave said.

"No. You come out here." Leo's voice was gruff and authoritative.

"If I leave the cave, then I will burn."

"It might be time for that."

His words cut through the air, and he could hear a whistle of breath in the cave but nothing else. The man in the cave was speechless.

The hand again. Then an ear-shattering pop rang out behind Leo. He jumped, and the willow hand returned to the cave. A woman stood in the grass before the hill sloped down to the sound, and she held a gun, standing over old Dad.

"Hi, little one," the woman said. "You don't know me, but we've met be—"

"You killed my mom," Leo said without emotion.

"I did not, but I was there. There is an evil man who forced me to be there. You are too young to under—"

"I understand. My old dad is"—Leo peered down at the blood pouring from his old dad's forehead—"was a bad man. Some do enough to deserve to die. It's okay." This time Leo was positive that his words were truthful.

"I am making up for my past. Trying to make up for it," the woman said.

Leo nodded as she ran out of the park and into the streets.

"Sometimes faces are not important," Leo said, turning back to the cave. "Your voice is a more important tool, but if there is no connection to a flesh-and-bone human, then you might as well be a computer."

There was no breath or voice from inside the cave. Leo turned to return to his new bed with his new and forever family.

"You are correct, Leonardo," the man in the cave said outside of the cave. He was behind Leo, and his willow hand passed through Leo's peripheral vision and slithered in front. Branches latched onto his arms and legs but left enough for Leo to spin and see the face of the man in the cave. "Faces make us part of who we are."

There was no pain as Leo screamed into the city where so much pain once lived.

ACKNOWLEDGEMENTS

A huge thank you to my editor, Sara Kelly. Sara has worked on each and every story I have released, and this book doesn't exist without her expertise. Everything right in this book is her fantastic work. Everything wrong in this book is my fault.

A shoutout to my forever cover designer, Elderlemon Designs. Knows exactly what I need and exceeds expectations each and every time.

A special shoutout for my friends in Bridgeport, Connecticut. As you maneuvered your way through this novel you recognized the many landmarks, street names, and my favorite diner. Bridgetown is a fictional city built on the foundation of Bridgeport. The story is completely fictional. The people of Bridgeport love and respect the city that is growing to be better every day. I know, I was born and raised there.

And last, but certainly not least, is my wife. Thank you for supporting me and allowing me the time to sit and write for hours. It means the world, as you do to me.

Joe Baldwin was born and raised in the idyllic state of Connecticut where he received his degree in Criminal Justice. When he is not nose-down in a book you can find him on a long walk beside the roar of traffic or attempting to befriend his pug-tailed tabby cat named Piranha. CHANGE is his debut novel.